Watch for a brand-new novel from

LAURA CALDWELL

Coming June 2006

Laura Caldwell

Look Closely

MIRA®

ISBN 0-7783-2183-5

LOOK CLOSELY

www.MIRABooks.com

Printed in U.S.A.

ACKNOWLEDGMENTS

My heartfelt thanks to the following people:
Margaret O'Neill Marbury, Maureen Walters,
everyone at MIRA Books (especially Dianne Moggy,
Donna Hayes, Laura Morris, Craig Swinwood,
Sarah Rundle, Margie Miller and Tara Kelly),
Mark Bragg, Pam Carroll, Jim Lupo,
Ginger Heyman, Trisha Woodson,
Ted McNabola and Joan Posch.

Thanks mostly to Jason Billups, purveyor of dreams.

Prologue

Seated at a table near the back, Caroline Ramsey lifted her champagne flute an inch off the table. "Cheers," she murmured halfheartedly, toasting the bride and groom for what seemed the fiftieth time. Almost immediately, she set the glass back down.

Her husband, Matt, leaned toward her. "Anything wrong?" he said. Through his glasses, his brown eyes looked only mildly concerned.

The groom was a distant relative of Matt's, and in order to compensate for knowing so few people, he'd gone into his social mode, dancing to every silly wedding song and striking up conversations around the room. He always became vivacious and outgoing in these situations, something Caroline loved about him, since she was more reserved. Yet now she almost wished that he were more of a watcher, like her, someone who hung on the fringes. If that were true, maybe he would wonder now, maybe he would look deeper.

"Nothing's wrong," she lied, because she didn't want him to wonder. She might not be strong enough. She might tell him what she'd planned. And if she told him, he would talk her out of it. This was something she had to do, though, just one more time. Hopefully, she would get the chance one day to explain.

Matt ruffled her hair, a gesture that usually annoyed her. Tonight, it somehow brought relief.

The wedding was being held in an eight-point tent on the lawn of a Charleston mansion, and the beleaguered jazz band struck up another number as the latest toastmaster finally gave up the microphone. Caroline and Matt both turned to watch the newlyweds take the dance floor, a surge of guests following and engulfing them. Caroline remembered her own wedding, just four years ago, at an inn on Mount Hood. It had been much smaller, with cheap ivory votive candles and wilted wildflowers instead of silver candelabras and elaborate white lily arrangements, but she'd been filled with promise just like the bride tonight. She'd stupidly assumed that her troubles were behind her, that her new life with Matt would obliterate the old.

"Should we join them?" Matt cocked his head at the dance floor.

She looked at those warm brown eyes, his soft curly hair, which was always a little too long, and the dimple he got in one cheek when he smiled, and she kissed him. He kissed her back, cupping her face. It reminded her of their wedding, except that it was beaming bright that day, the sun relentlessly striking their faces as they stood on the cliff. Matt's parents had been there, along with his brother and a few friends, but of course her family had been absent. Or maybe "absent" wasn't the right word, since she hadn't exactly invited anyone from her past.

"You want to go back to the hotel?" Matt murmured.

She shook her head, finding it hard to talk. "I have to use the restroom," she said at last.

"I'll be here." He stroked her cheek one more time.

She stood and turned away before she could change her mind, making her way across the flagstone path to the Trembly Mansion where the restrooms were located. According to the history printed on the back of the wedding program, the mansion had been built in 1856 by Arthur Trembly and his second wife, Meredith, who was only seventeen at the time of their marriage. Caroline glanced up at the mansion with its brick front, soaring white columns, wide veranda and leaded-glass windows, and she could almost imagine young Meredith stepping out onto that veranda, resplendent in a tightly bodiced gown of crimson taffeta, greeting the guests of their latest gala.

It was how Caroline had coped all those years—making up stories and images in her head, filling her mind with fascinating people and intriguing families to compensate for her own lack of friends and family. But she couldn't let herself go too far down the paths of those tales any longer. Instead of shielding her from reality as they used to, they now reminded her of the memories she'd worked so hard to bury. She quickened her pace and trotted up the side stairway, past a sign with an arrow reading Powder Room. The information about the Trembly Mansion also said that this side of the house had been temporarily converted into a catering kitchen and guest-bathroom facilities, while the remainder of the home was being renovated by a local historical society.

Caroline stepped into a well-lit kitchen. The shiny silver espresso makers sitting atop tan Formica counters gave nothing away about what the rest of the mansion might look like. She picked her way through a pack of tuxedoed servers, most of whom held trays of cut cake. One waiter nodded with his head to direct her toward the restroom.

When she came out of the bathroom, the kitchen was empty. There was no one to stop her from changing her direction and ducking under the blue velvet curtain that hung across the arched wood doorway, the one that led into the main part of the mansion. The renovations were supposedly in high gear, with too much dust and equipment to allow guests to view it, but Caroline didn't care much for rules. Why should she? Except for Matt, no one in her life had followed them.

As the curtain flapped closed behind her, she blinked to let her eyes grow accustomed to the darkness. The only light in the room came from the lanterns hanging in the trees outside, and there was a musty scent in the air. She could hear the tinkle of music from the band and the clatter of dishware from the waiters, who must have returned to the kitchen.

As the dark room became clearer, Caroline made out a massive, mahogany stairway that curled upward in scrolls from the center of the room. Nothing seemed to support the staircase, yet it gave the impression of solemn strength. Caroline felt a trembling inside her belly, a shakiness in her hand. The stairway reminded her of another staircase. One she hadn't seen in so very long, but one that had, in a way, started it all.

She had to do this. *One more time,* he'd said. *Just one more time.*

Caroline tried to draw her gaze away from the stairs but couldn't. And it didn't matter, because in her mind, she was seeing that other staircase so long ago.

The trembling deepened, the shaking in her hands grew stronger.

Finally wrenching her eyes away from the staircase, Caroline turned, found the front door and ran outside into the night.

The lights were blinking, weren't they? Blinking and flickering and then fading. Or maybe it was him.

Dan Singer stopped trudging and opened his eyes wide to stare at the lights. No. Not blinking. It was a Budweiser sign. Just a yellow and green neon beer sign hanging in a bar window. Jesus, he'd drunk too damn much, and after so many years of sobriety, it had hit him hard. He'd needed courage, and he'd convinced himself that this time the vodka might bring him some. Really, he was drinking to kill time. He was delaying the inevitable.

He'd been in and out of nearly every bar on this street. What was the name of it again? He turned and gazed at the street sign. "Division Street," it said. That was right. He knew that. Division Street in Chicago. He'd been at a convention here for the last few days, and he'd spent the time with other salespeople in the pharmaceutical industry, acting as if he still cared about the new cholesterol drug and his company's revenues. Yet, as uninterested as he was in the technicalities, he'd reveled in the normalcy of it all, knowing he might not have that for some time.

He turned to the nearest bar and pulled open the big oak door, a rush of laughter and music swelling out to greet him, along with the smell of stale beer. Strangely, the scent was comforting, a reminder of college—blurry days filled with classes and parties and bars and girls. He'd been able to escape for a while during those days.

He pushed his way to the bar, drawing a few irritated looks in the process. There were no available stools so he lodged himself between two patrons and waved at the bartender.

"Vodka with a splash of soda," he said when the bartender reached him.

He watched as she poured his drink. He liked the way she made a dipping motion with the bottle, her T-shirt lifting up and exposing a slice of tanned skin above her jeans. A week ago, he would have tried to flirt with her. He was finally getting back into the dating scene. But that wasn't an option now.

She slid the glass in front of him. "It's on me. You look like you could use it."

He tried to give a lighthearted smile, but her kindness put a lump in his throat, so he just nodded.

He tipped her and sipped the drink, trying not to think of Annie or how she must have felt when he hadn't picked her up today. His ex hadn't helped matters, he was sure. She'd probably told Annie, in a smug voice, that her dad didn't care enough. She wouldn't think about how hearing that would make Annie feel. She'd only know that it made her feel superior. His failure to show would confirm what she thought anyway—that he was irresponsible and not to be trusted. He'd never cheated on her when they were married, but he understood why she suspected it. It was his secretive manner that made her wonder, and when he wouldn't fill in any of the blanks, when they couldn't communicate the way she'd been taught on *Oprah,* she'd assumed the worst. He didn't try very hard to convince her otherwise. Annie was the loser in their divorce, caught between two people who wanted to move on with their lives. For that he was sorry. It was why he'd never missed any of his weekends or Wednesdays with her, until now.

He was jostled from behind by a group of women who were hugging and shrieking as if they hadn't seen each other in years. Soon, two of the women pushed in beside him, waving dollar bills at the bartender, who took their orders.

"You look amazing!" one woman said to the other, grabbing her friend by the forearm and looking her up and down. "You're so thin."

"Oh, stop," said the other, but she beamed.

They launched into a discussion about who they'd been in touch with, how much they'd missed everyone, how it had been way too long, and yet neither of them sounded particularly surprised to find themselves together again. It made Dan think about how empty his own life was, how devoid of any relationships like that. But it was too late to change. Way too late. And he had to make himself accept, again, that it had all been worth it. If he didn't get his mind around that, he would snap. He'd given up too much—his family, his hometown, his *history,* for Christ's sake. It *had* been worth it, he told himself, but his own voice sounded like that of a politician, trying to sugarcoat an international incident.

The ease of the women's reunion was depressing him, and the vodka seemed to have lost its power. He'd hit that point where he couldn't get any more loaded, no matter how hard he tried, his veins already coursing at their alcoholic capacity. He shot a halfhearted goodbye smile toward the bartender, then turned and elbowed through the girlfriends.

After he'd walked a few blocks, he saw cars up ahead, flashing by. In the spaces between the cars were intermittent glints of silvery light. He took a few more steps before it hit him. Lake Shore Drive, or LSD as he used to call it in high school, liking how saying that made him sound as if he might know a thing or two about illicit drugs. He had nearly reached Lake Shore Drive, which meant he was almost to Lake Michigan.

"Hey, buddy." The voice startled him so much he flinched. Spinning around, he saw a man crumpled on the sidewalk, against the side of a brownstone. Dan's first instinct was that the man was hurt and needed help, but in the next instant he saw the stuffed garbage bag at the man's side and his multiple layers of clothing, and realized he was homeless.

"Spare a couple bucks?" the man said, his voice a rough croak. "Gotta get some food."

"Yeah, sure." Dan extracted a ten-dollar bill from the few he had left and crumpled the rest in his pocket. He tossed the bill toward the man, but it caught a breeze, twisting and lilting in the air like a snowflake until the man snatched it.

"Thanks, bud." The man gave Dan a nod. "Appreciate it."

Dan stood a moment longer, looking at the man. He used to wonder how anyone could be homeless, how someone could shift from a house and a profession to a life on the street. But now he understood better. In fact, it was a possibility that occasionally loomed in his own future, because sometimes he just didn't care anymore. At those times, he could imagine letting it all go—his sales job, his apartment, his child-support payments—until he was fired, evicted and strapped with a restraining order. What scared him was that oftentimes that possibility appealed to him, because he saw it as a way to let go of the constraints in his life, and maybe that would allow him to let go of the secret, too. A secret that had somehow grown larger and larger over the years, when, in fact, some days he wondered whether it really needed to be hidden at all.

He turned away from the man and kept moving toward the lake. He'd avoided lakes his whole adult life, especially this one. It reminded him too much of the old days. But he felt its pull now, the water's tug. He kept walking. When he reached the poorly lit tunnel that would take him under LSD and to the lake, he hesitated, waiting for the alcohol to clear his head.

But the fear he expected didn't come. He took that as a good sign, and descended into the tunnel.

1

The short letter, a note really, arrived at my apartment on a Thursday. It was one of those random, end-of-April days in Manhattan when the temperature shot to eighty degrees, sending everyone to Central Park or the cafés that had rushed to set up their outdoor tables. A boisterous, electric feeling was in the air. I called Maddy from my cell phone as I walked home from the subway, and we decided to go for wine and dinner at Bryant Park Grill, a rooftop restaurant where Maddy knew the maître d'.

In the terminally slow elevator on the way to my apartment, I glanced at my mail. There was nothing interesting at first, just a bill and a few obvious pieces of junk, but I stopped when I came to the flat, business-size envelope with no return address. The envelope looked as if it had been printed on a personal computer, and there was a postage stamp with an antique car on it.

Inside my place, I dropped my purse, my brief-case and the rest of the mail on the front-hall table, then slit open the envelope. I pulled out a piece of folded white paper, and strangely, all my senses went on alert. The apartment was suddenly warm and stuffy. It smelled dusty and stale, and my skin itched from the uncharacteristic heat. Holding the envelope and the still-folded paper, I walked to the windows and cranked them open for the first time that year. Balmy, fresh air seeped into the room.

I sat on the couch and unfolded the paper. Only two typewritten lines appeared there.

There is no statute of limitations on murder.
Look closely.

"What?" I said the word out loud, but as I read the note again, some odd glimmer of comprehension began to ruffle my mind. It wasn't that I recognized the words or the type. I was sure I'd never heard those exact sentences before, and I had no idea who'd written them, yet there was a flicker of understanding.

The breeze from my windows felt too cool then, yet I didn't move to close them. In fact, I hoped the air would help me breathe. All at once, my chest and throat felt constricted, my lungs making shallow movements. I told myself to stay calm and put the note down. But I couldn't let go of the paper. I read the words over and over until I felt light-headed, and the words swam in front of me. *Murder, statute, closely...*

The ring of the phone rattled me away from the letter. I blinked rapidly, finally getting that deep breath, and grabbed the receiver off the end table.

"Hailey, it's me," Maddy said. "I'm early, and I'm two blocks from you, so I'm coming over."

I dropped the letter in my lap. "I need a few minutes."

"Why? What's wrong?"

"Nothing. It's... It's nothing."

"Whoa," she said. "I know that voice. I'll be right there."

Five minutes later, she buzzed from the lobby.

"What's up with you?" she said when I opened the door, the letter still in my hand. "What's wrong?"

I handed her the note. "I'm not sure." I felt both sick and elated, as if on the verge of some discovery.

Maddy read it. "What in the hell is this?"

I shook my head and took the note from her. I read it again, letting that flicker of comprehension grow brighter.

"Hailey, what's going on?" Maddy said, her voice cautious, slightly alarmed. She flicked her dark, ringletted hair over her shoulder.

"I just got it in the mail," I said inanely.

"Who sent it?"

I shrugged.

Maddy groaned. "Why are you being so difficult? Give me the envelope."

I turned toward the couch and pointed to where it had fallen off my lap. It was now almost hidden between the cushions. Maddy's heels tapped on the wood floor as she crossed the room. For some reason, I noticed that she was wearing an expensive-looking tan suit, one I hadn't seen before.

"The letter was sent from here in the city," she said, lifting the envelope and pointing to the postmark. "Do you have any idea who sent it to you?"

"No." I looked down at the page, although I knew the words by heart already.

"Well, who was murdered? I mean, do you know who it's referring to?"

I felt that nauseous elation again, a sick swoop and dive of my insides. "Yeah, I think so," I said. "My mom."

My lungs ached, but I ignored the feeling. I ran faster, heading south down Broadway, then rounding the corner at Union Square West, just barely avoiding a full-frontal collision with a falafel vendor. I kept running, my shoes making dull slaps on the concrete, until I hit University, where I turned toward my apartment. Almost there, almost there. My breath sounded ragged to my own ears, but I pushed past it. Just a few more blocks. I pumped my arms faster, increasing my speed, feeling my bangs stick to my forehead with sweat.

I reached Eleventh Street and dropped to a walk, letting my breath catch up with me. It was heaven to jog without all my winter layers, to let the breeze hit my bare legs, to let the run shake off the thoughts of that letter, those two sentences that I carried constantly in my brain. I'd spent the last few weeks obsessing about who had sent it to me. I wouldn't show it to my dad, and I had no guesses myself. On a long shot, I interrogated my mailman, but he could only tell me the bit of information I already knew—that the envelope had originally been sent from here in Manhattan. Which left me with millions of residents to consider, not to mention the millions of tourists.

I slowed even more when I reached the display of flowers on the sidewalk that signaled my favorite Korean grocery store. A few weeks ago there'd been prom carnations and roses that looked hairsprayed—winter flowers—but now there were tulips, bright-colored and fresh. Inside the crowded shop, I picked up a bottle of grapefruit juice and a mammoth Sunday *New York Times*. Buying that paper every weekend made me feel like a native, one of those people who acted as if it was no big deal to live here, in one of the largest, craziest cities in the world. Maddy was like that. So were many of the associates at my firm. Manhattan lingo rolled off their tongues with ease. They'd say, "I'm going to the Korean," instead of "the Korean deli," or "I'm heading to Seventy-sixth and Lex" not "Seventy-sixth Street and Lexington Avenue."

I, on the other hand, had never been truly comfortable in Manhattan, despite my three years there during law school and the last five years of private practice. I'd thought the accumulation of years, together with the fact that my father still lived in Manhasset on Long Island, would bring me a sense of contentment. But no matter how often I put myself in the thick of things, no matter how much I tried to convince myself, I always felt a little off, a little like an impostor. It was why I jogged the chaotic streets, picking my way past too many obstacles, like pedestrians and baby strollers and bicyclists, instead of heading for the river or Battery Park. I had this notion that if I constantly placed myself in the middle of the urban crunch it would soak in, and I'd finally feel as if I belonged.

I finished the juice while waiting in line to pay, picking the pulpy bits off my lips. I showed the bottle to the cashier when I reached him.

"How are you today, Hailey?" the cashier said. He was a short Korean man with a wide bald head.

"Good, Shin. How are you?" We had a few seconds of light chatter while he rang me up. Shin was the reason I went to that store; someone, other than my co-workers, who knew my name.

I threw the bottle in a trash can outside the store, feeling a cool trickle of sweat slide down my spine, then walked in the direction of Ninth Street. I balanced the paper on one arm, while I flipped to the business section.

"Shit!" I said. "Shit, shit, shit." The headline read, Online McKnight Store In Trouble?

McKnight Corporation was one of my clients—one of my newest, biggest clients—and I was scheduled to leave for Chicago that night to represent them at a federal arbitration. Until then, I hadn't been as nervous as I usually would be in an arbitration. I'd been more focused on that letter and the fact that Chicago was right across the lake from Woodland Dunes, the town where I'd lived until I was seven. The town where my mother, Leah Sutter, had died.

The night I had received the letter, Maddy and I split a bottle of wine, then another, talking for hours. Why, Maddy had demanded, did I think the stupid little note was about my mother? It was probably just a cruel prank, she said. By that time

I was sure that the letter was about Leah Sutter, but I had a hard time explaining my conviction, my absolute certainty. I couldn't remember much about that time, and I'd gotten used to ignoring it, yet now it had come back, a force to be reckoned with. The more I thought about it, a family shouldn't scatter the way mine did after someone died. One day I had a mother, a father, a sister and a brother. After my mom passed away, it was only my dad and me.

I've read stories of estranged families coming closer after someone dies. I don't know why that didn't happen to my family. We didn't stay long in Woodland Dunes, but during the few weeks that I'd returned to school, I saw the pointed stares of my classmates, a curious fear behind their eyes. So, I'd been glad when my dad said we were leaving. Caroline and Dan went their own ways—Caroline to boarding school, Dan to college and then both of them off into the world. I grew up without siblings, without knowing what I was missing. It wasn't until college, when I was away from my father for the first time, that I realized how strange that was.

Staring at the McKnight headline now, thinking of the publicity it would generate, my heart rate picked up again. I hurried to my apartment, and instead of waiting for the elevator, I took the stairs two at a time to my place on the sixth floor. During law school, I'd lived on the ground floor of the same building, in a small studio with a single window that had a lovely view of the Dumpster. Once I had a steady paycheck, I moved to the top floor and into a large one-bedroom. Instead of the Dumpster, my windows now overlooked an old church on the corner, which would have been quaint if it weren't for the couple of homeless guys who set up camp there every night and screamed obscenities at passersby.

Inside the apartment, I skimmed the article. The beginning gave information I already knew: McKnight Corporation owned department stores nationwide and had recently gotten into online retail, but they'd been sued by a competitor who claimed that McKnight copied its Web design and certain slogans. Their stock had gone down because of the suit, and if they lost the arbitration or a later trial, the article speculated, it could sound the death knell for the company. I knew the arbitration was important to McKnight's business, of course. What I hadn't known was that the company could go under if I didn't win.

"Christ," I said, slamming a hand on the table.

I stood up straight, embarrassed by my own temper, despite the fact that I was alone. It wasn't just the professional pressure that was getting to me, I knew. It was the thought that this development might steal away the time I'd planned to spend during my visit to Woodland Dunes.

The second half of the article gave a history of the company, something I was only vaguely familiar with. I skimmed most of it until I saw a teaser headline in the middle that read, Corporate Foul Play? The juice I'd drank felt like acid in my stomach.

According to the piece, Sean McKnight, the current CEO, had engineered a deal twenty years ago that allowed McKnight Corporation to buy another department-store company called Fieldings. Initially, the deal had all the makings of a hostile takeover, but suddenly Fieldings's board, made up of mostly Fieldings family members, had decided to sell. There was a rumor that McKnight had used personal information to blackmail his way into the sale. Charges were never brought, though, and McKnight Corporation had flourished until now.

I read the section again. I'd been told by McKnight's in-house counsel that there was no dirty laundry. I might be able to bar the plaintiff's attorney from questioning McKnight about this Fieldings takeover, but the rules of evidence were looser at arbitrations than at trials, so I would have to be prepared. The media surrounding the story would only make my job harder. Hopefully, Illinois didn't allow filming at arbitrations.

I picked up the phone and dialed Maddy's number. When I got her machine, I hung up and dialed her cell phone instead.

I had met Maddy on the first day of law school, and I liked her right away. I liked her loud, cheerful personality and her crazy, curly hair. Maddy, unlike me, was someone who told you her life story within the first twenty minutes of meeting her. When I wouldn't, or couldn't, do that, she seemed to understand. As we spent more and more time together—studying in the library, griping about exams, drinking too much merlot on the weekends—Maddy found subtle ways to draw me out.

One of her favorites was using magazines as props. We would study in the coffee-shop area of a large bookstore, and every few hours we'd take a break. Maddy would buy a stack of magazines, and we'd sit across from each other, steaming mugs of coffee in front of us, the magazines fanned out over the table. As we flipped the pages, Maddy would ask questions. They started mundane, or at least as mundane as Maddy could be. "Don't you think I'd look amazing in this dress?" she'd say, or "Can you believe how much these frickin' sneakers cost? They look like orthopedic shoes." But as we continued to talk, Maddy would sneak in slightly more substantial questions. "Did you have one of these hideous dolls when you were growing up?" or "Would you wear a wedding dress like this?"

I knew what Maddy was doing, but the questions didn't feel threatening, so eventually I began to talk, my eyes still looking at the magazines, my fingers still turning the glossy pages. The questions grew more pointed, and by the end of our first year in law school, Maddy knew everything about me. She knew about my mother. She knew what I knew anyway, which wasn't much. It was an odd freedom to release all those thoughts from the cage in my brain.

"I was just going to call you," she said as she answered her phone now. In the background, I heard the ticking of cash registers and women's voices. "I'm at Saks, and they're having an incredible shoe sale. Those strappy sandals you wanted are forty percent off. Get your ass over here."

"No, thanks. I think I'll get enough of department stores this week. Plus, I have to leave for the airport in a few hours."

"Oh, that's right. Your McKnight arb. You ready?"

"Check out the business section of the *Times,* and you'll know the answer to that one. Listen, I have a question about Illinois law. You had a few cases there, right?"

"Well, sure, but mostly I just carried the trial bags and ran for coffee." Maddy was also at a big law firm in Manhattan, and like many other young associates, she hadn't gotten much trial experience. I, on the other hand, had been lucky. Right out of law school, during the dot-com boom, I'd started a cyber-law division at my firm. I was young and determined. I had time to learn this new area of law, and I liked not being under the thumb of the other attorneys. To everyone's surprise, the division was a huge success, and the clients didn't stop coming even after many of the start-up companies failed. There was still so much business and very few firms who specialized in cyber law. Since my department was now pulling in lots of revenue, they pretty much let me do whatever I wanted. In fact, I was hoping to make partner soon.

"Do you remember if they allow TV cameras at arbitrations?" I asked.

"I know they're kept out of the courtroom. I don't know about an arb, though. Sorry I'm not more help."

"That's all right." I moved into the bedroom and took off my jogging shoes.

"How long will you be in Chicago?" Maddy said.

"A week or so."

"You'll be there next weekend, huh?"

"What are you getting at, Mad?" I pulled off my socks and slumped back on the bed. The satiny-smooth cotton felt cool under my legs.

"You know what I'm getting at. That bizarre letter. You're going to Woodland Dunes, aren't you?"

Like my father, Maddy knew me too well. Normally I loved her for it. "I'm just going to ask a few questions," I told her, trying to keep the irritation out of my voice.

"Not smart, girl. Someone who writes a letter like that is not someone you want to mess with."

"Right. Well." It had occurred to me that maybe the author meant to be helpful in some way, but I wasn't about to try to convince Maddy.

"Did you tell your dad?" she asked.

"Of course not." My dad was my other best friend. We even worked together at Gardner, State & Lord, but he worried about me too much as it was.

Maddy sighed. "You can be such a pain in the ass. Just leave it alone, okay?"

"I'll try."

"At least promise me you'll be careful."

"I will, I will."

"I'll tell you what. I'll buy those sandals for you, and I'll hold them hostage. You only get them if you're a good girl, and come home safely."

I laughed. "Deal."

I stripped off the rest of my clothes and took a quick shower. After I was dressed again, I loaded my laptop and the McKnight file into my large leather trial bag, the one that made me feel like a traveling salesman. Next, I packed a week's worth of suits, some running clothes and a couple pairs of jeans into a suitcase. I had everything I needed for the arbitration, everything I needed for a week away from home, but there was one thing left to pack.

I moved around my bed to the corner of the room where I'd set up a desk and computer. I opened the top drawer and took out the envelope. I lifted the flap to make sure the letter was still there, then I read it once more. *There is no statute of limitations on murder. Look closely.*

2

The opulent Chicago headquarters of McKnight Corporation were housed on the top floors of their State Street department store. Marble-decked with gold fixtures, I assumed that it was supposed to bring to mind old world elegance. Personally, I found the place overdone. It reminded me of some of the homes in my dad's neighborhood in Manhasset—all show and no warmth.

The receptionist escorted me to the top floor and into a conference room where paintings of the flagship store hung in gold-leafed frames. I was there to meet with Beth Halverson, McKnight Corporation's in-house counsel, and Sean McKnight whom I hadn't yet met. Then I would review my notes and get ready for opening arguments that afternoon.

I had the buzz, that taut, high-strung feeling I always got when I was on trial or in an arbitration. But now I was even more on edge since I'd been sideswiped with the new information about possible shady dealings in McKnight's takeover of Fieldings Company.

"Hi, Hailey, welcome to Chicago."

I stood to greet Beth Halverson, an impeccably dressed woman in her late thirties with stylish, short blond hair. I'd always found Beth competent and agreeable, and I was thrilled that she'd decided to give us McKnight's business, but I had a bone to pick with her this time.

She seemed to read my mind. "I want you to know that I found out about the Fieldings allegations the same way you did. By reading the paper yesterday."

"I mean no disrespect, but I find that hard to believe." On a side table, coffee, juices and pastries had been set out. I poured myself a cup of coffee and added a few drops of skim milk, exactly the way my mom used to.

"Look," Beth said. "I only came on as general counsel a year and a half ago."

I turned around to see her shutting the conference-room door.

"What I found," Beth said in a lowered voice, glancing at the closed door, "was that this place is run exactly the way Sean wants it."

I took my seat again. "And what does that mean?"

Beth walked around the table, coming closer to

me, and leaned on it with both arms. "It means that Sean doesn't want anyone to talk about the Fieldings takeover, so no one does. I wasn't apprised of the rumors. I never heard of any of the allegations until that article. Honestly, I wouldn't keep that from you."

I had only worked with Beth for a year or so, but she seemed like a straight shooter, and I believed her. "It's just that I don't know anything about that takeover," I said. "I don't know how to refute the allegations. I feel like I've been completely ambushed."

Beth slumped into a chair. "God, I feel the same way. I even thought about quitting, but this is a great job when I don't have to deal with the boss. I don't know what to tell you except what I've learned about the Fieldings deal since yesterday."

"I think I'd better hear it from McKnight himself. Where is he, by the way?"

Beth gave a shake of her blond head. "He should be here any minute. You've heard what he's like?"

"I've heard he's an asshole," I said, deciding that now wasn't the time to mince words.

I saw Beth's face go slack, then heard a rough laugh behind me. I swung around to see a man standing in the now open conference doorway. He must have been in his late fifties, but the trim body and the immaculate blue suit made him look younger. His salt-and-pepper hair was brushed away from his sharply angled face.

"I assume you're Ms. Sutter," the man said. He walked into the room and extended his hand. "I'm the asshole."

I stood, feeling heat rush to my face, but I was still angry about being kept in the dark, so I decided not to go overboard in my apology. I shook Mc-Knight's hand, feeling his strong, dry grip. His green eyes ran quickly over me, before they settled on my own eyes with a look of complete concentration.

"I'm sorry you heard that," I said. "I'm sure it's not true."

"Oh, I'm sure it is." He didn't let go of my hand. Instead, he stood there holding it, intently studying my face, until I pulled away.

I made a show of looking at my watch. "We need to get to work. Why don't you start by telling me about the Fieldings deal."

McKnight took a seat at the head of the conference table. "You're all business, aren't you?"

"Isn't that why you hired me?"

He gave me a tight smile. "Of course. What do you want to know?"

I flipped through my legal pad to the list of questions I'd prepared last night in my hotel room. The questions were those that the plaintiff's attorney might ask McKnight on cross-examination.

Once I got him talking, I found myself relaxing somewhat. Technically, the man would make an excellent witness with his obvious intelligence, his even more obvious good looks, and the way he never hemmed or hawed, never seemed edgy or defensive. He had brought with him a stack of documents, meticulously organized and tabbed, which he referred to every so often. He'd prepared well for the arbitration, and that impressed me. So many clients thought that I could—and should— do all the work for them.

His explanation of the Fieldings allegations sounded plausible, too, yet something still gnawed at me. The way he told the story, the Fieldings family members had been undecided over whether to sell to McKnight Corporation. Sean had had a talk with Walter Fieldings, the founder and eldest family member, and convinced him that it would be in the family's best financial interests to sell. Walter Fieldings had, in turn, convinced the rest of the family, and the deal went through. Yes, Mc-Knight said, there were some grumblings that he had pulled some kind of trick. The authorities had even questioned him, but everyone realized the blackmail allegations weren't true, and nothing came of it. He'd never been charged with any-thing, and he made the Fieldings family very rich.

"And that's it?" I said, the incredulity slipping

into my tone despite myself. "There's nothing more to the story? You just had a talk with Papa Fieldings, and the deal fell into place?"

"Essentially, yes." McKnight leaned forward on his elbows. His eyes held mine, and I wondered for a second if he was one of those older guys who hit on every woman under forty. For some reason, that thought didn't strike me exactly right. There were a handful of those types in my office, and they were much more overt—staring at your breasts, letting their hands run over your back as you passed them.

"Are you doubting me?" McKnight asked.

"I'm trained to doubt everyone."

"How interesting." He sat back in his chair, crossing his arms over his chest, as if waiting for me to make the next move.

"Look," I said. "I'm not trying to antagonize you, but if you want to avoid a trial, we need to win this week, and if we're going to win, we need to make sure you sound credible."

"Are you saying I don't seem credible?" McKnight's tone was low and, to be honest, scary.

"I'm simply saying that in case they're allowed in, you have to be ready for some intense questions on this issue. Your story needs to be perfect."

McKnight's gaze never left my face. "Well, Miss Sutter, what part of my 'story,' as you put it, don't you believe?"

I reviewed the notes I'd taken. It was a good question, because I couldn't exactly find fault with his rendition of the events. *He* was the problem, I realized. I didn't trust him, and that made me very anxious. Any lawyer's worst nightmare is a client you can't trust, who might hold things back or take matters into his own hands. McKnight struck me as that type, but I couldn't very well tell him that. In one month, the Gardner, State & Lord executive committee would vote on new partners. If I lost the McKnight account right before the vote, I might lose the partnership. I'd worked too hard to let this guy ruin it for me.

"It's nothing precise," I said, raising my head to meet his eyes again. "As I mentioned, I just want you to be ready."

"If there's one thing you should know about me, it's this. I am always, always ready." He closed the file folder in front of him as if the subject were also closed.

"All right then. Let's review what's going to happen this week."

I took them through what I expected of the arbitration step by step, and when we were finished, McKnight stood from the table and began moving toward the door. It was twelve o'clock, one hour before the arbitration started.

"Please call if you want lunch sent up," he said

to me. "You do eat, right? You do require regular human sustenance?"

I blinked a few times, confused at his hostility. "I've been known to eat once in a while," I said wryly.

"Good to hear it. I'll see you at the arbitration."

"I think we should walk over together so that we can talk some more about your testimony," I said.

He stopped and turned around. "I think you've taken up enough of my time." With that, he sailed out the door.

I looked at Beth. "What the hell?"

She rolled her eyes. "Don't take it personally. Supposedly, he wasn't always like this. I've heard that he used to be a decent guy until he got a divorce years ago. He was never the same after that."

"A divorce made him such a jerk? Are you kidding me?"

She shrugged. "You never know what can push a person over the edge."

A few days later, I sat at a scratched wooden table, alone in the arbitration room, getting ready to present McKnight's Web designer as my next witness. Since everyone else was at lunch, the room was cool and quiet. The proceeding was being held in a stately old government building near the federal courthouse, the place where Mc-

Knight Corporation would find itself in approximately six months for a trial if the arbitration didn't go well. The arbitrators had barred members of the press from the room, but journalists were always stationed outside, like vultures waiting to swoop, so most of the time I stayed put until I had to leave for the day.

It was hard when the room was so still. I wasn't as focused as I should have been. My thoughts kept straying from the notes and deposition transcripts piled in front of me to the letter tucked at the bottom of my trial bag. I kept counting the days until I could leave Chicago and drive to Woodland Dunes. Only two more now.

So far, the arbitration had been an odd mix, some parts better than I expected, others decidedly worse. I'd been pleased with my opening argument. I went into that zone where I wove my words easily, where I could read the arbitrators' faces and change my course when their interest waned. The only thing that threw me was the constant feel of Sean McKnight's eyes on me. It didn't seem like the lustful watch of a man interested in a May/December romance. That would have been simple, because I knew how to handle come-ons. No, his stare felt more like an ever-present evaluation. Every time I saw him observing me from the corner of my eye, I had to force myself to concentrate so that I could keep on the path of my statement.

Luckily, after the opening arguments, McKnight did as he said he would and disappeared until it was time for his testimony. Once he was on the stand, he became the charming person customers associated with McKnight department stores. I was surprised when the plaintiff's attorney, Evan Lamey, didn't hit McKnight hard with questions about the Fieldings takeover. I would've liked to think that Lamey was entranced by McKnight's good looks and smooth talking, but I knew better. Lamey was trying to cast a shadow of doubt over McKnight with his cross-examination, all the while saving his real zingers in case a trial was needed. As a result, McKnight finished his testimony at the end of the day with a smug look on his face.

"You see," he said, leaning toward me so the others wouldn't hear, "I didn't need the practice."

I clicked my trial bag shut. "Don't kid yourself. He went easy on you."

A flicker of doubt crossed McKnight's face, then disappeared. He didn't ask what I meant. Instead, he simply said, "When do I have to be back here?"

"Closing arguments. Friday at one o'clock. Unless of course you want to show support for your employee, who will be testifying tomorrow."

"And what do you do with your evenings here in Chicago?"

"I…" I faltered for a second, startled at the shift in topic. I wondered if I'd been wrong before, if he might be hitting on me. But his eyes were cold, and he had taken a step away, as if he found it difficult to be in my proximity.

"I don't think that's any of your business," I said.

"I think it is. I'm paying you to be here."

"You're not paying me for my time after hours."

"Yes, right." He studied my face with that way of his. Then he swiveled on the heels of his Italian-leather shoes and walked out of the room. I decided that he was, by far, the rudest and oddest client I'd ever had.

People started trickling into the arbitration room now, and I was finally able to get my mind on track. Unfortunately, the McKnight Web designer, a Jesus look-alike named Gary Sather, didn't fare as well as his boss that afternoon. My direct exam went smooth enough, although I had to constantly remind Gary to speak up and to respond to questions out loud instead of answering with a nod or a shake of his head. On cross-examination, he crumbled. Lamey didn't hold back this time. He went after Gary hard, his cross designed to show that the McKnight Web site stole ideas from its competitor, Lamey's client.

"Is it possible," Lamey said, prowling in front of Gary like a lion stalking its prey, the tails of his gray suit coat flapping behind him with the movement, "that the Easy Click and Shop system you said you designed for McKnight was actually a copy of technology you saw somewhere else?"

Gary blinked again. He looked at me for help, even though I'd told him not to. "I don't think so," he said.

Lamey stopped in front of him. "You're not sure, then?"

I tried to will the answer to Gary by mental telepathy. *Say you're sure, say you're absolutely positive that you created it on your own, just like we practiced.*

Gary missed my telepathy and lamely shrugged his shoulders.

"Let me ask it another way," Lamey said, taking a step toward the witness. "Is it possible that you'd seen something very similar to the Easy Click and Shop system on another Web site before you designed the McKnight site?"

Gary blinked again. "I guess it's possible."

"So, it's possible that you borrowed that technology and used it on the McKnight site." Lamey flipped through some papers as he said this, a trick designed to make Gary think that he had something in writing that could verify his statement.

Gary watched him and licked his lips. "Yeah," he said finally. "It's possible."

I resisted the urge to drop my head in my hands.

I opened the window and let the azure sky push a damp spring breeze through the rental car. I'd finally escaped the clog of cars that surrounded the Loop and was heading east on the Dan Ryan Expressway toward the Skyway. On the passenger seat, I had a bottle of water, a bag of pretzels and a map of the Midwest. Strangely, I didn't actually need the map. I knew the way, as if I could sense the streets and highways that would lead me to the past, to Woodland Dunes, and maybe to the truth about my mother.

Yesterday's closing argument had gone as well as possible, but afterward, when the arbitration room cleared, I'd broken the news to McKnight that Gary's testimony would almost certainly make the arbitrators find for the plaintiff.

McKnight listened, his unreadable eyes watching me, and then he said, "Fine. He'll be gone by this afternoon."

I looked at him incredulously. "You can't fire him!"

"I can, and I will."

"Don't you realize that terminating him is exactly what the plaintiffs want? At trial, they can make a huge issue of how you knew Gary had messed up, and that's why you sacked him. If you keep him on, though, you show confidence in your Web site and your belief that your employee did nothing wrong."

McKnight spread his lips in an insincere smile. "Point taken. He stays until the case is over. Although I suppose we could have avoided this conversation if you'd prepared him correctly."

I felt my jaw clench. The silence of the large room seemed to envelope us, although I could hear the murmurs outside the door; no doubt Lamey was spinning his tale of impending victory for the reporters.

"I worked with him for two days before his deposition, one day last week on the phone, and two nights this week," I said, trying to keep my voice low. "Gary is a very nice person, but he'll never be a good witness. No amount of prep can change that." I hefted my trial bag off the counsel's table, wishing I could launch the thing at McKnight's head. "The arbitrators will call me next week when they've reached a decision. I'll let you know immediately, and we'll come here together to hear it."

He nodded, his face slightly less haughty. "You did a good job. Other than that."

I didn't know whether to take that swing with

the trial bag or thank him, so I only nodded an acknowledgment.

"I mean that," he said. "You're obviously an excellent lawyer." He looked slightly embarrassed, and, for the first time since I met him, he seemed human. It was probably more than he could bear, because he turned and left without a word of goodbye.

Don't think about it, I told myself now, and I turned up the car radio so that it blared an Allman Brothers song. I dug my hand in the bag of pretzels and popped a few in my mouth, washing them down with a swig of water. I found that it wasn't hard to shift my thoughts as I made my way down the Skyway, a multilane raised road that hugged the lake and formed a bridge from Chicago into northern Indiana. Through the line of smokestacks and steel mills, I began to catch glimpses of the lake, a flat, watery carpet of deep blue, the lake that was my playground until my mom died.

Once across the Indiana border and into southern Michigan, I exited and got on a small highway that would take me even closer to the lake. The highway here was more scenic, lined with a couple of rural towns and then long patches of oak trees with nothing to interrupt them. It was odd how familiar it all seemed, how recent the memory. Finally, I reached a stop sign, so faded by the sun it was almost pink. Below it was another sign, black and rectangular with white lettering that read, Welcome To Woodland Dunes.

I didn't hesitate. I stepped on the gas and crossed the threshold. I was back.

3

I passed Franklin Park, a wide plot of green land filled with benches and swing sets and a white gazebo. On the other side of the park lay the softly lapping waves of Lake Michigan. After the park, there were small cottages on either side of the street. Soon, the houses became larger and grander, the old section of Woodland Dunes. I pulled over and checked the slip of paper where I'd written Della's address. I'd never been to her house before.

The street that Della lived on turned east, away from the lake, and coursed through the woods. This was where people built homes when they couldn't afford to live near the water, and as a result, the homes became smaller and closer together again.

Della's house was a trim ranch with brown aluminum siding and a small, unfinished wood porch with a lone rocker. An old blue station wagon was parked in the driveway. I pulled in behind it.

I climbed out of the car, not even pausing to

check my face in the mirror or grab my purse. I hadn't seen Della, the woman who'd been house-keeper and nanny to my family, in more than twenty years, but suddenly I couldn't wait.

There was no bell, so I rapped on the screen door, which rattled back and forth in its casing.

An older Hispanic man dressed in jeans and a golf shirt opened it.

"Is Della home?" I said.

He gave me a kind smile. "Are you Hailey?"

I nodded.

"Well, hello. I'm Martin, Della's husband. I met you years and years ago, but you probably don't remember."

"I'm sorry, I…"

"Don't be silly, you were a little girl. Della will be so happy to see you. She went out to the store. Wasn't sure when you'd be here. Would you like to come in?"

I tried not to show my disappointment. Now that I was there, I was impatient to talk to Della, to find out everything she knew and remembered, but I couldn't bear the thought of making small talk in the interim.

"Actually," I said, "I haven't been to Woodland Dunes in a long time. Maybe I'll just drive around, go by our old house. Do you know who lives there now?"

Martin looked a little surprised. "Oh, no one lives there. Not for a while. They call it the Marker Mansion, after the family that originally built the house at the turn of the century. It's been converted into a cultural center for the town."

"So I could go inside?"

"Sure. They'll even give you a tour."

I thanked him, promised to return in an hour, and headed for my car.

After a five-minute drive, I turned the corner and came face-to-face with the house, the image of my early childhood—its gables, its sloping black roofs, its wide dormered windows on the second floor and the tall oaks and pines that surround the house like a cape. I parked in a large concrete lot that used to be part of the front lawn.

Turning off the ignition, I stared at the house, taking in the Victorian shape and the broad porch with its white wood railing. The house was dove-gray instead of the creamy yellow that my parents always painted it, and there were tall bushes where my mother used to plant flowers. Otherwise, the outside looked much the same. It had resided in my memory for so long, a memory I didn't often visit, that it was strange to see it in person.

I got out of the car, and as I approached the front steps, I saw a small iron sign that read:

Woodland Dunes Cultural Center.
Formerly The Marker Mansion. Built 1905.
Tours Daily 10:00, 11:30, 1:00.

I glanced at my watch. I was just in time for the second tour.

When I stepped onto the porch, I had a sudden vision of a swing that used to hang in the corner. I could almost see my sister, Caroline, sitting there, her feet on the swing, her arms wrapped around her knees, her sandy, straight hair falling around her shoulders. She was always so quiet, so still, and in the summers, she spent much of her time on that swing. She never read or even hummed to herself. She just sat. I remembered myself, years younger than my newly teenage sister, coming out of the house to peek at her, wondering what tragedies she was mulling over. Although no one had given me that impression, I always imagined Caroline as a complicated and tragic figure.

"May I help you?" A voice startled me away from the memory. I turned to see a young woman in the doorway with dark hair twisted up in a loose knot.

"Hi. I'm here for the tour."

"Great. C'mon in." The woman stepped inside and held open the door. "We don't get too many visitors until the summer really starts, so I'm glad to have you."

My first thought when I stepped into the front hall, a wide foyer with molded plaster ceilings, was that the house was much darker now. Maybe I was mistaken or simply remembering poorly, but I always thought the house had been sun-filled and airy, even in the winter. Now the house had a shuttered, impersonal feel, a museum feel, which I supposed wasn't surprising, since it *was* a museum of sorts now.

"I'm Jan," the guide said, extending her hand. She was probably no older than twenty-one. She wore little makeup and a simple outfit of khaki pants and a blue T-shirt.

"Hailey." I shook her hand.

"Are you from around here?"

"No. New York." I didn't mention that I used to be from around here, that I used to *live* in this house. For now, I wanted to keep my memories to myself. It had been so long since I let them in.

"Let's start the tour over here." Jan led the way to the right, past open pocket doors and into the library.

The inlaid mahogany bookshelves were still in place, as were the Tiffany lamps, permanently installed at the top of each shelf. At the end of the room was a huge pink marble fireplace that my dad used to call the "bordello fireplace." It was so tall that I used to be able to walk directly into it without ducking. As I walked toward it now, I realized that I was a long way from that little girl. At five foot six, I could easily reach the mantel.

I took in the whole room, vaguely aware of Jan's talk about how the house had been completed for the Marker family in 1905, how craftsmen had needed the previous six years to complete it. Like the entryway, the library appeared much darker than I remembered, probably because it was now adorned with period furnishings from the early 1900s to make it look as it did back then—heavy red velvet drapes, brass candelabras, uncomfortable-looking high-back chairs. But I saw it as my mother had decorated it—with soft, stuffed chairs and ottomans, vases of fresh flowers, and the corner that was saved just for me, complete with a small child's chair, the replica of the larger ones, and my own miniature bookcases.

"How do you like it?" I heard Jan ask.

"Oh, it's lovely. I was just imagining what it would have been like to live here."

"Well, when the Markers were here, they had a full staff of servants to carry out their every whim, and they entertained often. The Markers were famous for their balls and their travels."

And what about the Sutter family? I wanted to ask. What were they famous for? Does anyone remember them?

Next, Jan led me to a large drawing room on the other side of the hallway. I listened to her speech about the oil paintings and the marble sculptures, because the room held few memories for me. I couldn't recall my family spending much time there.

But no, that wasn't quite right. A recollection came to me of my brother, Dan, seventeen years old when I was only seven, hunched over a scarred octagonal table, his straight blond hair falling over his forehead, writing furiously in his notebook, filling it with his stories. He'd used the room as an escape from the rest of the family, his teenage years making him crave privacy.

"Let's go upstairs now," Jan said.

I followed her back through the lobby and up the wide, dark wood stairway that was covered with a wine-colored carpet runner.

"You'll notice the tapestry on the landing here," Jan said, pausing, one hand resting on a carved wood globe that formed the top of the banister. Her other hand pointed to a silk wall-hanging in colors of gray and salmon. She described how the tapestry had been hand-woven in Italy, how the artist had visited the Markers. But I had quit listening.

I had returned to a moment that had lain buried until now. I saw my mother standing at the bottom of those stairs, dressed in a powder-blue suit, her feet in high heels I'd never seen before. She moved to the front door and opened it. She spoke to someone, their voices hushed, one voice much deeper than the other. A hand was on her blue shoulder. A large man's hand. A ring on his finger. The soft sounds of crying. Then my mother swayed, nearly fell.

I had watched this scene, I realized, from the landing where I now stood. I'd been dressed in my favorite pair of jeans and the shirt with the sunflower on the front, my face peering around the post at the top of the landing.

"Are you all right?"

I focused on Jan's face, her eyes wary. "Sure, sure. I'm fine." I looked back down the staircase again, but the vision was gone.

"Well, come on up this way. I'll show you the bedrooms."

I followed Jan again, surprised at the sudden, vivid flash of my mother. It had been ages since I'd really remembered her in any detail. There were the vague recollections, like how she ran every night, even if it was raining, sometimes coming in the house with her long hair dripping in sheets, her chest heaving as if she'd been chased and not out for a leisurely jog, and later the feel of that hair sweeping my cheek as she leaned over me, kissing me good-night, the smell of lavender on her skin.

"This bedroom belonged to Catherine, the Markers' only daughter," Jan said, leading me to the first bedroom at the top of the stairs.

I remembered it well. It used to be mine.

The walls were still painted peach, the fireplace still white, and a canopy bed still stood in the corner. The bed, though, which was made of dark wood, its canopy designed with heavy velvet, was different from the one I loved so much. Mine was white with an eyelet covering. Seeing the bed and the room brought back another flood of memories: myself in the bed, quilt up to my neck, reading until my mother insisted that the lights be turned off; my friend, Patsy, and I playing in front of the fireplace that was never lit; Caroline helping me with my homework at the desk against the wall.

How odd, I thought, that so few of those memories included my dad. But maybe it wasn't so strange, since he'd spent most of his weekdays working in Chicago and most of the weeknights at his apartment there. And yet, my memories after Woodland Dunes are exclusively of my father and me. No one else.

Jan showed me through three other bedrooms, two of which had been occupied twenty years ago by my siblings. She stopped in the hallway before the master bedroom and pointed out an intercom system that had been installed by the Markers in order to talk to their servants.

"The intercom hasn't worked in a long time," Jan said. "At least not since the cultural center moved in here."

"And when was that?"

"The early eighties."

"Really?" The early eighties were when my family moved away from Woodland Dunes. "Why did the town want this specific house?"

"Well, I don't know that they actually wanted this particular home, but from what I heard, they got it at a great price. The people who'd lived here before couldn't sell it."

"Why was that?"

Jan made a show of looking around, even though there was no one else near us. "We're not supposed to talk about this," she said in a conspiratorial whisper, "but a lady died here."

I was quiet. I felt as if I was holding my breath and didn't know how to let it out. I'd never known where my mom was when she died or exactly how it had happened. I was only seven at the time, and I didn't remember anything—nothing at all— which had always troubled me. And yet my father and I rarely talked about the subject. When we did, or I should say when *I* did, it was too painful for him. *She became ill,* he would say, tapping his head as if to indicate some injury or disease in the brain. His eyes would cloud over, making me fearful he might cry. I knew I looked like her in some ways—my slim build, my wide shoulders, my long sandy hair. I always assumed that resemblance, combined with the horrible memories, made it too painful for him to talk about her death. And so I never stayed on the topic for long. What difference did it make, really? Eventually, I managed to ignore the issue altogether. But that letter had let loose the wonderings again.

"There was some talk, I guess," Jan said. "The rumor was that someone had done something to her. I got this all secondhand, of course. I was just a baby when it happened." She checked her watch. "Anyway, let's finish up."

She started to take a step away, but I grabbed her arm. She looked at my hand, then at me in surprise.

"I'm sorry." I took my hand away. "I didn't mean to startle you, but can you tell me what you mean by the rumors. I mean, what were the rumors, exactly?"

Jan gave me another wary look and rubbed at the spot on her arm. "I don't know really. Like I said, we're not supposed to talk about this on the tour, and I wasn't around to hear about it at the time."

"I understand." I tried to make my voice easy, conversational. "But what have you heard? I'm just curious."

Jan paused a moment, then shrugged. "Well, to be honest, I heard someone killed her, but no one was ever charged, so I'm sure it's one of those old wives' tales. Now let me show you the master."

I trailed behind, her words reverberating in my mind. *Someone killed her.*

We entered the master bedroom, a large space with a huge bay window of curved glass at the opposite end. A secretary's desk was tucked into the bay, but I remembered how my mother had installed a long bench under that window and covered it with pillows. I would often find her there, writing in her journal or just looking through the glass onto the front lawn.

I studied the rest of the room, and the cold feeling returned. I remembered so many things all of a sudden—my parent's king-size bed against the right wall, a bureau of cherrywood with a mirror over it, more flowers, my mother's yellow sweater hanging over a chair, an armoire to match the dresser, paperbacks and tissue on one nightstand, a lone alarm clock on the other. Recollections poured into my brain with such speed that they startled me. And yet, there was something else about the room that I couldn't recall.

"Thank you," I said, interrupting Jan's remarks. "I have to be going."

I turned and left the room.

"Is something wrong?" Her voice followed me.

I hurried down the stairs, distantly hearing Jan's feet pounding behind me, until I made myself stop on the landing. *Be calm,* I told myself. *Be calm.* It wouldn't be good to act crazy when I'd come here seeking answers.

I opened my mouth to say something, but as I gazed down the stairs, I saw my mother again in the powder-blue suit. She was struggling to stand, holding a hand to the back of her head. The doorbell rang once, then again, then pounding came from the door. My mother moved slowly, inching toward the doorway, the white of her hand never leaving her head, holding it gingerly, as if she was keeping her hairstyle in place.

"Is something wrong?" I heard Jan say again.

"No. Nothing at all." And I turned away, because if I said anything else, I might have told her what I suddenly knew—that my mother, Leah Sutter, died in this house.

4

After leaving the Marker Mansion, formerly the Sutter home—my home—I drove slowly, not sure where I was going, letting the sights of Woodland Dunes fill my head and refresh my memories of the place. I passed the town's riding stables, matching white barns with green roofs resting on a large field, a white fence surrounding the property. Patsy and I used to ride there on Saturdays, eating brown-bag lunches in the long grass behind the barns when we were done. The town's championship golf course with its rolling greens and intermittent circles of sand appeared the same as it did years ago, just like the lighthouse at Murphy's Point.

I turned left on the outskirts of town, then left again toward the lake. And suddenly, there it was. A square plot of land on a hillside dotted with trees and sprinkled with gray and white headstones. The Woodland Dunes Cemetery. I hadn't realized I was so close. In fact, I didn't know if I could have found it if I tried.

I pulled into the lot, the tires of the rental car crunching over the gravel. As I got out, I remembered where to go. My dad had brought me here a few times before we moved. I walked toward the far left corner, the heels of my loafers sinking into the damp, spongy ground. I passed an older man in jogging clothes squatting over a small, simple headstone. He pulled stray weeds with a quick hand as if accustomed to the movement.

I stopped when I came to the tall white column made of stone, an angel on either side looking down, protecting the grave. A grayish-green film had made its home in some of the crevices of my mother's memorial, around the angel's wings and in the edges of the lettering that read: Leah Rose Sutter, Beloved Wife and Mother, 1942–1982. The rest of the grave site was remarkably clean. No weeds or sand on it like some of the others nearby.

Then I noticed it. A single yellow tulip lying at the base of the monument. I stood completely still, staring at it, my mind latching onto our old house again, wandering the rooms inside, seeing it the way my mother had always kept it. Flowers below the porch, blooms in the vases in the library, and more flowers in her bedroom. In the spring, when the air was new and clean as it was now, those flowers were usually tulips, mostly yellow.

I wrapped my arms around myself. The fact that my mother loved yellow tulips, and the fact that this one had been placed by her headstone had to be a coincidence. I wasn't aware of anyone who visited her grave. My mother's own parents had died a few years after her, and she had no siblings. Once we moved away, my father and I never returned. As far as Dan and Caroline were concerned, I didn't know where they were. They had both been so much older than me. After my mom died, Caroline had gone off to boarding school and Dan to college. We never really saw them after that. My dad and I moved all over for his work at the firm—San Francisco, London, Paris, Long Island—and when I asked about Caroline and Dan, he said that they had their own lives and families. He gave the impression that they didn't want to be a part of ours any longer.

Maybe the flower had come loose from a nearby bouquet. I glanced at the other grave sites. Some were untended and nearly overgrown. A few had small flower arrangements but no tulips.

When I looked back at my mother's grave, I had the odd feeling that someone was watching me. A few more glances around told me that I imagined it. The man in the jogging clothes had turned away, walking back to the parking lot.

I bent down and lifted the bud. It looked fairly new, only two of the petals showing signs of droop, probably no more than a day or two old. I laid it gently on the cool stone again, wondering who could have left it here. No matter. I was grateful to the person for honoring my mother, for remembering her.

This time, there were two cars parked in Della's driveway. As I pulled in behind them, the front door flew open, and a short woman dressed in gray slacks and a sleeveless white blouse rushed down the sidewalk. I got out of the car and opened my arms to hug Della, the woman who'd helped raise me until we moved away from Woodland Dunes, and someone I recalled well, as if there was nothing to fear from my memories of her.

"Oh, Hailey." Della held a warm hand to my cheek. "You're so grown-up. You look so much like your mom."

"Thank you." Other than my father, I didn't come across many people who knew my mom, and I liked hearing about the resemblance.

Della took me by the hand and led me around the back of the house where she had a pitcher of iced tea and a tray of cookies waiting on a metal patio table. The branches from a tall oak tree formed a canopy of shade, the breeze making its leaves ruffle and whisper.

Della fussed over me, telling me to sit in one of the chairs. While she spooned ice into our glasses and placed a few cookies on a paper plate, I noticed how little she had changed. Her olive skin was still smooth, her cheeks still full with a pink glow. Her hair, though obviously dyed to keep its black color, still lay in crinkled waves to her chin. She'd put on a few pounds, but they only made her seem more like the comforting figure of my memories.

"Tell me," Della said, settling into the chair next to me. "Tell me everything about you."

I talked about law school, my job, my apartment in Manhattan. When I finally slowed down, I took a bite of an oatmeal-raisin cookie, the soft, sweet taste raising a recollection of Della in our old house, lifting a baking sheet out of the oven, placing a hand on my head, telling me to wait until they were cool.

"And you're not married?" Della said. She bit into her own cookie, but her eyes watched me, waiting for an answer.

"No. I'm a long way from married."

"No one special then?"

I shook my head. "A few years ago, I was dating someone seriously." I thought of Michael, sitting bare-chested in his bed, eyes playful, holding firm to my hand, trying to pull me back under the covers.

"And what happened to that?"

I shrugged. The therapist I'd seen after Michael and I broke up had nodded her head at the end of our first and only session and said in a grave tone, "Abandonment issues," as if she was making a horrible diagnosis like, "Permanent facial disfigurement." It was natural, she said, for a child who lost a parent so young to have such feelings, but I couldn't carry them over into my adult relationships and push people away. I knew she had a point, but I had never learned how to avoid keeping most people at arm's length. I got busy with the bar exam, and I didn't keep up with the prescribed weekly appointments. Michael met someone at his firm our first year out of law school, and he slid away from me the way the others had. I didn't think I was ever really in love with Michael, or with any of them for that matter.

I felt that I'd know true love when a kiss could make everything, the rest of the world, disappear. I kept waiting for that moment with Michael. I didn't expect it to happen right away, but I hoped each time. I'd close my eyes, feel his lips settle over mine, and while I enjoyed it, I was always still right there. Nothing ever disappeared, not the Miles Davis music Michael always played or his high-rise apartment where we often stayed. I began to wonder if maybe I was incapable of feeling that kind of love, or maybe I was laboring beneath an unattainable fantasy.

Della asked me about college at UCLA, about high school on Long Island, about the tutors in Europe and grade school before that in San Francisco. And then we were back to Woodland Dunes, to the year my father and I left.

"I missed you all so much when you were gone," Della said. She raised a paper napkin to her eyes, and I wondered for a second if she was going to cry. "It was like a part of my family had left." Her voice creaked, betraying her age. "Of course, I had my own family to take care of. Max was twelve and Delphine ten. My husband said I had to get over it. I had to get over Leah's death and get a new job."

"And did you?"

"Oh, I got other jobs, although never as a housekeeper or a nanny again. I cleaned office buildings for a janitorial service, and I cooked meals for the sick." Della tsked, as if none of that had mattered much. "I never got over Leah."

"You two were close," I said. An image drifted back of my mom and Della in the kitchen, sun slanting through the high window over the sink, the two of them laughing as they washed dishes. It seemed to me now that my mother probably kept Della around as much for her company as her housekeeping skills. I couldn't remember my mom having any other close friends.

"She was a wonderful woman." Della's voice was softer now. "A good friend. And I miss her every day."

I stayed silent, and tilted my head up for a moment, watching a squirrel above me racing from branch to branch. I had missed my mom every day, too, but not in the same way. I longed for the vague concept of my mother, of *a* mother in my life. I missed her especially when I was learning about boys, shopping for prom dresses, graduating from college, from law school. I had my dad for all those things, and he tried to be everything— father, mother, friend—but sometimes I craved female guidance and companionship. My friendship with Maddy had filled some of that void, yet no one could totally replace a mother.

"How did she die?" It was the question I came to ask, the one that had been haunting me since I read that letter, but I hadn't meant to say it so abruptly.

Della sat straighter in her chair, then raised a hand to her lips. She lifted her shoulders, then let them fall again. "It's hard to say. What do you remember?"

I pushed my mind back to that time when I was seven years old. I remember not needing to ask the question of how she had died, as if I had known the answer and didn't want to be reminded. But somewhere along the way, I lost the knowledge.

"I don't really remember anything specific," I said. "That's the problem. And I need to know."

Della pushed her plate away and leaned on the table. "Do you remember talking to the police?"

I felt a strange pulse beating in my neck. "The police? I talked to the police?"

"We all did."

I tried to conjure up some sense of my seven-year-old self, in a police station, sitting across from a detective, swinging my legs underneath the table. "I don't remember."

"Well, they never made any decisions. They never drew any conclusions. Just looked into her death and closed the file. It got people to talking, though."

"I remember the whispering and the looks," I said, slightly agitated now that I was getting close to the topic, yet not learning anything. "But why did the police look into it?"

A gust of wind blew through the backyard, pushing Della's hair into her face. She brushed it away; she sighed loud enough that I heard it over the breeze. "Oh, sweetie, your mother died from a blow to the head. They wanted to find out if someone had done that to her on purpose."

5

I checked into the Long Beach Inn, an aptly named bed-and-breakfast perched above a lengthy stretch of tawny sand that hemmed Lake Michigan. Because the summer season hadn't yet started, I was able to get an upstairs room. It was the largest one, I'd been told by the housekeeper, who was filling in for the owner. The room took up half the third floor, a sunny space painted white, like a summer cottage. A large canopy bed covered in pillows sat in the center. The French doors on the other side led to a balcony and, beyond that, the beach. I had always dreamed of a balcony off my bedroom overlooking the water, but I was too preoccupied now to enjoy it.

I unpacked the way I always did in hotels. I traveled so often that I liked to try to create a semblance of home for myself, even if it was a fictional and transient one. Once my clothes were in the closet and my makeup in the bathroom cabinet, I called Maddy to tell her what I'd learned. For once I got no answer at either her home or cell phone. There was no one else I could tell about what I was doing, what I'd discovered.

I closed my eyes and let myself hear Della's words again.

Your mother died from a blow to the head. They wanted to find out if someone had done that to her on purpose.

It only confirmed what I'd thought—that something strange surrounded my mother's death. What did it mean that my mom had died of a head injury? Did that necessarily mean that someone had purposefully hurt her? I had asked Della those questions before I bolted, but she had shrugged. "There were lots of stories about what happened, but mostly people said it was an accident," she'd said. "No one really knows."

But someone knew. The person who'd sent the letter knew. Or at least they thought they did.

The sound of a vacuum downstairs made me realize I was standing in the middle of the room, motionless. I'd had so much momentum all day. What to do now? Though the room was cozy, a huge step up from the impersonal hotel where I'd stayed in Chicago, I wished for my own apartment right then, for my comfy sweatpants and the taupe chenille blanket my father had given me. Under different circumstances, I would have loved to curl up on the canopy bed here with a book, but I couldn't just sit around. Not now. I couldn't stand the thought of being in Woodland Dunes and not be moving, remembering, doing. I wasn't here for a weekend getaway. I was here for my mother.

The thought drew me to the French doors, but for a moment, I didn't open them. I stared out at the wide beach, the gray-blue water licking the sand. As I watched the rush and recede of the water, I remembered the feel of my small hand in my father's as he led me down the unfinished wood pathway to the lake. I must have been about six or seven years old. He had come home to Woodland Dunes that day, a treat for the middle of the week.

"Where's Mom?" he'd said when he was inside the front door. He crouched down and held open his arms. "Is she taking her walk on the beach?"

I nodded and charged into him, wrapping myself around his neck, breathing in the slightly stale scent of the city he always brought with him.

"Let's find her," he said.

We walked the two blocks to the lakefront and then down the wood sidewalk to the sand. We pulled off our shoes, my dad rolling up the bottoms of his suit pants.

"Which way?" he said, his voice playful. "You pick."

I bounced on my toes with excitement. I looked both ways down the beach. The sun was growing gold and heavy, but it wasn't dark yet. To my right, the houses were grand, some of them as big as hotels. To the left, they grew smaller and friendlier, and there were usually more kids that way, so I raised my left arm and pointed.

"You got it, Hailey-girl," my dad said.

We walked along the water where it was packed wet and hard, looking for beach glass, the colored shards of glass, rounded and smoothed by years spent in the water.

"Here's a great one," my dad said, bending down to lift a green piece the size of a quarter.

I held out my hand, but just then I saw a flash of pink farther down the beach. I looked closer, and I could see my mother's pink T-shirt, the length of her sandy blond hair.

"Mom!" I called.

My father stood in one quick motion, the glass falling from his hand. I knelt to pick it up. When I stood again, I saw my mother hadn't heard me. She was standing a few hundred yards away, her back to us, and she was talking to someone.

"Let's go see Mom," I said, tugging my father's hand, but he refused to move. He was frozen, it seemed, with his pants rolled up, his suit coat over his arm, staring at his wife.

I looked at my mom again, too. I couldn't see who she was talking to, but I could tell it was a man, someone a little taller than her, and for a second, I saw the man reach out and put a hand on my mom's shoulder.

"Let's go." My dad pulled my hand so hard I almost cried out. He marched me back the way we came, pulling me down the beach. In my other hand, I gripped tight to the beach glass, trying not to drop it. When I looked up, my father's jaw was hard, his eyes narrow. A few times, I almost stumbled as he propelled us over the sand.

When we reached the wood walk that would take us back to the street, he slowed so we could sit and pull on our shoes.

"Did I do something wrong?" I asked.

He looked at me as if I'd said a terrible thing, then he pulled me to him, hugging me so close it was difficult to breathe.

"Everything's all right." He released me, but I thought for a moment he might cry because of the way his eyes were pulled down, the way his mouth seemed ready to tremble. "Let's go home."

We walked back quickly, not strolling as we had on the way to the beach. When we reached the house, he said he loved me very much but he'd forgotten something at the office. He needed to go back that night.

I sat on the window bench in my room, watching him pull out of the driveway. The bench reminded me of the larger one in my parents' room where my mother often rested and wrote in her journals. Usually, when I sat on my own bench, it made me feel a little like my mom, and that made me happy. That night, though, staring out at the now dark lawn, I didn't want to be my mother. She'd made my dad leave, and I only wanted him to come back.

When my mother came in the room, I was still there. "You made him go away," I said.

"What?" My mother raised a hand and smoothed the pink cotton front of her T-shirt.

"Dad was here. We saw you on the beach, and he left."

My forehead was touching the glass of the French doors. Still, I peered at the beach, thinking over this new memory the way I studied a witness's testimony after a deposition.

I'd always assumed my parents were happy together, from the devastation my father experienced after she passed away. But was my mother involved with someone else? I knew my father had been upset with her that day, but I'd been too young to draw any conclusions. Now it seemed possible my mother was having an affair.

I opened the French doors and went onto the balcony. The spring air was balmy and light. I leaned on the painted white railing and gazed at the beach, trying to bring back more of the memory, the parts that had happened before and later, but nothing else came.

Just a few blocks to my left was where my father and I had taken our walk, where my mother had stood with the man. Just because he was a man, though, didn't mean my mother was involved with him. Why was I so quick to jump to the conclusion that my mother had been unfaithful? The hand on my mother's shoulder, the way she'd smoothed down her pink shirt when she'd come to my room, that was why.

I sank down on the Adirondack chair, painted white to match the railing. The hand had reminded me of the vision I'd had on the stairs today, of the hand that I had seen steady my mother at the door. The lawyer in me confronted myself. How can you assume it was the same person? And even if it *were* true, who was he? Did it matter? He might not have anything to do with her death.

I ran a hand through my hair. I was going in circles. This happened to me sometimes during a big case. My mind wound around too many details, unable to see the important things.

I threw on a pair of khaki shorts, a long-sleeved

shirt and sandals. Once down on the beach, I walked to the left, the way my mother had headed that day, the way I'd followed with my father. A soft breeze blew, playing with my hair, pushing it in my eyes. There were only a few people on the beach—a jogger and an older couple who were camped out with chairs and a cooler. The couple gave me a happy wave.

As I walked, I gazed across the lake toward Chicago. If I narrowed my eyes, I could see the blocky outlines of the Sears Tower and the Hancock Building through the hazy sun. Somewhere over there, probably on Monday morning the arbitrators would come to their decision on the McKnight case, or maybe it was done already. Either way, it seemed a lose/lose situation. If I lost the arb, I'd have to work with Sean McKnight during a trial, and if I won, he might hire me again. The thought of dealing with his arrogant attitude on another case was not pleasant. I made myself find the bright side. If I won, it might be what I needed to ensure I would make partner. Some associates thought I was a shoo-in, knowing my father was on the executive committee, but the reality was that the higher-ups were so afraid of nepotism accusations that I had to prove myself more than the average attorney. Winning the McKnight case could help seal the deal.

I stopped walking when I saw a glint in the sand. Reaching down, I wrapped my fingers around a piece of clear beach glass, rounded to a perfect oval. I rubbed it between my fingers, caressing its smooth, dusty surface. It had the same feel as the green beach glass I'd found with my dad that day.

When I got back to the inn, I looked at the clock over the front desk, surprised it was almost three in the afternoon. I hadn't eaten anything for lunch except those few cookies at Della's.

"Can I help you?" A man in his late twenties or early thirties came out of the back room. He grabbed a handful of the rusty hair that had fallen over his eyes and pushed it away, but it fell right back again.

"Oh no," I said. "I'm already checked in." I pointed uselessly with my finger toward my room upstairs as if that might provide some explanation.

"I'm Ty." He held his hand over the desk. "Ty Manning."

He wasn't much taller than me, but he had a presence about him. When he smiled, his blue eyes crinkled a little around the corners.

"Hailey." I shook his hand. "That's an interesting name—Ty."

"It's short for Tyler, which is too preppy–East Coast–boarding school, don't you think?"

"Sure," I said, unable to imagine this guy who wore old jeans and an olive T-shirt going to a boarding school on the East Coast or being called Tyler. I knew a million of those types from Manhattan, and unlike my first impression of Ty, they were much more arrogant, much more reserved. "So, do you work here?"

"I own the place."

I could feel my eyebrows rise. "You own the inn?"

"Yeah. My parents bought it years ago. Their plan was to rehab it and run it as a B and B for an early retirement. My dad can't seem to retire though, so I bought it from them."

"I'm impressed."

"You are?" He gave me a disarming smile, and again, his eyes crinkled with his grin. "Thanks. Which room do you have?"

"Third floor on the right. It's beautiful."

"I call it the nap room because I feel like lying down every time I'm in there."

I laughed. "I can understand that."

Ty turned around and reached into a multileveled box where they kept the keys. "You said your name was Hailey, so your last name must be—" he lifted out a piece of paper with my check-in information, "—Sutter."

"Right."

He glanced up at me. "That sounds familiar."

"I used to be from around here."

"Ah."

"Do you know someplace I can get lunch?" I said. "It's been a while since I've been in Woodland Dunes."

"Sure. I can make a few recommendations." He looked at the check-in slip a moment longer before he put it back in the box, then turned back to me, his lazy hair falling farther over one eye. "Mind if I join you?"

"Oh." I hadn't expected him to ask that, although it wasn't a totally unappealing thought. "Don't you have to stay here?"

"Nah, everyone's checked in, and Elaine, my housekeeper, she's like my right hand. She can deal with anything." He paused a second. "But if you'd rather be alone, I can tell you where to go." He pulled a map out from under the desk and placed in on the counter.

Alone. I thought about it a minute. It might be the best thing since I needed to keep looking, to keep pushing in corners until I found out what happened to my mother. Yet I wasn't sure what my next step was, and it would be helpful to have someone who knew the area.

Truth was, I was feeling a little rattled. I didn't want to be alone right now.

I smiled at Ty. "Let's go."

* * *

Ty took me to a diner called Bingham's, where we could sit in the sun. The restaurant was in the downtown section of town. It still boasted quaint shingled buildings and bricked sidewalks, just as it used to when my family had lived there, but the stores that used to sell hardware, flowers and crafts had been replaced with a designer boutique, a coffee shop and an upscale delicatessen.

I suppose I shouldn't have been surprised at the change. Decades had passed since we'd left. During that time, Woodland Dunes and the surrounding towns had morphed into sort of a Midwest version of the Hamptons—a summer enclave for those looking to escape the city. When my parents had originally bought here, they too used the place as a summer retreat, but my mom had fallen in love with it. They had two children then, Dan and Caroline, both of whom adored the space and the freedom they couldn't get in the city, so my parents made the house near the lake their permanent home. My dad bought an apartment in Chicago for the nights he couldn't get home during the week.

My dad had told me this much. He'd always been willing to talk about the early days, about the afternoon he met my mom at University of Chicago, their wedding at the Palmer House, and how they'd moved to Woodland Dunes. But I learned not to ask questions about anything after that. Seeing the pain in my father's eyes was too difficult. He was the only family I had, and I wasn't willing to risk losing him, as well. So I learned to push away the wonderings. The letter had brought all those questions back, though, and I didn't have the power to bury them again.

We placed our orders, Ty joking with the owner, who gave him two complimentary lemonades.

Sitting under the red-and-white-striped awning, I bit into my turkey sandwich, suddenly starving. "Good?" I asked Ty, watching him dig into his food.

"Excellent," he said between mouthfuls of a broccoli and cheddar omelet. "I love breakfast foods after breakfast. I eat weird stuff first thing in the morning, too, like sushi and pasta."

"Cold pizza. That's a good breakfast."

Ty's fork stopped in midair, and he smiled wide. "Exactly."

We talked, and I told him about my job and my life in Manhattan. Ty explained the work he'd done on Long Beach Inn before it opened.

"How did you know how to do all that stuff?" I asked. I finished the last bit of my sandwich and sank back into my chair.

"After I got out of college, I came home and worked construction. I was pretty lost during that time. No idea what I wanted to do, but the construction paid off. I learned a hell of a lot. Because of that, I was able to either do the work at the inn myself or find someone fast who knew how."

"How do you like living in Woodland Dunes?" I said. "I vaguely remember living here as a kid, but now that I'm in New York, it's hard for me to imagine."

"You know what? I love it here. When I first came home after school, I thought I'd just get my act together and head out again. I didn't think I'd stay for good, but once I took a breather and looked around, I loved a lot about this town."

"Like what?"

"Oh, geez," Ty said, as if there were too many things. "I love the beach, the people, the way everybody knows me and the way anyone would help me if I needed it. I love the crazy summers when the bars are packed and people are crawling all over my place, and I love it when the fall ends too, and it gets quiet. It's like having the best of both worlds—parties and crowds for five months, R & R the rest of the year."

I nodded. I liked the picture he painted. There was never a respite from the teeming people or the noise in Manhattan.

Ty waved to a woman walking her dog on the other side of the street, then shifted in his chair so he faced me directly. The sun picked up the freckles that dotted his cheekbones. "So you were how old when you lived here?" he said.

"We left when I was seven. I remember school the most. The playground and Mrs. Howard, my first-grade teacher. I went to Dunes Primary." It occurred to me that maybe I'd been at the same school as Ty. "Maybe we were there together?"

"No, I went to St. Bonaventure, or St. Bonnie's as we called it. Twelve years of Catholic repression for this kid." Ty glanced down for a second. "I think I remember you, though, or at least hearing about you."

"You do?" Despite the sun on my skin, I felt goose bumps prickle the back of my arms.

Ty watched me. "Your mom died, didn't she? When you lived here?"

"That's right."

"I remember that. I saw a picture of your family that was taken at the funeral."

"Where did you see it?" Maybe it had been in the paper, something I could dig up.

Ty scratched his jaw, looking a little uncomfortable for the first time since I met him. "I saw it in my dad's office."

"Your dad? Who's your dad?"

"He's the chief of police."

"Wait a minute," I said, after a moment spent digesting Ty's words. My stomach felt slightly ill, but there was a tickle of excitement. "This picture you saw was in the police station?"

Ty nodded.

"Why?" I asked.

"I don't know all the details. I was just a kid too, but…" He trailed off.

"Look, I don't know much about my mom's death," I said. "It's why I'm here. So please, just tell me what you know."

A look of surprise came over Ty's face, and I realized I might have spoken a little harshly.

"I'm sorry." I leaned toward him. "I had a case in Chicago last week. I'm an attorney. But the point is, I came here to see what I could find out about my mother's death. Anything you could tell me would be a help."

"Wow." Ty shook his head. "That's tough. But as I said, I don't know much. What I recall is waiting for my dad in his office at the station. It was a big day for me because he was going to take me to get my uniform and equipment so I could start football. My dad wasn't the chief then. He was assistant chief. Anyway, I was playing around his desk, and when he came in, I was holding that picture. There was a coffin being moved into the ground, and your family stood around it. You had on a long yellow coat."

I nodded. My Easter coat, the one my mom had picked out for me.

"When my dad saw me with the picture," Ty continued, "he stopped, pointed to the coffin and said, 'Do you know what that is?' I told him there was somebody who was dead in there. He said, 'That's right. A dead lady, and I'm going to find out who killed her.'"

I took a breath. "But they never charged anyone, did they?"

He shook his head again. "My dad told me sometime later that he'd been wrong, that no one had killed her or meant for her to die."

I felt a little gust of relief. If the police had ruled out murder, then maybe whoever had sent me the letter was simply mistaken. "Would your dad talk about this?"

"I think so. I mean, I don't see why not. He's fishing this weekend. He won't be back until tomorrow night. Will you still be around?"

I didn't answer right away. I'd been planning on going back to Chicago Sunday night so I could wait for the arbitration decision that should come sometime Monday or Tuesday. But talking to the police might be just what I needed to set my mind straight, and I could follow up on some other questions in the meantime. And then there was Ty with his freckles.

"Can I keep my room at the hotel?" I asked.

He made a face like he was thinking hard about it. "For you, I'll make it happen."

"Yeah?" I said, surprised to hear the coy tone of my voice.

"Definitely."

"I'll be around," I told him.

6

For the third time that day, I pulled into Della's driveway, still thinking about my lunch with Ty. Over lemonade, I had told him what I knew about my mom's death, about the letter, and about my visit with Della this morning. I hadn't meant to spill the whole tale—it was so unlike me—but I was unusually comfortable with him, and once I started talking, it was cathartic to get the story out.

Ty had asked me if I'd spoken to my brother or sister. They would be obvious places to start, he said. Obvious, yes, but I had no idea where either of them were, a fact that had always gnawed at me, confused me. When I got up the nerve to ask my dad about either of my siblings, he became visibly upset, telling me that they had their own lives now. During college, I went through a period when I longed for companionship, for family, and I made a halfhearted attempt at finding them. I called Information in different cities where I thought they might be. The Internet wasn't widely used then, but I had a friend who was adept at computers do some digging. Neither of us could find a Caroline or Dan Sutter. And so I eventually gave up.

Ty thought I should call my father right then and ask him, point-blank, what had happened and where my brother and sister were, but I wasn't ready for that yet. Old habits weren't easy to kill, and I still abhorred the idea of distressing my father, of picking at old wounds.

The last time I raised the issue was shortly after I met Maddy in law school. It was so weird, she had said over and over, that I didn't know how my mom had died, that I didn't know what had happened to my brother and sister.

"I *know*," I'd said, irritated that I'd told her to begin with.

But Maddy's questions stayed with me, and so I brought up the topic a few weeks later on a Sunday afternoon. I was with my dad on his patio, sipping a glass of cabernet while he grilled steaks for us.

"Do you ever think about Mom?" I said, apropos of nothing.

He dropped the grill tongs he was holding. They clattered on the stone patio tiles. He bent over to pick them up, and when he stood, he looked like a confused old man instead of a confident trial lawyer. His face was slack.

"Of course," he said quietly, his gaze asking me how I could ask such a question.

But still I pushed. "Really?" I said. "Do you really?"

"Yes, Hailey. I think about your mother all the time." He blinked.

"Well, you never talk about her. You never talk about when she died."

A strange, garbled sound erupted from inside my father's throat, making me stop my words. I could have sworn he was about to cry, something I had never seen, and I bailed.

"I'm sorry," I said. I stood and took the tongs from him. "Let me do that."

And, like an old man, he feebly handed them to me, wiping the grease from his hands on his immaculate khaki pants before he went into the house.

I had never brought up the issue again. If I could find my own answers, without confronting the parent who raised me on his own, I wanted to do that.

Which brought me back to Della's.

"Sweetie!" Della said when she opened the front door now, a dish towel thrown over one shoulder. "Come in, come in."

"Thanks." I accepted a quick hug. "I hope I'm not bothering you."

"Not at all." Della led me into the kitchen, a large, green-painted room smelling of garlic and

crowded with plants, knickknacks and crocheted
pot holders. It was the type of warm, homey
kitchen I'd always hoped my father and I would
have, one that was lived in, that was used to cook
for a large family. My dad wasn't much of a chef,
though, and so although our homes were lovely
and expensive, the kitchens always had cold tiles
and stainless-steel appliances, and I never spent
much time there.

"Martin has poker tonight," Della said, "but I'm
making enchiladas and salsa, so you're just in time.
I'm glad you're here, because I was worried about
you when you left. I hope I didn't upset you."

I leaned against a countertop while Della picked
up a carving knife on the butcher-block island. "I
was startled, that's all."

Della nodded and began chopping cilantro,
sending the scent of it into the air to mix with the
garlic. "You all moved away so fast when Leah
died. I always wondered if that was the best thing
for you kids after losing your mom."

"I guess my dad thought it was right." At least
I assumed that's what my father thought. We had
never talked about his rationalization for that first
move out of Woodland Dunes and over the ocean
to London and Paris or the next to San Francisco,
except that my dad said the firm needed him in
those particular cities. When I was fourteen, and

he told me we were moving again, I put my foot down, telling him this had to be the last move, that I wanted to go to high school in the same place for all four years. So we moved one more time to Long Island, and my father hasn't left New York since.

"Oh, I don't mean to second-guess your father," Della said. "Part of my thinking was probably because I missed you all so much. Danny was ready to go off to college, but I don't know that Caroline was quite prepared for boarding school."

I stood away from the counter and blurted out the questions I'd returned to ask. "Do you hear from them? Do you know where they are now?"

Della abruptly stopped dicing cilantro, and it was a moment before she looked up at me. "You don't talk to your brother and sister?"

I shook my head, aware of a ticking clock somewhere in the room.

Della opened her mouth as if to say something, but she paused first. "You don't keep in touch at all?"

"I did get a few letters from Caroline when she was in boarding school, but I haven't seen either of them since my mom died."

Della laid the knife on the butcher block and came around to me. "Let's sit down." She led me to a polished wood table.

We both sat, and I leaned forward, ready to listen, to learn anything I could. "Do you know where they are now?"

Della took the dish towel off her shoulder and slowly rubbed her hands. "I don't know if your father would want me to talk about this. Shouldn't you ask him these questions?"

"Look, Della," I said. "My dad and I are very, very close, but there's one thing we don't talk about, which is the time when my mom died. And I'd really like to find my brother and sister. It's been way too long for a family not to see each other."

Della's concerned face watched me as I spoke, then she looked down and kept rubbing her hands with the towel. I forced myself to endure the silence even though I didn't understand it.

"Wait here," Della said. She left the room for a minute or so. When she returned, she was carrying two stacks of envelopes, one thin, the other thicker.

"I used to hear from Caroline regularly, maybe once a year," she said, placing the larger pile of envelopes before me. "These are most of the letters. A few I misplaced or threw away. I haven't heard from her for a year or two now. The last place she wrote me from was Portland."

I ran my finger over the top envelope made of thin, peach paper. In the left corner was a label that read "Caroline Ramsey" and an address on Northeast Jarrett Street in Portland.

"So she's married?" I said, looking up at Della.

Della nodded. "She sounds very happy. I think there's even a picture in there." She placed the other stack before me. There were only four envelopes. "I've saved everything I've received from Dan, but again it's been a while. Last I heard he was out in Santa Fe."

The top letter was in a plain, white envelope, and just as Della had said, it bore a return address from Santa Fe, New Mexico.

"Can I keep these?" I asked. "Just for a few days, I mean."

"Don't worry. That's why I brought them out. You can have them."

She put her hand on my head, stroking my bangs back, making me remember the way she had done that same thing once when I was a small child. I'd been sick, I remembered, and Della had carried my lunch on a white tray to my room. I hadn't been able to eat, so she sat on the side of my bed and stroked my hair until I fell asleep.

Odd, I thought, that it should have been Della taking care of me that day and not my mother, but I had the distinct recollection of my mother being absent, of Della coming to get me from school, Della taking my temperature and helping me into cool sheets.

"You've always been so good to our family," I said.

"Well, of course. I love you all. I've always done what I've been asked."

"You've been wonderful." I paused. "I do have another question for you. As far as you know, did the police find anything after her death?"

"No," Della said, sitting in a chair next to me. "They talked to everyone once or twice, and they decided that whatever happened was an accident, and that's what I came to believe, too." She nodded as if to reassure herself. "No one would've wanted to hurt your mama. Everyone loved her."

"Everyone?" I said, thinking of the letter implying murder, and Ty's recollection of his father's words that he was going to "find out who killed her."

"Well, sweetie, if you're thinking about your father, he always loved your mom. Even when they separated and he was living in Chicago, he still loved her."

I sat without moving. The word *separated* battered my memory. Had I known this and buried it along with so many other things? Nothing came to me. Not even a shred of recognition.

"Separated?" I said, my voice coming out a little high.

Della looked at me, her face slightly alarmed. "Yes. Your parents had broken up. You don't remember that, either?"

7

"Hey, you're back," Ty said, looking up from the front desk, where he was sorting through a stack of papers. "How'd it go?"

"Okay." I shifted my purse to the other shoulder. Although the letters from my brother and sister added no real weight, I thought I could feel them inside my purse, waiting.

Ty pushed aside his paperwork and leaned on the counter. "Want to tell me about it?"

I did. I wanted to blurt, "My parents were separated!" But more than anything I wanted to read the letters and see if I could find Dan and Caroline. "Not just yet. Thanks, though."

A sconce shone behind Ty's head, making his hair look redder, making him seem younger somehow. "How about going out later?" he said. "I could show you some of the Woodland Dunes hot spots." He rolled his eyes as he said the phrase "hot spots."

"Yeah, maybe. I've got to read over some things first, and I think I'll do it on my balcony. Is there any way to get a glass of white wine sent up to my room?"

"I'll take care of it."

"Thanks. I appreciate it." Ty and I stood still a moment, smiling at each other, but then I touched my purse and felt the imagined heft of the letters. "Bye for now," I said and headed for the stairs.

Fifteen minutes later, I was settled on the chaise lounge on the balcony. On the table at my side was a wedge of Gruyère cheese, a small loaf of bread and a bottle of pinot grigio in a tan plastic bucket that read "Long Beach Inn" on the side. Elaine, the housekeeper, had brought it up, saying it was compliments of the house. A small note had been tucked under the napkin that read, *"Hope you find what you're looking for. Let me know if I can help. Ty."*

The note touched me more than I'd have thought possible, and I kept picking it up, reading it again, running my finger over the blue ink. It was something about the kindness, the offer of assistance without getting anything in return. I had no one in my life who made offers like that except my dad and Maddy. Other associates at work might ask if they could help me, maybe take a court call or a deposition from me. But their offers were more about moving up in the firm, getting in good with the young woman who had started the new department and whose dad was on the executive committee, forcing me to build a shield around myself that protected me from alleged friends looking for something other than friendship.

Ty's gestures, on the other hand, felt genuine. His open smile and watchful eyes made me want to keep in touch with him even after I'd left Woodland Dunes. He wasn't bad-looking either, the olive T-shirt barely hid a solid chest and strong arms. Then again, he lived in the Midwest, a thousand miles away from Manhattan.

I stared out at the softly lapping waves, aware that I still hadn't absorbed the news that my parents had split up before my mother's death. I must have known that at some point, although Della said that they had lived apart only a few weeks before my mom died. But why hadn't my father ever mentioned this? And why had he seemed like the grieving widower if they'd broken up?

To distract myself, I got up and checked my voice mail in case there was an SOS call from McKnight Corporation or someone from my office. Nothing.

The letters, I decided. *Focus on the letters for now.* I went back onto the balcony. I put Caroline's letters in chronological order, using the postmarks on the outside of the envelopes, then I opened and stacked them, so that the earliest rested on top. The first five letters were written on lined paper, the round holes and frayed edges on the left side making it clear they'd been ripped from a notebook. Tiny cursive handwriting, afraid to take up too much space, covered the pages. The words *Brighton Academy* were stamped on the top right corner of each sheet of paper.

One afternoon, a few days before our mom died, I had sat on the front porch swing with Caroline, and I asked her what it would be like to go to high school. At the time, she was supposed to attend the local high school in town. Caroline rubbed a hand on my back and said, "You'll be great when you go to high school. You're pretty and happy, just the way they like 'em. For me, it'll be hell."

"But you're pretty," I'd said. Caroline wore no makeup over her peach-toned skin and always had on loose clothes that could have been worn by a boy, but she couldn't hide the dark eyelashes or her new breasts or the long, thin legs that seemed to have sprouted from her body over the last year.

"But I'm not happy." Caroline pulled her hand away from my back, wrapping her arms around her knees.

"Why?"

Caroline shrugged. "I never have been. I don't know how."

A month later, with our mother dead, and Dan gone to college, Caroline was sent to Brighton Academy, a boarding school outside Detroit. The letter I held in my hand had been written in September 1982, Caroline's first year there.

Dear Della, I hate it here,

the first letter started.

The other girls are assholes. I know I'm not supposed to swear, but there's no one around to stop me anymore. The classes are fine, I guess. Algebra is my favorite, because if you learn the rules and stick by them, everything works out the way it's supposed to. I don't know why people think math is so hard. I hope things are good with you in Woodland Dunes. I miss you a lot.

Caroline wrote Della once or twice a year from Brighton Academy, and the majority of the letters were in a similar vein. *I hate this place,* she said. *I hate the other girls.* It seemed she hated everything—the teachers, the food, her roommate—everything except a few classes. And she was lonely.

In the spring of what I figured should have been her senior year, Caroline wrote:

Well, I'm staying here for one more go-around. I flunked three classes accidentally. It was better than the alternative.

What, I wondered, was the alternative? Graduating and moving on to college or out into the world? Why wouldn't she have wanted that if she hated the place so much?

The next letter came in the spring of the following year, Caroline's fifth at Brighton.

They passed me, and now I'm slated to walk the plank so I can leave. I don't think I actually did better in class. In fact, I think they passed me to get rid of me, or maybe my father paid them. Wouldn't surprise me. He's supposed to be here tomorrow. Nice of him, don't you think?

I put the letter facedown on my lap. Caroline's sarcasm made me anxious and confused. I took a sip of my wine, but it tasted too warm and citrusy now. The sun was starting to slide into a thicker, yellow color, threatening to turn rust-red and hot-pink, but I couldn't appreciate it. Why, why, why,

I kept thinking, why hadn't I been allowed to see
Caroline? Why hadn't my father and I *both* gone
to her graduation? Was Caroline's resentment
based solely on her being sent away to boarding
school? Or was it the result of something more?

I lifted the knife off the tray to cut a piece of
cheese, more for something to do than out of any
real hunger, but as I sliced through the brick of
Gruyère, my hand slipped and the knife made a
sharp scrape on the bottom of the silver tray, nearly
missing the index finger of my other hand. I put
the finger to my mouth, as though I had cut myself, feeling jumpy, nervous.

I managed to cut a slice of cheese, and then
lifted the stack of mail from Caroline again. The
next letter on the pile was written on lavender sta-
tionery and was dated seven months after Caroline's high-school graduation.

Dear Della,
Merry Christmas. Sorry I haven't written
sooner. They asked me not to contact anyone
for a while, so that I could stay "in touch"
with myself instead. I keep telling them how
ironic that request is. I'm already too in touch
with myself. Oh well. It's not all bad here.
Hope you are happy in Woodland Dunes.
You can write me at the address on the en-

velope, and if you feel like sending some of your oatmeal cookies, I would be thrilled. Miss you, Caroline.

I found the envelope the card had been in and looked at the return address. Caroline's name was listed there and below that, "Crestwood Home" and an address in "Holly Knolls, Connecticut." Crestwood Home? I swallowed hard on a piece of cheese.

I went inside and turned on my laptop. I could hear a peal of laughter from downstairs and the low rumble of voices. Probably the happy hour Ty had told me about. Every Friday and Saturday from May to October, he opened the small bar on the deck and treated guests to a few cocktails. Normally, it was the kind of gathering I would have joined with optimism, hoping to meet a few nice people, hoping for that rush of belonging, even if it was just for a few hours. Right now, though, I wasn't feeling very social.

Once my computer was powered up, I got on the Internet, clicked on "Web Search," then typed in "Crestwood Home." The search brought up a number of results that I had to scroll through, including a few Crestwood Inns and B and Bs. Finally, I found a Web site for Crestwood Home in Holly Knolls, Connecticut. Under a banner with the Crestwood name hung a photo of a beautiful estate on a green lawn. Below that, in scrolling script it said, *At the Crestwood Home and Psychiatric Institute, we are devoted to the restoration of well-balanced mental health. Our residents live in the peaceful harmony of Connecticut horse country until that restoration is achieved.*

Oh, God. I sat back, away from the laptop, staring back and forth between the photo of the lovely brick mansion that looked more like a country inn and the words *Psychiatric Institute.* I pushed the laptop away and leaned on the desk, cupping my face in my hands. Why had Caroline been there? Because she had seen something too awful, because she had known something too painful?

Or maybe, I thought, because she had done something too horrible.

8

I pried open one eye and groaned. Even that minor movement caused a lurch of pain in my head so severe it blinded me for a second. There was light. Way too much light.

I blinked repeatedly until the other eye opened and focused. A small, black alarm clock was on a nightstand, I could see that much, but it didn't tell me anything except that I was in a hotel, not an uncommon event. I opened my eyes wider and moved my head toward the clock. Now I could see that it was on a white wicker nightstand instead of the usual lacquered wood veneer of most hotel tables. I continued to stare at the clock until the numbers made sense. Finally, I grasped that it was 11:00 a.m., an ungodly late hour for me. I forced my eyes past the nightstand to the source of the light—sun streaming through white-trimmed French doors. That's when I remembered that I was in Woodland Dunes. And as I pushed myself up on my arms and took in my clothes scattered in a trail toward the bed, I realized that I was very hungover.

Last night, Ty had called and told me that I should get out of the room. "You need something to eat, and c'mon, you can't work all night," he said.

I laughed. I wanted to say, "Tell that to the people at my firm," but he was right. I was famished, and the text of Caroline's letters had begun to swim and merge in front of my eyes. I wanted an excuse to escape.

"Great," Ty said when I accepted. "We'll get you something to eat, and we'll have a few beers."

But a few beers had turned into six. Or seven. Okay, possibly eight. I lost count. What I did remember was Ty shaking his head at some point, saying, "You don't need another one," and me grabbing the beer out of his hand, saying, "I sure as hell do."

I rarely get drunk, and if I do, it's with Maddy, someone I can let down my guard with, no one else. But it turned out that I felt I could relax with Ty. It was something about the kind eyes that watched my face as I talked, the way he held the barstool out for me, the way he tried to get me to slow down on the alcohol. And he had danced with me to "Brown Eyed Girl" when I'd played it on the jukebox, even though there was no dance floor, even though some guys he knew jeered at us.

I found some ibuprofen in my bag and took two. Then another one for good measure. I lay down again, waiting for the drug to take the edge off. I buried my head under the pillow, but still the light from the beach forced its way into the room.

That's what I should do, I realized, go running on the beach. I wanted to get back to the letters, but more than anything, I wanted to sweat out some of the alcohol.

I changed into running shorts and a T-shirt, trying to ignore my parched throat and the throbbing blood vessel in my temple. I trod lightly down the back stairs and out onto the beach, wanting to avoid Ty for the moment. I was sure I looked like absolute hell, and I was embarrassed about my drunken conduct last night. As I stepped onto the sand, the sunlight pierced my eyes like a thousand needles, almost making me turn around and scrap the run. Then a thought struck me—had I kissed Ty last night? Some slobbering attempt at comfort? Mentally, I scrolled through the end of the night. He had walked me to my room, letting me lean on his shoulder after I stumbled twice on the stairs. Finally, he'd unlocked the door with my key, which he gave back to me, and told me he'd had a good time, that he would see me tomorrow. Then he left. Thank God. Thank God I hadn't made an even bigger ass of myself.

I made my feet move over the sand, down toward the water where the sand would be packed and firm. I turned right and walked for the first few minutes, letting my muscles and my brain warm up. No clouds hid the absurd brightness of the sun, which had brought all types onto the beach for the first taste of summer—parents with armies of little kids, a few teenage girls in bikinis, their towels angled away from the lake but toward the sun.

This side of the beach housed the larger, grander homes, and they seemed to grow with each step. From Mediterranean villas to Cape Cod clapboard houses, there was no set style requirement except for jaw-droppingly big. I forced my reluctant feet into a run. Every jolt of my heel sent an equally jolting clang to my head, but eventually, I found my running void. I watched the sand, the water, the homes, but I didn't process much anymore.

I ran like that for at least twenty minutes before I made a wide turn and headed back. As I did, something familiar shook me out of my zone. An odd feeling like the one I'd had at the cemetery, the sensation that someone was watching me. A tingle of fear ticked its way up the back of my neck, making me light-headed and dizzy. Or maybe it was the hangover.

I jogged in place for a moment, taking time to breathe, to look around. There were no other joggers near me, and the closest person on the beach was a man a few hundred feet away, his head in a paperback. I glanced out at the water. A couple of boats bobbed in the distance, but they were so far away I couldn't even make out what type of crafts they were. I turned my attention to the houses lining the beach. Immediately behind me, sitting high on a dune, was a massive, white contemporary home with flat roofs and walls of glass that faced the beach. The boxy structure made it look cold and unappealing, but it had probably cost millions.

The reflective glare of the glass made it impossible to see if anyone was inside, and I was just about to begin running again, when an image snagged my attention. I continued jogging in place, squinting up at the house, until I could determine what it was. On the far right side, a figure stood at the corner of the deck. I couldn't tell if it was a man or a woman. I could only make out a baseball hat, an orange windbreaker, and arms that were holding something up to the person's face. I stopped running, and without the bouncing I could see that it was a pair of binoculars. And the binoculars were facing toward the lake and down to the beach. Right at me.

I looked both ways, but there was no one close to me, no one else that the person could be focusing on. *Doesn't matter,* I told myself. It must be a home owner simply checking out the beach. But the person didn't sweep the water or the length of the sand with the binoculars. Instead, the orange-clad arms held fast, the body facing mine, not wavering, frozen.

I took off running back the way I'd come. I was moving too fast, and the speed would soon tire me, I knew, but I had an irrational desire to get away from the house, from that person, quickly. Yet I couldn't outrun the feeling of being under surveillance, and when I stopped and looked back, I thought I could still see the figure, turned toward me.

When I got back, I peeked in at the front desk. The housekeeper was on the phone taking a reservation. Ty was nowhere in sight. Then I remembered he'd said that he spent most Sundays at his parents' until high season. He had told me that he would come back to the inn in the early evening to pick me up for dinner, a dinner where I would meet his father and, hopefully, find out what the police knew about my mother's death.

I was glad Ty wasn't at the desk. I didn't want him to see me right now, looking sweaty and smelling as if I'd bathed in a pool of beer, but at the same time, I couldn't stop the feeling of wanting him around, wanting that ease.

"Excuse me, Elaine?" I said, stepping into the lobby.

The housekeeper looked up and gave me a smile. "Good morning."

"I was wondering if you know who owns that big white house down the beach."

"Down to the right, you mean? The one with all the windows?"

"Right."

"Ah, probably just some summer resident. I can't keep them all straight. Sorry."

I thanked her and went to my room.

After a shower, two more ibuprofen and a raid of the minibar that included every bottle of water and miniature bag of chips, I felt somewhat human. I padded barefoot out onto the deck and again settled into the Adirondack chair with Caroline's and Dan's letters.

I began with the next few from Caroline. She had, it seemed, stayed at Crestwood Home for five years. Five years, *five years,* I kept thinking. Surely that was a hell of a long stay for inpatient treatment. I tried to think of every reason that a nine-teen-year-old girl might be in a psychiatric clinic for that length of a time—anorexia, bulimia, depression, drugs—but did any of those require five years of inpatient treatment? I wanted to believe that Caroline had just needed some help, that she needed counseling and had gotten it, but my mind kept coming back to the same thought, that her stay at Crestwood had something to do with my mom's death, what Caroline knew about it or what part she'd played in it.

I couldn't stand thinking like that. I had to find her and figure out the real story. That was the simplest route to answering the nagging questions in my head. And it was time, after all, just as I'd told Della. So I kept reading. Five years after that first letter from Crestwood Home, Caroline wrote Della that she had left Connecticut and moved to Portland.

I'm crazy about this city. I have no money, but I don't care. I'm going to school at some crappy community college to get an accounting degree. On the weekends, I head to Mount Hood or Tillamook where I can hike or swim or just sit outside by myself. I finally feel like I've gotten past my problems. I feel like I can move on with my life.

A year later, Caroline wrote that she had gotten a job at an accounting firm. *They're paying for part of my school, can you believe it? And they'll hire me full-time when I graduate!*

In November, a few years after that, she wrote

that she was still at the accounting firm, that she liked it very much, and best of all she'd met someone special.

> His name is Matt Ramsey, and Della, you would adore him as much as I do. He's the kindest, most gentle soul you've ever met, and you know what? He loves me, too. He loves me like crazy. Sometimes I can't believe it, and sometimes I think it will all fall apart the way everything else did, but I've learned how to get myself past those thoughts, and so most of the time I'm just content. That's a word I'd never think to apply to myself. But there it is.

The next letter on the stack wasn't actually a letter, but a wedding announcement that appeared to have been printed on a home computer.

> Caroline and Matt Ramsey are pleased to announce that they made it official on August 12.

Below that, a new address was listed, and Caroline had handwritten:

Dear Della,
Sorry I didn't tell you about this ahead of time, but it was just us and a few friends on

the mountain. I'm sending you a picture.
Miss you, Caroline.

No mention of any parents, I noticed. I wondered
if my father had received one of these, if he had
studied it, silently, while I was in the other room.

I flipped the announcement over. Fixed to the
back with a pink paper clip was a photo. I un-
clipped it and raised it to my face, and there was
Caroline, a little older but not much different than
I'd remembered. She was standing, holding a bouquet of wildflowers, wearing a loose ivory cotton
dress. The hair around her face was streaked blond
from the sun, the same way mine got in the summer. She was tilting her head to one side, and the
man behind her, who must have been Matt Ramsey, had leaned in and put his face next to hers.
They were both smiling broadly, with smiles in
their eyes, as well. Matt had longish, thick brown
hair and brown eyes under bronze wire glasses.
One of his hands was squeezing Caroline's bare
arm, his new gold wedding band glinting in the sun.

Matt looked kind, I thought, and very much in
love with my sister. I felt a rush of happiness for
both of them, for the sister who had gone off to
boarding school alone and then on to some clinic.
I continued looking at the picture, at Caroline in
particular, silently asking, "Do you know what

happened? Did you have anything to do with it?"
But now, faced with the picture of Caroline's adult
face, rather than the vague image of her teenage
self, I found it harder to place on Caroline the suspicion I'd been so quick to adopt.

I read the last of Caroline's letters. There were
only a few more, and they were usually brief, telling Della about her job at the accounting firm or
how she and Matt had gone rafting or skiing or
camping over the weekend. The return addresses
on the last letters were all the same, on Northeast
Jarrett in Portland.

Caroline could be at her home in Portland right
now. The last letter had been written over a year and
a half ago, but she could easily still live there. She
might be sitting in the sun, too. She might be in her
backyard, her husband at her side, and she might be
pleased, excited even, to hear from the little sister she
hadn't seen in over twenty years. Or she might not.

I went back and forth, reminding myself how
miserable Caroline had seemed in her letters until
she'd moved to Portland and married Matt, until
she'd gotten past her problems, as she put it. And
so maybe she didn't want to be reminded of any
part of her old life. Maybe it would cause some
kind of setback in her mental condition, and I
didn't want to be responsible for that. Yet at the
same time, I found it harder and harder to be still,

knowing a phone sat only twenty feet away. If I couldn't find the number from Portland Information, I could search the Web, or I could get databases of addresses and phone numbers from my Internet clients and search those, as well.

I took the letters and photograph inside and sat down at the small desk. I picked up the phone, the plastic of the receiver cool against my hand. The line seemed to ring interminably. I stared at the pile of letters on the desk, Caroline's tiny handwriting blending into a series of small loops and slashes as I gazed unblinkingly. Finally, the pleasant voice of a woman answered, and I gave her the names of Caroline and Matt Ramsey in Portland, Oregon, on Northeast Jarrett Street.

"Checking," the woman said.

There was a long pause, during which I heard the clicking of a keyboard through the phone.

"Yes," the woman said at last. "I have an M. Ramsey on Northeast Jarrett."

In the middle of the first ring, the phone was answered, snatched up it seemed, and a gruff male voice said, "Hello?"

I was startled by the quick answer. "Um…is this Matt Ramsey?"

"Yes. Who's this?" Again, the man was abrupt, and this surprised me. I glanced at the picture of

Matt and Caroline that I held in my hand. I had expected someone kind, someone gentle like the man my sister had written about.

"This is…" I faltered for a second, wishing I'd taken more time to plan what I would say. It seemed ludicrous to say, *Hello, this is your wife's sister who she hasn't talked to in at least twenty years.* But there was no easy way, so I just said my name.

"Excuse me?" It was Matt who sounded startled now.

"I'm Hailey Sutter. Are you married to Caroline?"

"Yes."

I ran my finger over the photo of Caroline as if I could smooth the fold of my sister's dress where it creased at her shoulder. "I'm her sister. Is she there? Could I talk to her?"

Matt let out a laugh that sounded bitter. "She was making you a quilt."

"What?" I couldn't be sure I had heard him right.

"She was making you a quilt. She's been going to these lessons for years. It takes her forever to get a square right, the way she wants it." He laughed again, and it came out softer, more genuine this time. "I didn't know if she would ever finish it, but she always said she'd like to give it to you someday."

"Oh." I was struck by an image of Caroline, the grown-up Caroline from the picture, sitting on a couch, legs curled under her, stitching a quilt square by lamplight. For me. That was the truly striking part.

"Can I speak with her?" I said.

Matt cleared his throat. "She's not here."

"Well, can you have her call me? I live in New York, but I'm out of town right now. I could give you my numbers."

"I wouldn't know where to reach her."

"Excuse me?" I had the sensation of falling backward, zooming far away from that dream of Caroline on her couch.

"Look, I can't say much else. I don't even know if you really are her sister, and even if that's true, I…" He trailed off.

"Has something happened?"

"You could say that." The gruff tone had returned. "You haven't heard from her, have you?" He said this last bit as if the thought had just occurred to him.

"No, I haven't talked to Caroline since I was a kid. If you could just tell me where she is. I don't mean to bother her. I just want to talk."

There was a pause, as if Matt was thinking. "Look. I'll be honest with you. Caroline is missing. And I have no idea when, or if, she'll be back."

9

They'd been in Charleston, Matt said, at his cousin's wedding. Caroline was quiet, but she got that way sometimes. She'd gone to the bathroom inside the mansion, and she never came back. He went looking for her. At the hotel, he found a note from Caroline saying she was fine, but she needed a break and she would be in touch. But she hadn't called. It had been two weeks.

If only, I thought, if only I'd looked for her a few weeks ago. I could have talked to her. Maybe she wouldn't have taken off.

"Why would she have left like that?" I asked.

"I thought maybe you could tell me," Matt said.

"Me? What could I tell you when I haven't seen Caroline since I was seven?"

"You're in contact with your father, aren't you?"

I felt defensiveness and apprehension roll up my spine. "Yes," I said cautiously.

"Well, maybe you should see if he knows something."

"What's that supposed to mean?" But of course, I had an idea. Caroline's letters implied that she'd had some contact with our father, but I had chosen to believe that such contact had drifted off after a while, that what my father told me was true—Caroline and Dan didn't want to be part of the family anymore.

I heard Matt breathing on the other end.

I pushed my chair back and stood up. The sunlight was slanting through the open French doors now, right into the room. It was too bright.

"Look, I can't talk about this," Matt said, "I want to leave the line open. I mean we've got call waiting and all that, but I can't take any chances. So unless you can help me out, I've got to go." He paused. "It's just that I miss her so much."

It was the tenderness in that last sentence that made me sit down again. Caroline was missing. I couldn't simply turn my back and head out for lunch as if I hadn't learned anything, as if I hadn't done all this to learn *everything*.

"What if I come there?" It was out of my mouth as soon as I had the thought.

"You'd do that?" He sounded hopeful.

I calculated the beginning of my week in my head. If the arbitrators had their decision tomorrow, I might be able to leave for Portland in the afternoon, and if the decision wasn't ready until Tuesday, maybe I could leave that day.

"I have some work to take care of," I said. "I'm near Chicago right now, but I'll get a flight out in the next day or two. I'll be there."

Ty knocked on my door at 5:00 p.m., just as he said he would. He wore khaki shorts and a navy-blue sweater with a white T-shirt peeking out at the neck. He seemed to have even more freckles around his eyes, as if he had been in the sun.

"Hi," he said. He stood in the doorway, seeming like he didn't own the place and he needed to be invited in. "How're you feeling?"

"Better than this morning. I'm really, really sorry I was such an ass."

He grinned as though he might make fun of me for my drunken state, but he only said, "You weren't. Ready for dinner?"

"One second. I just need to throw some things in my purse."

I walked to the desk and began collecting my wallet, my compact, my cell phone.

"What did you do today?" Ty asked.

"Oh, not much." I would tell him eventually. I would tell him what I'd learned, but right now, my siblings' letters were too vivid and raw.

I hadn't stopped thinking about Caroline all afternoon. Had she run away? Or had she disappeared against her will? And what did my father know about it?

I had picked up the phone at least five times, wanting to call my dad. I knew that on a Sunday afternoon, the one day he didn't work, he would be in his home in Manhasset, reading his three Sunday papers and drinking coffee from a pot in the middle of the kitchen table. He would spend hours like that, absorbing everything he read, making notes on a small yellow legal pad by his side whenever he came across something that could affect one of his cases. I knew he would be happy to hear from me, that he would ask me about the arbitration, and he would hear in my voice that something was wrong. I would have to ask him then what he knew about Caroline, about my mother's death.

And so I'd put the phone gently back on the cradle, wanting to pretend I hadn't picked it up, because I couldn't confront him yet. I couldn't risk being wrong. If I lost him, I lost my whole family.

"Damn," I heard Ty say from the doorway. "I just remembered I have to call a guest who's checking in this week. I'll meet you at the front desk, okay?"

I glanced at him over my shoulder. "No problem."

I turned around again, and my eyes fell on the pile of Dan's letters I had arranged after reading them this afternoon. I picked them up and flipped through them once more, turning over the envelopes to look for some writing on the back, some scribble of a phrase that might tell me more than the letters had. There were only four of them, and although Dan chatted about his surroundings and his activities, he didn't let his emotions seep out the way Caroline had. The letters seemed to have been written out of a sense of duty, as if Dan was writing to a distant grandmother who sent money occasionally.

The oldest letter had been postmarked from East Lansing, Michigan, where Dan was attending Michigan State University. He talked about football games and late nights and the crisp fall campus, but not much else.

The next letter was written a few years later, postmarked from Detroit:

Dear Della,
I graduated a few months ago, and I've landed a sales job. I'm sharing an apartment with a few friends from school.

He wrote a few anecdotes about people at work and the slovenliness of his roommates. He closed with,

I don't like Detroit that much. How's everything with you?

The letter was devoid of real details. Nothing there that I could follow up on.

The next two letters were similar in their descriptions, as well as their lack of emotional substance. The first was postmarked from Santa Fe, a place I'd never been. Dan reported that his company had transferred him, that he was finding he liked the open brown plains of the Southwest. The last letter was also postmarked from Santa Fe and had been written over six years ago. I figured that Dan would have been thirty-two at that time.

I tried to imagine my brother, who was permanently seventeen in my mind, in his late thirties now. I imagined that his sandy blond hair, which he had worn long during high school, was now clipped short. Maybe he was even balding. Maybe he wore glasses over his light blue eyes. I tried to envision him in a distinguished suit, but I couldn't seem to get him out of the faded jeans and black T-shirts that had been his teenage uniform. I wondered if he still wrote stories, if he carried around small notebooks that he filled with his stocky scribble. I hoped so because it was something he had in common with my mom.

I could remember Dan, so often in the parlor room that no one else used, sitting at the octagonal table. He would hunch over his notebooks, his hand pushing across the page. I used to try to spy on him. I'd sneak in from the kitchen, crawling stealthily, I always thought, until I reached the far couch or the big leather chair, something I could hide behind. I would peek my head out and watch him, trying to figure him out, this brother who was part man, part boy. But almost immediately, and without looking up from his notebook, Dan would say something like, "Hey, kid. I know you're there." Usually, I wouldn't respond. I would hold my breath, hoping he was just guessing, that he had an inkling but maybe didn't really know I was in the room. But he always knew. He would tiptoe over to me, and although I couldn't see him, I could sense the shift in the room, and the anticipation made me shake. Then he would scream to scare me, and I would scream back, and he would tickle my stomach until I begged him to stop.

I knew I should go downstairs to meet Ty, but I kept looking at the envelopes from Dan, turning them over and over. I took out the letters, then returned them to their places, hoping I would see something different, something that might make it simpler to find him.

I had called the Santa Fe directory today, just as I had Portland, and I'd gone through the same process, but there was no Dan Sutter or D. Sutter listed anywhere in that city. He might have left by now. Who knew what had happened to him over the last six years? It struck me that he could have died. People got cancer. People got hit by cars. Why not my brother? But I couldn't believe that. Somehow I would have known, I told myself. I would have been able to tell if my brother had died. There was no logical basis for that conclusion, just something I felt in my gut.

As I studied the envelopes from Santa Fe, I noticed something different from the first two envelopes Dan had sent to Della. The addresses were different, but that wasn't it. It was the way he'd written his name that was off somehow.

I put the letters side by side on the desk and looked at the top left corners where Dan had written his return addresses—East Lansing, Detroit, Santa Fe, and Santa Fe again. I studied the first two. Dan had scratchy, short handwriting, and he didn't make an effort to be legible, but I could tell that he'd written, "D. Sutter" in the corners. On the last two, the ones from Santa Fe, again there was the initial *D,* but the last name looked odd. I could tell it started with an *S,* ended with an *R,* and had roughly six letters, so maybe Dan's handwriting had simply changed a little. That wasn't it, though. It was definitely different.

I picked up the last letter and held it close to my face. There was a dot right above the second letter of the name, as if he'd written an *I,* but there was no slash as there had been through the *T*'s in the other letters. Instead, the fourth letter dipped down below the word. Was it a *J* or a *Y?* I stared some more until the word began to shape. "Singer," it said. I picked up the other letter from Santa Fe and saw that I was right.

My brother had apparently changed his name to Singer.

10

I locked the room and ran down the stairs, excited about the "Singer" discovery, yet trying to prime my mind for my meeting with Sheriff Manning. This wasn't just a nice Sunday dinner.

When I got to the front desk, Ty was behind it with a young woman, a friend who helped out occasionally. Ty had instituted a late Sunday checkout of four o'clock, but he said he still didn't push people to get out on time, so sometimes they had a rush on Sunday afternoons. It looked like one of those days. Both Ty and the woman, who had a cute upturned nose and bobbed brown hair, were leaning over the counter, handing out credit-card slips, taking keys from guests.

"Sorry," Ty mouthed to me over the head of a man who was signing his slip. "Two seconds."

I smiled and shook my head, and as I did, I saw that the woman behind the desk had seen our exchange. The woman looked quickly from Ty to me and back again.

When all the guests were gone, Ty waved me over. "Sorry about that," he said. "This is Molly." He gestured to the woman.

"Hey," Molly said, offering me a short smile and reaching over the desk to shake my hand. "Nice to meet you."

"Molly is one of my best buddies in the world," Ty said in a proud voice while he ruffled the back of Molly's hair.

Molly raised her hand to smooth her hair. As she did so, she shot another glance at me, one that sized me up in a short sweep of her eyes. I knew right then that Molly wasn't happy to be simply one of Ty's buddies, and the thought bothered me.

"Well, it was nice to meet you," I said.

"Same," Molly said. She turned to Ty then. "If you're having burgers tonight, tell Chief not to use too much steak sauce. He drowns them every time."

Ty laughed. "Will do."

Point taken, I thought. *You've been to their house for dinner before me.* I made myself smile again at Molly and followed Ty to his car, which was parked out front.

It was an old Chevy with green nylon seats and pop cans rattling in the back.

"I keep my house and the inn immaculate," Ty said as he opened the door for me, "but I can't seem to get my act together with my car. It's some teenage-regression thing. I'm getting serious therapy very soon."

I chuckled, but then my mind flew to Caroline because of the word *therapy*. What had she been dealing with?

Ty pulled out of the inn's circular front driveway, the whole Chevy leaning as he maneuvered the curves.

"So is your head still pounding from last night?" Ty asked.

"I've started to feel a little better."

"You want to tell me what got you in such a mood that you had to drink me and every guy in Woodland Dunes under the table?"

"I'm sorry about that."

"Don't be sorry. I'm just glad I was there to mop you up, but something tells me that's not everyday drinking for you."

"Ha," I said. "Definitely not."

"So what was it? This thing with your mom?"

I watched the larger beach homes give way to smaller ranch-style houses as Ty turned the car away from the lake. "It was so many things," I said, suddenly tired and wishing this was just an easy dinner with a guy I liked.

"You don't have to tell me," Ty said when I didn't explain.

"I do want to tell you. It's just that it's complicated. Being back here, dealing with the memories. It's been bizarre to say the least. But the thing that pushed me over the edge was this stack of letters I got from Della."

"Yeah?"

"Actually, talking about it would probably help me to sort through it all. How soon until we get to your parents'?" We were heading into town now, and we passed the deli where Ty had taken me for lunch.

"About two minutes, but I can take the long way."

"That would be great."

Ty looped around the neighborhood, passing a park, an old pharmacy and a rash of small, aluminum-sided houses. By the time we pulled into the Mannings' blond brick home, I had explained about Caroline's disappearance and Dan's last two envelopes that bore the name Singer instead of Sutter.

"So where does that leave you?" Ty asked as he turned off the ignition. "I mean, it seems like you've learned more but you still don't know anything definite, right? And your sister… Shit, that's scary."

"I know, but I'm hoping your dad will add some more to the mix. Maybe he'll be able to explain everything. Even if that happens, I'm still going to Portland to see Caroline's husband. I want to help him if I can. And I want to meet my sister again."

Just then a woman appeared in the doorway of the Mannings' house and waved at the car. She had short hair the same rust color as Ty's and wore jeans with a sleeveless mint-green sweater.

"That's my mom," Ty said with a laugh. "And she'll come out to the car and get us if we don't move."

I glanced at Ty, at the affection on his face while he looked at his mother, and I felt a pang of envy. I would never get my mother back, but maybe I would be recovering members of my family soon. "Let's go then," I said.

The Mannings' house felt like a quaint, seaside cottage, even though it was miles from the lake. Wood furniture painted white was mixed with quilts, embroidered pillows and decorative flowerpots. Ty had told me that his mom was instrumental in decorating Long Beach Inn, and I could tell that she must have done the room where I was staying.

"Hailey, how are you? It's so nice to meet you," Mrs. Manning said. She squeezed my forearm. "Now, please call me Bert. My real name is Roberta, but I hate it. Let's get you a glass of wine."

Bert looked as though she might be in her forties, rather than approaching sixty as Ty had told me. She was the kind of mother I'd always wished for, one I could have fun with, who I could have a drink with and confide in. It was obvious that Bert and Ty were close judging by the glances and private jokes that passed between them.

"Your father's late," Bert said, removing a tray of lasagna from the oven.

"Surprise, surprise," Ty said.

"So we're going to let this cool and start on the salads without him."

The three of us sat down at a whitewashed kitchen table with leaves hand-painted in the corners. I passed on the wine that Bert offered. The thought of it made my stomach shriek. Over a large salad and a loaf of garlic bread, Ty and his mother talked about Ty's older brother, who was a computer programmer in Chicago, and his younger sister, who was getting a master's degree in child psychology at Northwestern.

"She said she's definitely going for the Ph.D. after this," Bert said. "Can you believe it?"

"Of course," Ty said, eating his salad, "and she'll probably run for president after that."

Ty and Bert both laughed, and I felt a wave of longing again for a family like this, the kind that knew each other so well.

"So, Hailey," Bert said, offering me the basket of bread again. "Ty said you're from Manhattan, is that right?"

I took a slice. "I've lived in New York for years now, but my family used to live here—a long time ago."

"Oh!" Bert said. Apparently Ty hadn't told her that much, and it confirmed my feelings that I could trust him. I had asked Ty not to let his parents know why I wanted to meet them. I hoped to bring the conversation around naturally and see what came up. Experience taught me that I often got more information from witnesses when they didn't know what I was going to ask them.

"Would I have known your parents?" Bert asked.

"I'm not sure. Will and Leah Sutter?"

Bert made a thoughtful face. "Sure, I remember them. Your dad was the lawyer for this town for a number of years."

"That's right," I said. "I'd forgotten that, because he doesn't do municipal work anymore."

"I remember everyone was so proud that we had a big Chicago lawyer representing us. And I remember your mom, too, honey." Bert's tone was lower now. "I didn't know her well, but what I knew of her I liked, and I was so sorry to hear that she'd died."

"Thank you," I said, although it felt odd to accept

condolences over a woman who'd passed away so long ago, a woman I had a hard time remembering.

"Did your father ever remarry?"

"Oh, no." It was the same answer I always gave. Often I would go on, explaining that my father had been too in love with my mom to ever replace her, but this time I fell silent because of the separation. I had no idea whose decision that had been. Was it a mutual one because they had fallen out of love? Or had one of them done something to the other, something they couldn't forgive?

There was a second of silence and then the sound of a car pulling into the garage. A minute later, the garage door leading into the kitchen opened.

"Hi, honey," Bert called without even looking at the door. "How were the fish?"

Lou Manning stepped into the room, carrying a large duffel bag over his shoulder. Like Ty, he wasn't a large man, but there was a presence about him. His brown-gray hair was thinning, and he had intense dark eyes. When he smiled at his wife, though, the solemn face broke.

"Hi, doll," he said in a quiet voice. He nodded at his son, and said, "Ty." Then his eyes turned to me. He gave another nod of his head.

"Dad, this is Hailey Sutter," Ty said.

I crossed the room to shake his hand. "Nice to meet you, Chief."

His face had returned to its serious cast, and he didn't meet my hand. "Call me Lou. I'm filthy from fishing. I'll just grab a shower." He moved around me and into the next room, and soon we could hear him climbing the stairs.

I let my hand fall to my side and took my seat again.

"His bark is worse than his bite," Ty said.

"That's for sure," Bert said. She picked up her glass. "You definitely won't have any wine, Hailey?"

"Oh, no," I said, and I could almost feel Ty's smirk. "I had a little too much to drink last night."

"Well then, you'll need more bread," Bert said. She put a few more pieces on my plate. "Soak it all up."

Chief Manning returned ten minutes later with comb marks in his wet hair, dressed in a flannel shirt and jeans. He walked to his wife and kissed her on the top of her head.

"Did you bring us any fish?" Bert asked him.

He nodded. "It's in the freezer in the garage."

"Good. Then we'll have a fish fry this week. Hailey, maybe you could come back for dinner again?" Bert got up from the table and began cutting the lasagna.

"I wish I could," I said, "but I'm leaving tomorrow. I may be coming back to Chicago for business, but I'm not sure when."

I looked at Ty's face as I said this and saw him glance down at his plate. I couldn't read his expression, but I hoped it was a little sadness over me leaving. Under different circumstances, I could get very interested in a guy like Ty, someone undeniably attractive, someone who wanted to understand where I came from, who wanted to support me. But these weren't different circumstances. I still lived in Manhattan, and I still had to leave tomorrow. I would go to Portland to meet Matt, and then get back to New York the next day. I'd have tons of work piled up by then.

I felt someone's eyes on me, and I turned my head to see that Chief Manning had taken the seat to my left and was watching me closely.

"Chief Manning—Lou, I mean," I said. It was hard to imagine being on a first-name basis with this imposing man. "My family used to live here in town, and Ty mentioned you might have worked on a case that involved my mother."

He didn't say anything, but he gave a single nod of his head. I wasn't sure if this was an acknowledgment that I was right, or encouragement to keep talking.

"My mother passed away," I continued, nervous now, "when I was seven. Ty said you might have looked into the matter."

"Leah Sutter." He said this matter-of-factly, not as a question.

"Yes, that's right. Do you remember this at all?"

Another nod.

"Dad, how about helping her out a little bit?" Ty said.

Lou glanced at his son, then back to me. "It was a long time ago, but I remember. What do you need to know?"

The kitchen went silent, and I had the sense that even Bert, standing over the lasagna at the stove, was waiting for my answer.

"It's just that I was so little," I said. I tried to make my words light and chatty, as if I had this conversation often. "And I don't know much about how she died. I'm curious."

"Well, let's see." Lou put his hand to the collar of his flannel shirt and slowly pulled at it. "Your mother died from blunt trauma to the head. She fell down the stairs, if I'm not mistaken."

I felt a strange disappointment. "That's it? She fell down the stairs?"

He nodded.

"Then why were you looking into the case?"

"Standard procedure."

"But Dad," Ty cut in. "I remember you saying

that she'd been killed, and you were going to find out who did that to her. That sounds like you thought there was more going on."

Chief Manning sent his son a look I couldn't interpret. "Quite often, when family members say something like 'She fell down the stairs,' it means a possible abuse situation. So we have to look into it. We have to interview the family members, anyone else who was around, and we make a determination whether to pursue the case. When your mother died, we did consider whether she'd been physically abused. Maybe that's when I made that comment to Ty."

Bert made a tutting sound as she put the pan of lasagna in the center of the table and took her seat. "If I knew you were saying such things to the kids, I never would have let them come to the office."

Chief Manning glanced at his wife and let a grin cross his mouth, then looked back at me. His gaze was disconcerting, his brown eyes unblinking, focused solely on my face. I had the brief thought that he should have been a lawyer instead of a policeman. I'd hate to go up against him in court.

It was hard to ask my next question, but I forced myself. "Who did you suspect of abusing her? I mean, when you had suspicions."

There was another quiet moment, during which

Ty began helping Bert dole pieces of lasagna onto the plates.

"We suspected your father," Chief Manning said. "That's standard, to look to the spouse first."

"But they were separated. Doesn't that remove the spouse from suspicion?"

"Actually, that usually makes us more suspicious. There's often a lot of unresolved animosity in separations."

That seemed obvious now that he'd said it, but I couldn't imagine my father being abusive to my mom or anyone else for that matter. Yet what did I really know? "You ruled him out eventually?"

"I guess you could say that."

"Did you suspect anyone else?" I asked.

"You had an older brother, right?"

"That's right," I said. I cut my lasagna with my fork. "Dan."

"Well, we thought about him, of course. He was old enough and big enough, but he had an alibi. Seems he was gone all night with his friends, taking advantage of your dad being out of the house, I suppose. And he came home to find you all."

"What do you mean, 'you all'?"

Chief Manning glanced at me. "You were with your mama. You and your sister. Your brother came home early in the morning and found you three in your parents' room."

The lasagna caught in my throat, and I grabbed for my water. The light that hung over the table seemed too harsh, reminding me of a light in a police interrogation room.

And then I remembered something. *The sound of pounding.* Far away, like the sound in a dream. It became louder, then louder still, until I'd had to leave the dream and wake up. And when I did, I was in my mother's bed. She was asleep. Her head was turned to one side. Her sandy-blond hair fell like a panel over her face. The pounding again. It was coming from the door. I untangled my legs from the sheets. I noticed that I had slept in my jeans and my shirt with the big yellow flower on it.

I was almost to the door when I heard my name. "Hailey!"

I stopped. I looked at the bed. My mother was still asleep.

"Hailey!" I heard again. It was coming from the door. I walked toward it, rubbing the sleep out of my eyes. "Hailey, it's me!" I heard.

"Danny?" I said.

"Hailey, open the door."

I stepped toward the door and reached for the handle. It wouldn't turn. "I can't open it. It's locked."

"Unlock it then." His voice sounded mad.

I scrambled with the handle, trying to figure

out how the lock worked. It still wouldn't open. Why wouldn't it open? We were trapped. "I can't," I said, scared now. Maybe I should wake Mom.

"Is Caroline in there?" I heard Dan ask.

I started to say no, just me and Mom, but I glanced around the room to make sure. And there was Caroline. Hunched in a corner, knees up to her chest. The same way she sat on the porch swing. It seemed she might be asleep, too. Then I saw her eyes were open, staring at me.

"You all right?" Ty said, leaning toward me now, jarring me away from the memory.

Bert jumped up from the table and refilled my water glass. Chief Manning, on the other hand, hadn't moved, his eyes still on me.

I blinked a few times, focusing on the line of freckles over Ty's cheekbones, unable to bring back that moment in my mom's bedroom.

"Fine, fine," I said. I took a sip of the water, then another, grateful for the cool slickness on my throat. "I didn't remember that," I said. I glanced at Chief Manning. "That morning, I mean, not until now."

I tried to get my mind away from the image of Caroline, eyes wide, her back pushed into that corner. I tried to force myself into the detached clinical-questioning mode I went into during depositions, but I found it difficult to come up with something to say.

Again there was a hush at the table, and I considered changing the subject for good. Instead, I took a deep breath and asked, "And had my mother passed away? I mean, was she dead by the time Dan found us?" I tried to make this sound like normal conversation, but I already knew the answer.

"Correct," Chief Manning said. His fork clanked on his plate as he cut a piece of lasagna. "She'd passed by then. Maybe she would have lived if she'd gotten immediate medical attention after she fell down the stairs."

"Lou," Bert said in a chastising tone.

He put his fork down and looked at his wife, then returned his attention to his plate. "That's just speculation, though. She had a big head injury, and internal bleeding in the head can be nasty to treat. Sometimes there's nothing they can do for it."

"She died in her sleep then?" I found this concept oddly comforting.

"Seems so."

"But how did she fall down the stairs?" I supposed people tripped and fell all the time, but my mom had been a runner, a graceful woman, and it seemed strange that she would accidentally fall.

Chief Manning turned his head toward me, a wondering expression on his face. "She just slipped. At least that's what you told us."

11

The alarm went off at 5:00 a.m. I staggered to the bathroom and stood under a hot shower. I told myself to hurry. I had to get on the road to Chicago before the traffic hit. I had to find out whether my arbitration decision was back. And then I would meet with the McKnight people, which hopefully wouldn't include Sean McKnight.

But my body refused to be rushed, and my mind rebelled against the thought of leaving Woodland Dunes, so I leaned against the tiled wall, letting the water envelop me, letting my mind wake and sift through my dinner with the Mannings last night.

Chief Manning had said that he had interviewed me personally after my mom died. He'd interviewed all of my family, in fact, and both Caroline and I said that we had been talking to my mom by the stairs when she tripped and fell. Afterward, my mother said she was fine but that she wanted to lie down, so we helped her to bed. And it was in that bed, with her daughters in the same room, that she died.

I listened to Chief Manning talk, trying to remain impassive, to pretend he was just a witness at one of my many depositions. And all along I was willing more of my memories to spring into my mind. Yet as hard as I tried, I couldn't recall my mother falling down the stairs. Was I not able to remember because it hadn't happened, because Caroline and I had been covering for someone, maybe our father? Or could I have been lying to save my big sister, the one who needed lengthy psychiatric attention years later?

The thought that I'd been there that night had jolted me. I was seeking answers, when all along they might simply be hibernating in my mind, waiting to be awakened.

As the water pelted me, I kept thinking about that morning when I awoke with my mother next to me—dead, I now knew—and Dan calling from the other side of the door, Caroline curled in the corner. I had been wearing the same clothes I had on when I saw my mother stumbling to the door, her hand on her head, talking to someone. That scene with my mother at the door must have happened the night before I'd woken up in her bed, which meant it must have happened after she fell, and that was why she was clutching her head.

I squeezed my eyes shut in frustration. If only I could fill in the details of the fall, then I could be sure it was an accident, not murder as the letter had suggested.

I turned off the taps and dried myself with a fluffy white bath sheet, thinking that the only person who could help me remember, the only one who was there that night, was Caroline, and Caroline had disappeared. I wrapped the towel around me and looked in the mirror, combing my hair with a brush. My eyes, a muddy green, were unlike my mother's or my siblings', but my long, wet hair reminded me of my mom, of those nights she would run in the rain and come home with her hair soaked flat. Was that all she was doing on those nights? Or was she meeting a lover, that man on the beach, that man at the door that night?

I stopped brushing my hair. That man at the door. He might be able to help me, too. He might have seen something, heard something. My mother might have told him something.

I gripped the cool porcelain of the sink and squeezed my eyes shut once more, trying to bring back any details of him that would make him easier to find. But I could only see his hand, brown from the sun, resting on my mother's blue shoulder, then gripping it, and I could hear the low rumble of his voice. I could feel myself holding on to the banister, peering around it. And then I remembered something new. I became my younger self, watching my mother at the door, watching that hand clutch her shoulder, and I saw that the man had worn a ring, because something glittered, catching the porch light through the open doorway. A gold ring with a large black diamond shape on the face. And then my mother swayed, pitched sideways, but the man caught her. I could see the back of his dark hair bending over her.

A knock interrupted me. I jumped, dropping the towel. The knock sounded again. I slipped into a hotel robe, glancing at the clock on my way to the door: 5:30 a.m. Who else was up this early? I had said goodbye to Ty last night, promising to keep in touch.

"Who is it?" I called, strangely afraid to open the door.

"Ty."

He stood outside, holding a tray covered in white linen, and sitting atop that, a basket of rolls, a white ceramic pot of coffee and a plate of neatly sliced cantaloupe.

"I thought you should eat something before you leave." He gestured with his head toward the tray, his copper hair falling over one eye. "I would have brought you cold pizza, but we were out."

"You're a sweetheart," I said, giddy that it was him, not… Not who?

Ty brought the tray into the room, put it on the desk and poured me a cup of coffee. "Let me guess, skim milk?"

"I'm that predictable?"

Ty poured a little milk into my cup. "I don't think I would ever use the word *predictable* to describe you." He turned and handed me the mug.

"Will you stay and have one with me?" I smoothed my wet hair with my hand, aware that I was wearing only a robe.

"Nah. I know you have to get going."

I took a sip of the coffee. It tasted like warm, roasted hazelnut. "Thank you," I said. "This is a treat."

"So was meeting you."

We both smiled awkwardly. My grin felt stupid and too big for this time of the morning.

Ty glanced at his watch. "Well, I know you wanted to be gone by six. Let me know what happens, okay? And let me know if I can do anything else from this end."

"Great. Thanks."

Ty took a step forward, leaning toward me, until he kissed me softly on the cheek. "I'll see you," he said, and then he left.

I stood there, holding my coffee, wanting to

call Matt in Portland and tell him I wouldn't be coming, to call McKnight Corporation and tell someone else to check with the arbitrators. I could just stay here for a few more days, maybe longer.

But that wasn't going to happen. I had work to do, obligations to fulfill, both in Chicago and in New York, and I had to get to Portland to see Matt. He was the only link to Caroline. Except for my father. The thought hit me like a slap. When I got back to Manhattan, I would have to face him.

Fifteen minutes later, I drove away from Long Beach Inn and headed out of Woodland Dunes, trying to ignore the feeling that I was leaving something behind.

12

At 7:30 a.m., I reached the Chicago branch of Gardner, State & Lord, a cozy suite of rooms, so different from the huge, impersonal office in Manhattan. I used a spare office to log on to the firm's network and check my e-mail. Immediately, I saw one from my father.

Hi, Sweetie,
I hope your arb went well, and you're enjoying Chicago. It's funny how I've been at this firm for nearly forty years, but now it doesn't seem the same without you here. Give me a call and let me know when you're returning. Love, Dad.

I read it over a few times. I searched for any hidden meanings, any hints that he knew what I was up to, but I only saw the words of the man who had raised me by himself.

When I was done checking e-mail, I called my

secretary, Amy, who happened to be the most efficient twenty-year-old on the planet.

Amy had started working for me six months out of high school, after finishing a short secretarial course. Some evil person in Human Resources, who was irritated at having to give me my own secretary, when most associates had to share one, foisted Amy on me, figuring she would be horrid. She wasn't. She was conscientious and funny and detail-oriented. And after I had trained her on my terrible shorthand and all my anal-retentive work habits—like diarying every court date five times (in my personal book, the firm book, the secretary book, the computer and my Palm Pilot)—Amy was secretarial perfection. I always encouraged her to go to college, but I secretly hoped she wouldn't follow my advice. I would be lost without her.

"Well, you've got a million things here," Amy said, "but three biggies."

"Hit me."

"Numero uno—Werner wants to know where your essay is."

I groaned. Lev Werner was the head of the partnership-election committee, and he had been calling for weeks, asking me to write an essay on what it would mean to make partner. I thought that this sounded suspiciously like a beauty-contest question and wondered whether other candidates were being asked to write something similar.

"Tell him I'll get it to him this week," I said.

"Got it. Number two, your father called. Like, thirty times since you left, and four times since I talked to you Friday morning."

"What did you tell him?" I had let Amy know that I'd be in Woodland Dunes, and I'd given her the number of Long Beach Inn just in case there were any emergencies, but I had asked her not to tell my father, or anyone else, where I was.

"I said you'd changed hotels in Chicago, and I'd lost the number of the second one." Amy giggled at the thought that she could be so irresponsible.

"Great. Let him know I'll be back tomorrow, and I'll call him then." I tried to wipe the thought of that from my mind. "What's next?"

"The people from Your New Home called about that dep next week."

I groaned. Your New Home was a big Internet client that was being sued for cybersquatting. One of their executives needed to be presented for his deposition next week in Delaware, but now that I was discovering information about my mom, I wanted to keep my schedule open if possible.

"Give it to Magoo," I said, referring to Miguel Barragan, one of the cyber-law attorneys.

"No problem. What else do you need?"

I sighed. "An extra year."

"You're coming back today?"

"Today or tomorrow." I was purposefully vague. I wasn't ready to tell anyone I was going to Portland.

"All right. I'll hold down the fort."

Ten minutes after I hung up with Amy, I received a call from the arbitrators asking me to appear that morning for a reading of the decision. I felt that flicker of anticipation in my belly, that excitement I experienced whenever a verdict was back. In this case, I had a feeling that I might lose, and I would have to take the case to trial, but the nervous stomach was still there. These moments of anticipation were one of the reasons I loved being a trial attorney. You never knew what the outcome could be. It made for sleepless nights, but it was fun just the same.

I called Beth Halverson and asked her to bring Sean McKnight to the arbitration building.

I logged on to the Internet. Using a travel site, I checked the day's flights from Chicago to Portland. There was one that left at 1:00 p.m. Perfect, I thought, checking my watch. The arbitration decision would be read at ten, which would only take a few minutes. We could return to McKnight headquarters and discuss our next move, which should take until no later than eleven-thirty, and then I could grab a cab to O'Hare. It was cutting it close, but I would make do. Matt wouldn't talk to me over the phone about it, but he was clearly suspicious of my father. I wanted to know why. I wanted to meet my sister's husband, and I wanted to help find her.

I clicked on the one-o'clock flight, then selected a red-eye return flight that left around midnight and would put me back in New York at seven in the morning. I could grab an hour or two of sleep and be in the office before lunch.

I fed my credit-card information into the computer, thinking I would be exhausted tomorrow, but it would be worth it. Today, I would meet my sister's husband, and that was closer to Caroline than I'd been in two decades.

Someone had leaked the news of the arbitrators' decision to the press, and a number of reporters, cameramen and photographers were loitering outside the room. When they saw me they went from bored chitchat directly into action, pressing microphones and camera lenses to my face, shouting questions. I pushed past them, elbowing a few in the process, thinking inanely that I was glad I had worn my red suit, but I wished I'd put on some more makeup at the office.

"How do you think your case went?" they yelled. "Are you expecting a victory?" "What will you do if the decision goes against you?" "Do you think the rumors of Sean McKnight's problems with the Fieldings company will affect the decision?"

"All right!" I yelled, because they were starting to frighten me. Luckily, my outburst worked the same way; it scared them into silence like a pack of dogs. "I'll make a brief statement," I said.

Cameramen steadied their equipment, their lights blinking red; reporters pushed their microphones into position.

"The Fieldings allegations," I said, "are just that—baseless allegations that have absolutely no merit and no bearing on this case. McKnight Corporation is an outstanding company with an outstanding record and nothing to hide. We look forward to the reading of the decision."

When I was done, I pushed through them, refusing to answer any other questions. As soon as I got into the room, I called Beth on her cell and warned her about the press.

Five minutes later, she came into the room with Sean McKnight, the sounds of reporters' questions following them. Beth looked a little rattled, but McKnight was cool as ever in a light gray springweight suit and silvery tie.

"Hailey," Beth said. "How are you?"

"Fine." I stood and shook both their hands. Sean McKnight looked me over, as if he would have to give a report later about precisely what I was wearing that day. He seem to grimace at the red of my suit, before he took a seat and pulled out the *Wall Street Journal.* I shot a look of exasperation at Beth, who rolled her eyes.

At exactly ten o'clock, the three arbitrators came into the room, greeted the participants and took their seats.

"As you know," said the lead arbitrator, an older gentleman with a rumpled suit and white hair, "once we've rendered our decision, it is final. However, either party may file a notice of rejection of the award within fourteen days. If you choose to do so, you must pay the statutory fee and this case will be placed back on the trial call with the federal court. Any questions?"

I glanced at Evan Lamey sitting at the opposing counsel's table. He shook his head, and I did the same. This was it. The excited tickle in my stomach grew.

The lead arbitrator opened a folder and read, "In the matter of Kingston Marketing Company versus McKnight Corporation, we find in favor of the plaintiff, Kingston Marketing, and award the sum of five-hundred-thousand dollars."

I let my breath ease out of my lungs, disappointed but not entirely unhappy. I had lost, just as I suspected, but the award was much lower than

Kingston had asked for. In Lamey's closing argument, he'd asserted that the company had lost millions because of the copyright and trademark infringement and asked for forty million in damages. So, essentially, this was a victory for McKnight Corporation. If they wanted to, McKnight could pay the award easily and the whole thing would go away, although I had a feeling that Evan Lamey would reject the award if I didn't.

I turned to Beth and McKnight. Beth raised her eyebrows and mouthed the words "Not bad," but McKnight had his mouth set in a steely line. I should have known that he would be happy with nothing but total domination.

"Let's go back to the office to talk," I said.

"I'll meet you there," Sean said, and then he was out of his seat and out the door, pushing through the reporters without a word.

Once Beth and I reached McKnight headquarters, Sean McKnight was not there to meet us as promised. Instead, Beth and I holed up in a conference room, going over the arbitration award, the effect it would have on the company if they paid it, and the pros and cons of advancing to trial. I kept looking at my watch, irritated that McKnight couldn't be bothered to grace us with his presence, then growing more anxious than annoyed as the time crept past eleven and toward eleven-thirty. I had to leave for the airport by twelve at the latest. Even then, I was giving myself probably only thirty minutes to get through security and on the flight.

"So what do you think, Hailey?" Beth said, interrupting my thoughts. "Pay it or play it?"

"It's not a bad judgment," I said for the third time that day.

I wasn't sure if I was trying to convince myself or Beth. The award was minimal compared to the millions the company had, but while paying it could get McKnight Corporation and its CEO out of my life, it could also make the company look guilty and affect future earnings. Beyond that, I was growing concerned again about what the verdict would do to my chances of making partner at the firm. Any partners opposed to the thought of me making their ranks too soon could just point to a recent loss on behalf of a big client and use it as an excuse.

"A trial would drag this thing out," I said to Beth, "but maybe that's for the best. The public has a short attention span these days."

The door opened then, and Sean McKnight walked in without comment. He strode to the head of the conference table. "Well?" he said. He took a seat at least five places away from where Beth and I were.

Beth ducked her head as if trying to stay out of the line of fire.

"Well, what?" I said. I hated this guy more and more by the minute.

"What happened?"

"I'm not sure what you're referring to, but if you're talking about the judgment, it's exactly what I told you to expect. Arbitrators often find for the plaintiff and award an amount they think the defendant can afford in order to get rid of a case. With Gary's testimony, we knew this would probably happen, and I advised you of that on Friday."

There was silence at the table, one I refused to break, so McKnight and I sat staring at each other until he opened his mouth again.

"And so what shall we do now, Hailey?" It was the first time he'd used my name, and a chill went through my shoulders.

"If the award won't hurt your reputation too badly, you could pay it and be done with it. You'd have to change the Web site, too, of course."

"Well, the award *would* hurt our reputation, and I don't think our stockholders would be happy. So trial is the other option?"

"That's right." I pulled my gaze away from his odd stare and snuck another look at my watch. Only an hour and fifteen minutes until the flight left.

"What makes you think you could win at trial,

when you couldn't win at an arbitration?" McKnight shifted his weight back in his chair and crossed his leg, his dove-gray pants barely creasing with the movement.

I swallowed a lump of anger that rose in my throat like bile. "We'd do a few things differently at trial."

"Like what? Gary is still a liability."

"As I said, he'll never be a good witness, but I'll work on him some more. I'd also like to hire a trial consultant to work with him."

"Anything else?" McKnight crossed his arms, and I was scared suddenly that he would fire me. I despised the guy, but I couldn't lose his business, not now.

I decided to give him exactly what he wanted to hear. "Yes, there's something else."

He cocked his head as if to say, "Continue."

"We start playing hardball," I said. I went on to describe investigations we would undertake into Kingston's own history to try to ward off any reminder of the Fieldings allegations. And I described the exhaustive research we'd conduct to find other Web sites with similar marks and technology to prove that Kingston wasn't so unique in its own site.

"I like it, Hailey," he said when I had finished, and again, his use of my first name made me nearly cringe. "Why didn't we do this before?"

"We decided to keep costs down and see if we could win at the arbitration level."

McKnight looked to Beth Halverson, who nodded to confirm that this had been the plan. Then he returned his gaze to me.

"This will be a much more expensive route," I continued. "Trial consultants and investigators cost a lot of money. Plus, I'll have to put at least one or two associates on the case to research the trademark and technology issues. As you may know, we bill at an average of three hundred and fifty dollars an hour. So it's partly an economic decision. Are you willing to pay to get the dirt?"

McKnight gave me a cold smile. "I'd like a budget plan. As well as a letter from you analyzing our trial strategy."

I didn't even blink. "Fine."

"Fine." Another silence descended over the table.

What is his goddamn problem? I wondered again. I didn't let myself linger on the question for long, though, since I saw that the time was now advancing on twelve o'clock.

"I'll call the arbitrators and Evan Lamey to notify them of our decision, and Beth will file the rejection of the award when she attends the status conference in court today." I looked to Beth, who nodded again.

McKnight exhaled, as if tired of the conversation. "I want that budget plan and analysis within the next few days." He rose from his chair and headed for the door.

I held myself back from making a comment about the fact that I had other clients, that I had a life. "Fine," I said one more time.

He stood at the door, looking at me as if he might speak again. Beth and I both waited for whatever he would say. But he was silent, and for what seemed like a full minute, his gaze never left mine. Then without another word, he turned and left.

As soon as he closed the door, I looked at Beth.

"He's a freak," she said. "Don't let him get to you."

"You're right." I shoved my papers and laptop into my briefcase. "Look, I've got a plane to catch. I'll call the arbitrators and Evan from the cab. You can handle the status conference, right?"

"No problem." She shrugged her arms into a suit coat. "And just so you know, I think you did a great job at the arb."

"At least someone around here does."

Beth groaned. "I know. I wish I could make an excuse for him."

"There's no excuse for someone like that."

I made it to the airport with only thirty minutes to spare. I rushed to the front of the security line, begging the agents to let me cut in, then ran to the gate and was rewarded with a nearly empty flight and an upgrade to first class because of all the miles I had. I tried to relax once the flight took off, letting the layer of white clouds outside my window block out whatever lay below, but there were too many tasks, too many nagging voices in my head.

I pulled out my laptop and went to work on the ludicrous essay on why I wanted to be a partner. I was tempted to write, *"For the money, of course,"* but instead I went on about how I wanted to be a permanent part of a firm that was a bastion of excellent legal skills and about the way the cyber-law department had increased the firm's revenues. And then I put my fingers to the keyboard, ready to write about my father and how I wanted to follow his legacy, but suddenly I couldn't get my hands to type the words. I'd planned this part of the essay for weeks, figuring it would play on the sentiment of the election committee while reminding them that my father had helped put the firm on the map. Yet, although I wanted the partnership more than anything, I felt unsure now whether I wanted to follow the path my dad had walked in life.

I turned off my computer and called Beth Halverson from the plane phone to see how the status conference had gone. I hadn't been able to reach

Evan Lamey from the cab, and I wanted to see how he'd taken the news.

Beth answered on the first ring. "Oh, Hailey," she said, "I've left two messages for you on your cell phone. You are not going to believe this."

I felt a prickling on the back of my neck. "What is it?"

"The judge expedited the trial. We've got four weeks."

"Are you kidding me?" My voice was so loud I drew a sharp look from a flight attendant making her way down the aisle.

"Unfortunately, no. He's sick of the press and said there's no reason to wait since we're done with most of our discovery."

"But we're not. We've got all sorts of new discovery we want to do now."

"I told him that, but he wouldn't take no for an answer. He said he had cleared his schedule, and we need to finish everything up within the month."

"Jesus." I rapped my knuckles on my closed computer, ticking off in my mind everything we would need to accomplish. "I'll get some associates researching the marks and stuff. Can you make a few calls?"

I gave Beth the names of two investigators to look into Kingston's background. I couldn't help thinking about everything I'd have to put on the back burner, namely my investigation into my mother's death. I should probably get a flight to New York as soon as I landed. But I knew I wouldn't. I was too close to Caroline.

13

Once in the rental car, I made a distress call to Amy and fired a million directions at her about the McKnight trial. Next, I reached two associates who were free and asked them if they could drop everything in favor of some initial research into Kingston's technology. When I got back, I would decide who to officially appoint to the case.

It began to rain. Sparkling droplets cut through the sheet-gray sky to splash on the windshield. Instead of depressing me, as rain often did, I found it soothing, so I didn't close the window. I let the mist inside the car. It sprayed my face; it cleansed me. Every lawn I passed, every landscaped park, was lushly green with soaring trees and bursting shrubs.

I drove for twenty minutes, following the directions that Matt had given me. Finally, I found Northeast Jarrett Street, where Caroline and Matt lived. It was a residential street lined with small, trim houses. I slowed and craned my neck to see the addresses, wondering if this had been a good idea. For all I knew, Matt was lying. He could have harmed my sister or pulled a cruel trick as part of a divorce. What did I know about their marriage or their lives? Nothing. I knew nothing about my own sister and that was exactly why I was here.

Fear wouldn't make me turn a blind eye anymore.

I pulled into Caroline's short driveway, which led to a brick bungalow with a white roof. The wind caused blossoms to drop from an apple tree onto the front lawn. A row of bushes protected the house, and a wind chime hung from the front door, tinkling softly. The chime made the house seem calm, a place friends would want to visit, but I knew from talking to Matt that this spot had been anything but calm for the last few weeks.

A pang of nervousness hit my stomach as I made my way up the curved concrete walk to the door. I hadn't gotten over my fantasies that this search would lead to a happy ending. We would all be a family again. In the future, Matt and I would drink too much eggnog on Christmas Eve, exchange funny e-mails from work.

I rapped on the door with my fist. It opened immediately.

Matt Ramsey looked like the picture he had taken with Caroline on their wedding day—

slightly long brown hair, bronzed-wire glasses—but beneath the glasses his eyes appeared red, the skin below them bruised.

"You look like her," he said without introducing himself. "Your eyes are different, but the hair…" He trailed off.

I nodded. "Can I come in?"

"Oh yeah, sure. Sorry." He raised his hands, a helpless gesture, before he backed away from the door.

This is where she lives, I thought. Caroline must have picked out that tan-and-white-striped couch, and she probably made the quilt thrown over it. She might have painted the bricks of the fireplace yellow, and those daisies long dead in a vase—she bought those, or maybe she'd gone out in her backyard and picked them.

"Sorry about the mess," I heard Matt say behind me, and it was then I noticed the layer of dust over everything in the room and the restaurant carryout boxes stacked on the coffee table.

"No problem."

"Sit down, please. Can I get you something to drink? I really only have water, but I could make some tea. Or if you're hungry I could make you soup, something."

I sat on the couch and shook my head no, smiling a little at Matt's sweetness, at his desire to make me feel comfortable when his wife was missing.

"This is a great house," I said.

He looked around. "Yeah. It's small, but we love it. We bought it right after we got married. As soon as we saw it, we knew it was home. You know what I mean?"

"Sure," I said, but I didn't know.

There had never been a place in my life that was home. Well, maybe the house in Woodland Dunes had felt like that once, but I had only been a child, and I had tried for so long to forget that part of my life that it didn't resonate anymore. My father was the only symbol of home for me.

"I saw your wedding picture," I said, desperate for safe conversation. "You both looked so happy."

"That one?" Matt gestured to a wood-framed photo on the mantel, the same photo I had in my briefcase.

"That's it."

"Where'd you get it?" He looked confused and, for the first time, mistrustful. "We didn't send many of those out."

"Oh, I…" I stumbled with my words, feeling guilty that I had read Della's letters, that I had been prying in someone's life.

"Did you get it from your father?"

"No," I answered immediately. And then the

next logical question occurred to me. "Does he have that picture?"

Matt sat in a wood chair to my right, but then he pushed it back a little as if afraid to come too close. "I don't know. If Caroline sent him an announcement, she didn't tell me, but then Caroline never really talked about her family. When we first met, she told me that her mom had died when she was about to start high school, and that she didn't get along with her father. She only told me about you after she started making that last quilt, the one she wanted to give you, but I know that she's had some contact with your father since we've been married."

"She told you that?"

Matt shook his head. "When we first started dating, she said she hated Will. She always called him by his first name. Said she never talked to him, that she didn't want to ever see him, didn't want to invite him to the wedding. She seemed fine about it, and I never pushed her. But one day a few years ago, I came home from work and heard her talking on the phone. Her voice was strange, really tight and controlled. I don't know how else to describe it. She was talking very formal, saying she was fine and yes, she was happy. She got off quick when she saw that I was in the house, and when I asked her who she was talking to, she said no one. She left the house then and went for a walk."

Matt stopped for a moment, removed his glasses and rubbed the bridge of his nose. I heard the wind chime trill from the front door again, making me aware of how silent everything else was.

"What happened then?" I said. I couldn't bear the quiet.

Matt slid his glasses back onto his face. "I checked the caller ID when she left. The name listed there was W. Sutter, and it said, 'cellular call.' I confronted Caroline when she came back. I was probably too harsh on her, but I felt like she'd been holding something back from me. Finally, she told me that her father kept tabs on her."

"Were those the words she used?" I asked. "Kept tabs?" How odd that sounded, not at all like a normal father-daughter relationship, but more like a warden and a paroled prisoner.

"Yeah. She told me that she'd tried to stay away from him because that's what he told her he wanted. But he always found her, so she'd given up hiding from him. She talked to him every once in a while to make him go away again."

I sat back and rested my head against the sofa.

"I take it you didn't know any of this?" Matt said.

"No." I raised my head. "I haven't seen Caroline since I was little, and my dad and I don't really talk about her. Do you know why she didn't want to see him or why she thought he didn't want to see her?"

"She refused to tell me about it. I finally accepted that it was the one part of her life she wouldn't let me into."

"That must have been hard."

"I hated it." Matt shifted his gaze away momentarily. "I hated the thought that we would have any secrets from each other. And it scared me, because she always acted so strange whenever the subject came up. But I had to get over it. I thought it was for the best. Now I wish I'd made her tell me about your dad. She might still be here."

"Why do you think my dad had anything to do with Caroline taking off? Isn't it possible that she has other problems or issues that might have made her leave?"

A look of annoyance took over Matt's face. "Like what?"

Should I mention Crestwood Home? Maybe my sister hadn't told Matt about that either. Maybe she wouldn't want him to know. For all I knew, it could have been Caroline who'd caused my mother's death.

"Depression, maybe?" I said.

"If you haven't seen or talked to Caroline since you were seven, what are you getting at?"

I was silent, then I felt my face grow pink. I didn't want to be evasive, but I didn't want to betray my sister.

"Look, Hailey, I need to find my wife. I need to know she's safe," Matt said. "I'm doing most of the talking here, and yet I don't know anything about you. I get the feeling we both care for Caroline and both want what's good for her, but you're going to have to tell me what you know. Anything might help."

His face fell as he spoke the last sentence, and I knew he was right. I couldn't expect him to contribute everything.

"I don't know much," I said, "but I've been looking into how my mom died." *Look closely.* "So I've been asking around, trying to find out what happened and where my brother and sister are."

"Why not ask dear old dad?"

I shot him a cool look. "Because it upsets him too much."

"Oh, I bet." Matt's voice rang with sarcasm.

"What is it with you and my father?" My voice rose a little despite myself. "So what if your wife had a bad relationship with him? So what if she talks to him once in a while?" As I asked these questions, my mind echoed with another: Why didn't my father tell me he kept in touch with Caroline?

Matt leaned forward, his eyes awake now, hard. "Will Sutter clearly terrified Caroline. That was obvious every time I found her speaking to him.

But I could live with that. What I can't live with is my wife disappearing. I have good reason to believe your father was the cause of that."

"Why?" Immediately, I wished I could take the question back. I wanted to leave that sunny, dusty room. I wanted to forget Caroline's quilt and the daisies and the apple tree outside.

But I didn't move. I sat still, listening to a breeze blow the wind chime into song again.

"He called the day before we left for Charleston," Matt said. "I was barbecuing in the backyard, and I came inside to get the garlic salt. Caroline likes that on everything." He paused for a second, his eyes elsewhere, before he looked at me again. "Anyway, it was just like that other phone call. I found Caroline sitting at the kitchen table on the phone. She was hunched over. She was talking like a little girl. She was saying, yes, no, I understand, stuff like that. When she saw me, she hung up fast, and I asked her who it was."

Matt stopped and stared past me to the kitchen, the room where it had all happened.

"And," I said, prompting him.

Matt returned his gaze to me. "And," he said, the emotion gone from his voice, "she said it was Will. Two days later she was gone."

Matt remained still, looking at me, as if daring

me to challenge his assumption. Something trembled inside me, and yet I ignored it. I did what I'd been trained to do, to analyze the situation. It wasn't necessarily a logical assumption, I decided, to think that the phone call was somehow a precursor to Caroline's disappearance days later. Yet nothing about the last few weeks was logical. I had received the letter and started investigating my mom's death. Around the same time, my father called my sister, and then my sister disappeared.

"Maybe you're looking for someone to blame?" I said weakly.

"Are you kidding me?" He nearly shouted the question, and I flinched involuntarily. He pulled his glasses off again, and I thought he might cry. "I'm not looking to blame someone. I just want her back, and I've done everything I can think of. I've talked to the police here and in Charleston. I've been sitting around here every minute like the police told me, in case she calls."

"I'm sorry," I said softly. "Is there anything I can do? I'd like to help."

Matt replaced his glasses and stood up. "I've got to get out of here. Even if it's just for half an hour. Do you want to get a bite? I haven't eaten all day."

I glanced at my watch: 5:00 p.m. There was no sense in checking into a hotel and trying to sleep before my flight. "Sure," I said, and then as an afterthought, "Are you sure you want to leave? What if she calls?"

Matt opened his mouth then closed it again, his eyes roaming his house as if he was searching for something. "I've been holed up here since I got back from Charleston. I haven't gone to work, nothing. I'm about to get fired. But once in a while, I have to get out. There's an old schoolhouse a few blocks away that's been converted into a hotel and restaurant. It's quick."

I picked up my purse and followed him out the door.

We walked without speaking down Matt's street, around a park, and along another street. I was acutely aware of Matt at my side, aware that he was family to me. Matt walked with his hands in his pockets, his head hung low as if it was an effort to keep it on his shoulders. I could almost feel how exhausted he was.

The rain had stopped but the air felt heavy with moisture. And I sensed something else, too, a feeling I'd had before, one that was growing familiar. I looked around and saw a black car as it turned a corner. A midsize sedan, an Alamo rental sticker on the bumper; a gray strap flapped from the trunk as if it had been closed too fast and had caught the handle of a bag. There were probably a million black rental cars cruising around Portland right now, yet I remembered that one in particular because of the Alamo sticker and the gray strap. The car had been in front of me for a few blocks on the way to Matt's house, before it turned off. And I remembered seeing a black car behind me a minute or two later, but then I had begun to look for Matt's address, and I forgot about it.

I shook my head. I was being paranoid.

I was about to make conversation with Matt, but as I began searching for a neutral topic, we reached the restaurant. It was a large, yellow stucco building, with arched windows and doorways. There were stone reliefs of carved cherubs in the corners. We walked up the steps, and Matt swung open the heavy wood door and held it for me. I was about to step inside, when I saw it again. The black car. It was parked a half block away. Glare on the windshield prevented me from seeing inside, so I stayed where I was, waiting for the car to move. But the car sat there, so that the sedan and I seemed in some type of standoff.

"Hailey?" I heard Matt say. "Ready?"

I felt foolish suddenly. "Sure, sure." With one last look at the still car, I walked through the door.

Inside the old schoolhouse, all the rooms were still intact, so that what had once been the classrooms and offices were now bars, dining rooms and hotel rooms.

I remarked about how great the restaurant was, but Matt barely managed a smile in return. He led me down the old wood hallway to a courtyard that held a large fireplace pit in the center.

Once we were seated, Matt pushed the menu away. "The Caesar is excellent if you like salads, and the burgers are my favorite."

"Sounds good," I said. I ordered a chicken Caesar, while Matt asked for a turkey sandwich. "No burger for you?"

"I normally would, but…" He scratched his jaw. "I guess I don't want to enjoy myself."

I nodded. "I was wondering, if it isn't too painful, if could you tell me what Caroline was like. I mean, *is* like." I wanted to shoot myself for using the past tense.

Matt made a short exhale, almost like a laugh. "How do I describe Caroline? It's so hard to come up with the words. What was she like when you were a kid?"

"Beautiful, quiet, sad, or at least I always thought she was sad."

Matt nodded. "Caroline does carry around a certain amount of melancholy. One of the reasons she moved here was for the rain. Most people just put up with it, but she said it's comforting to her, and that it's the sunny skies that depress her. My friends were surprised when we started dating because she wasn't the outgoing party type I usually brought around, but they came to love her, too."

"How did you meet?"

"We met in Astoria. It's a small town on the Oregon coast. My hometown, actually. Caroline was taking a weekend trip there."

"By herself?"

"Yeah."

I knew he was going to say that. I was struck by the first similarity, other than physical, between my sister and me—loneliness had been a companion to us both.

"I met her in a diner there," Matt said. "We started talking, and we were there for four hours. I knew by the end of that day that I was in love with her."

Our food was delivered, and Matt looked relieved.

I began to eat my salad. "So I have to ask you. What did the police say?"

"I called the Charleston police the night of the wedding, but they told me I needed to wait twenty-four hours. Then I got back to the hotel and found the note from her." He put his sandwich down. "I was up all night, just waiting. And I waited all the next day. I wandered around looking for her. Finally, when night came I contacted the local police again, but when I showed them the note, they weren't interested. Gave me some line about how women do that sometimes." He laughed scornfully.

"And that's it? They wouldn't help you?"

"Nope. I called the Portland police, too. They were a little nicer, and they looked into her disappearance for a few days, but they kept coming back to the note, and eventually they dropped their investigation. It was the same song and dance about letting her have a little space. I've been trying to find your father, but the number's not listed. How about giving me that?"

His question startled me. My father was a private man, and I wasn't sure what to do. "Do you still have the note?" I said, ignoring his question for the time being.

Matt sighed. He stared at me. Finally, as if he'd made a decision, he nodded, then leaned back and reached into the pocket of his jeans. He pulled out a small, worn piece of white notepaper and handed it to me. Across the top, in green italic printing, it read, *Planters Inn.* Under that, in blue ballpoint ink and tiny cursive handwriting, Caroline had written:

Matty, I love you so much, and I'm sorry to just take off like this, but I need a break. Please, please, please don't worry about me. I'll be fine. I'll be in touch. Love, Caro.

I read it once more and felt a tug in my heart at the nicknames.

I handed the paper back to Matt. "Has she done this before?"

"Never." He ran a finger over the note before he folded it and put it back into his pocket.

"And you haven't heard anything from her?"

"No."

"Have you called her friends?"

Matt smiled. "You're looking at him."

I felt that tug again. "She doesn't have any girlfriends?"

"Not really." He must have caught the surprise on my face. "Don't look so sad. She became pretty good friends with my buddies, and I'm her best friend. We've been happy, until your father screwed it up for us."

The lettuce in my mouth felt dry and sticky. I had to force myself to chew and swallow it. I was angry at my father for keeping me away from Caroline, but I still hated to hear someone malign him. Will Sutter was an organized, cerebral man who always had a reason for his actions. He did nothing by accident. I wanted to believe that he had a good motive for keeping in touch with Caroline and not telling his youngest daughter about it.

"I'm sorry," Matt said. "I know you lived with your dad, and you probably believe he's perfect, but if you'd seen Caroline that day…" His words died away for a moment, as if the memory was too painful. "I should have made her talk then. I should have forced her to tell me what was making her act like that and look so scared. But Caroline got jumpy when she was pushed, and I thought there was time. I thought…" He trailed off again, and shoved his plate away. He'd eaten only half his sandwich.

"Shouldn't you try to eat more?" I asked. "You need to keep your strength up."

Matt smiled, the first genuine smile I had seen since I met him. "That's what Caro always used to say. 'You need to keep your strength up.'"

I returned the smile. It was something I said frequently, too, clichéd words of wisdom I gave to my father when he was on trial or to Maddy when she was drinking too much wine. A glimmer of a memory then. My mom in a pair of shorts and a peach T-shirt, bringing a basket of rolls to the table.

"Della made them special," she'd said, placing the basket on the table. "Eat, kids. You need to keep your strength up."

Suppers during the week were laid-back affairs, with all of us in casual clothes—shorts in the spring and summer, jeans and sweaters during the colder months. The food was brought in whenever it was ready, Della sticking her head in the dining room to say goodbye before she hurried home to her own family. But on Fridays, when my dad came home, dinner was transformed.

It was as if our father was a celebrity, the one we were all waiting to see. My mother dressed up, put on makeup, and made elaborate dinners without Della's help. She even set the dining-room table with linens. In my earliest memories, those dinners were the highlight of everyone's week, a festive feel lingering at the table.

By the time I was five or six, Dan had become sullen and sat in hostile silence. Caroline, who had always been quiet, was more withdrawn, too. In retrospect, I could see that there was something different about my family during those last years. Or was I filtering my memory because of the news that they'd been separated? No, I didn't think so. When I'd been much younger, maybe four or five, my parents would kiss in the front hall when Dad came home, and they would hold hands over the table. But later, during the few years before my mother's death, they made polite small talk while I chatted on and on about school, hating the odd silence in the room.

And I remembered something else. In the months before my mom died, the Friday dinners didn't happen anymore. I was allowed to have a grilled-cheese sandwich in front of the television, while Caroline escaped to her room or the porch swing, and Dan fled with his friends in an old Jeep.

I heard a small cough, and I realized that Matt was watching me, waiting.

"Want to let me in?" he said.

"It's nothing really. I was just remembering how my mom used to say the same thing about keeping your strength up, and that made me think about the times when she was still around, when I was little."

"And that's it?" Matt looked doubtful.

"Actually, I was thinking about family dinners and how we didn't have them anymore before she died. I found out recently that my parents were separated in the months before her death."

"Well, that's interesting, isn't it?" he said. "All these women running from Will Sutter."

"One has nothing to do with the other," I said in a haughty tone.

Matt shot me a disbelieving look, and I dropped my eyes. I wasn't so sure, either.

"Did Caroline keep in touch with our brother, Dan?" I asked Matt.

"Not often that I know of. She told me her brother had sent money a few times when she first moved to Portland, but I can't remember them having any contact since we've been married. We made our wedding plans at the last minute, and I asked her if she wanted to wait so that she could invite some family. She said no."

"Did she say why?"

The corners of Matt's mouth raised a little. "She said that I was her family now." He looked around the restaurant. He seemed to remember again that his wife wasn't here, that his family was gone, and the happy expression evaporated.

14

The next morning, back in Manhattan, I treated myself to a cab to work, figuring that if I went into the bowels of the subway, the darkness would send me straight to sleep. The red-eye had left on time the night before, but I couldn't rest on the plane. My mind churned with too much information, too many things to do and the lingering memory of my brother-in-law's haunted face.

Matt and I had talked for a few more hours. We filled in the details of our lives, got to know each other better. At times, the conversation veered to Caroline, to where she might be, to what we could do to find her. Matt kept asking me for my father's number. I told him I would have better luck speaking with my father than he would, and I promised to do that. I dreaded it.

Framed in the cab's window, the city flew past. The morning sun hid some of the dirt; the high-rises climbed upward. I organized the day's to-do list in my head. First, I would put out fires on any cases other than McKnight. Next, I would call an emergency meeting about McKnight, and I'd ask two attorneys to be permanently assigned to the case, including Magoo Barragan and at least one other lawyer who could devote a crazy number of hours over the next month. But there were other things I had to do today, things that didn't involve my quickly spinning legal world. I had to talk to my father and I would try to find my brother, Dan. Learning that Caroline was missing had come too soon on the heels of getting that letter—*Look closely*—and now my family wouldn't or couldn't leave my brain.

"Morning, Hailey," the receptionist said as I walked out of the elevator and onto the thirty-third floor. Behind the woman's high, mahogany desk, the words Gardner, State & Lord were spelled in burnished gold on the glass wall that overlooked a large conference room. Soothing classical music played from hidden speakers. This was the image our firm wanted outsiders to see.

"Hey, Tina," I said.

I slipped my key card in the slot by the side door and stepped into the true Gardner offices, where secretaries clacked away on computers, swore at printers and answered constantly ringing phones. The attorneys' doors were all open and the sound of their phone conversations blended with the other voices. Meanwhile, mail and copy people hurried through the hallways, making deliveries and picking up stacks of documents.

I called hello to a number of employees as I made my way down the hall. Everyone looked pale to me today, as if they hadn't seen the outside of this building in years. It was nearly true.

I was lucky enough to have what was considered a large associate office with a window, which, unfortunately, looked upon nothing but the building next to it. But at least I had some fugitive sunlight sneaking in, unlike some of the other associates who were strapped with internal offices and nothing but a fluorescent glare for their twelve-hour workdays. I even had room for a small love seat, although now it was stacked with large red McKnight file jackets.

Amy, a small woman with a cap of dark hair, bustled in after me. As usual, she wore a too-short skirt with a trim, matching jacket. "You look tired," she said, frowning.

"Thanks," I said in a sarcastic tone. But both Amy and I knew that I needed occasional mothering, that I liked it.

"Eat breakfast yet?"

"It's almost eleven." I unpacked my laptop and files. "I'll wait for lunch."

"Nope. I'll get you a bagel."

I didn't argue. I told Amy to bring in the Your New Home files and any other cases that had to be dealt with immediately, and then to schedule a lunch meeting with all the cyber-law attorneys for one o'clock.

I worked for the next couple hours, absently picked at a cinnamon-and-raison bagel between interruptions. My phone rang incessantly, as if clients and other attorneys had sensed I was back in town.

I had just picked up my Dictaphone to dictate a Motion to Dismiss on a new file, when I heard Amy speaking to someone outside my office. "Hailey's busy," she said.

"Oh, I'll just pop in," said a sugary voice.

I groaned.

Paige Amboy, my least favorite attorney at the firm, stuck her head in my office. Her lustrous blond hair swung with the movement. "Welcome back, Hailey."

"Hi, Paige." I refrained from sighing, and sat up in my chair, aware that I'd worn my oldest, most unflattering gray pantsuit. Paige, meanwhile, looked stunning in a lemon-yellow dress just tight enough to be sexy but still conservative enough for Gardner, State & Lord. I was rarely able to pull off that effect.

"I heard about your arb," Paige said in an overly

sympathetic voice. She advanced into the room, eyeing my clutter with disdain. "You win some, you lose some, I guess."

"I consider this a win."

Paige's eyebrows shot skyward. "Of course," she said soothingly.

"What can I do for you, Paige?"

"Oh, I just wanted to check up on you." She said this as if she were babysitting a four-year-old in a sandbox.

"Everything's just fine, thanks."

"Getting ready for the partnership election?" She had finally stopped prowling and now stood in front of my desk.

I didn't ask her to sit. "Sure."

"Did you write the essay yet?"

"What essay?" I said this to see if I could draw a reaction. Paige, two years my senior, was also up for partner this year, and she'd probably wondered, as I had, if she was the only one who had to craft such a silly document.

"You weren't asked to write an essay about what it would mean to be partner?" Paige's face tightened, her eyes narrowed.

I took a moment to think and draw out Paige's confusion. "Oh, *that* thing," I said at last.

Paige recovered her composure. "Well, have you done it yet?"

"Weeks ago," I lied.

"Really?"

"You should get yours to Werner soon. I heard they're taking timeliness into account."

Paige's mouth formed a small O before it was taken over by a distrustful frown. Paige was always concerned that I was getting inside information from my father. "I better get going on that then," Paige said.

"Yes. You better." I was too tired to spar anymore, so I glanced down at the documents on my desk. Luckily, she took the hint and left.

I forced myself to ignore my sagging eyelids and continued to plod through the work on my desk. At twelve forty-five, I pulled out the McKnight file again, and began to get ready for the lunch meeting.

"Oh, hi, Mr. Sutter," I heard Amy say. My stomach lurched.

"Call me Will," my father said, as he always did.

"I'll try," she said.

My father stepped into my office, and for a second, the sight of his silver hair, his kind eyes and his warm smile made me forget the last few days and everything I'd learned.

"Welcome back," he said. The smooth tones of his voice filled the office, carrying to all parts of the room. The perfect voice for a trial lawyer. He wore an olive suit with a creamy shirt and lightly patterned tie. His cuff links matched his tie clip, his brown loafers buffed to a high shine. He always dressed to perfection, even on weekends.

"Hi, Dad," I said, nervous.

He walked to my desk and held out his right hand. I grasped it with my left, and we squeezed. It was the greeting we had developed when I started working at the firm. We decided it wouldn't be professional for us to hug in the office, and so the handclasp was our secret sign of affection. I held on a little longer than usual, not wanting to break the bond.

"Anything wrong?" He looked down at our still-gripped hands.

I let mine drop. "No. Of course not."

"Congrats on the arbitration award." He sat on one of the chairs in front of my desk.

Finally, someone who understood. "Thanks."

"Tell me about it."

This was our usual custom—rehashing a dep, a trial, a mediation. Picking over the testimony, deciding what could have been done differently, what other choices there were to make. My father agreed that Gary's testimony had hurt, but nothing I could have done would have changed it. He liked my trial strategy, and gave me the names of some recent law-review articles that discussed intellectual property in the Internet world.

This bantering of ours, this legal give-and-take, comforted me. I let myself get lost in it. I pretended that this was any other day.

Too soon, our talk slowed.

"Well," my father said, "I better get going. I've got a settlement conference in half an hour." He moved forward in his seat.

"Dad," I said, a little too loudly apparently, because he turned his head to the side ever so slightly, as if he'd heard a sound outside. It was a mild gesture to anyone unfamiliar with him, but I knew it as a look of wariness.

He sat back in the chair and nodded, an invitation to continue.

"I need to know something." My eyes were down toward my desk, not meeting his. I forced myself to look up and saw him staring at my hands. I was uncurling a paper clip and twisting it around my finger. I dropped the clip and folded my hands together.

"Dad…" Again I faltered, unsure what to ask him first. "Why didn't you ever—" How hard it was to form a single coherent question from all those battling in my head.

My father gave me another nod.

"I need for you to tell me—"

"Time for the meeting," Amy said, sticking her head in the door. "Everyone is already in the conference room."

I exhaled. "I'll be right there."

Amy left, and my father leaned forward in his seat. "What is it?"

I shook my head. This wasn't the time or the place. I couldn't start and finish this conversation in five minutes.

"Nothing." I rose from my chair. "I need to get to that meeting."

My father stood, too. "You're sure?" His forehead creased with worry, a look that meant he was concerned about me, that he probably wouldn't sleep tonight.

Whenever I'd had a rough spot in my life, or at least what I perceived as rough at the time—like when Rob Bradshaw asked someone else to the prom or when I failed to make law review by only a few points—my father got that look, and he wouldn't sleep for days until I was over it. I would hear him walking around the house at night and the soft murmur of the TV. In the morning, I would find him in his study, the stacks of work telling me he had been at it all night. He wasn't the type of parent to try and solve my problems. He offered advice if asked, and held my hand if I wanted, but he fretted and paced and stayed awake until I was back to normal. I hated to see him like that, hated that I caused his reaction, and yet his reaction was a silent gesture of love. I knew he would worry about me now. He would lay awake at night until I asked the questions or told him I was fine, but this time, the thought of his worry didn't bother me as much. In fact, maybe it was a good thing, because it would force me to ask him the tough questions in order to erase it. Things would have to come to a head. It was time.

I told him I would find him later, and he left my office with those worry lines still crossing his face.

"Are you trying to kill me?" Magoo Barragan said as I walked into the conference room. Magoo, an olive-skinned man with wavy, dark brown hair, was standing by the buffet table with the four other attorneys that made up the cyber-law department. They were all choosing from the sandwiches and salads Amy had ordered. Unlike my office, this room had a view of the river. Outside the glass, the sun gleaming off buildings made me wish I was back on the stretch of sand behind Long Beach Inn rather than breathing the artificial air of a sealed room.

"Magoo," I said in a jokey, plaintive voice. "You know I love you, so why would I want to kill you?"

He carried a sandwich to the table. "Then what are you doing giving me the Your New Home dep in Delaware *and* dragging me into this McKnight monstrosity?"

I'd left him a voice mail earlier, officially asking him to help on McKnight.

"I need you desperately," I said. I put the files down on the table and walked over to the buffet.

"Yeah, yeah," I heard Magoo say behind me. "All the women in this firm need me."

As I helped myself to a turkey sandwich and a scoop of pasta salad, I greeted the other attorneys. Ellis Radwell, a tall, African American man two years out of law school, was loading his plate full of food and said, "Hey, Hailey," through a mouthful of potato chips. Ellis was an excellent lawyer and an even better writer. I knew the McKnight trial would require extensive motions and briefs, so normally I would seek his help, but Ellis's wife had recently given birth to their first child, and I felt bad asking too much during this time. McKnight was going to require some very late nights.

I talked with the three other associates, trying to decide who would be the best to help on the case. Michelle Headly, or Mickey as we called her, was the youngest of the bunch, coming up on her one-year anniversary at the firm. A beautiful, fair-skinned woman who didn't seem aware of her good looks, she was eager to take on any work, but I needed someone with a little more experience. That left Natalie Decker, a true New Yorker with a very serious demeanor, or Jim Siderski, a jovial, football-loving guy. I preferred Jim, since we would all be spending a lot of time together, and Jim tended to make things fun, but Natalie had extensive intellectual-property experience that would be invaluable. As I picked up a fork—real silver here at Gardner, State & Lord no plastic stuff—I asked Natalie to help out.

"Whatever," Natalie said, sweeping her blunt-cut hair out of her face. That was Natalie's reaction to everything: whatever. It seemed that after living in this city all her life, nothing could impress, nothing could shock.

That decision made, I took my seat, and after we chatted, I briefed them on the McKnight case, the work that Magoo, Natalie and I would need to do in the next month and the overflow of cases the others would have to pick up. With the exception of Natalie, they all jumped in with suggestions and insights, and I came out of the meeting feeling as if we had a plan. It would be crazy, but we would get it done.

Back in my office, I called Beth Halverson at McKnight headquarters to update her, then closed my door.

"Amy," I said over the intercom, "can you take my calls for a while? I want to get some work done."

I turned off my ringer. I didn't like lying to Amy, but I wasn't about to tell her that I was trying to track down the brother I hadn't seen in more than twenty years.

I had already called Santa Fe information when I was at the Long Beach Inn. Now I logged on to the Internet. I typed the name Singer into the on-line Santa Fe phone book and found that the Singers took up almost a whole page. There were listings for David Singer, Don Singer and Dierdre Singer, but no Dan.

Next, I ran a people search on the Internet and came up with a list of twenty-one Daniel Singers around the country. Of course, there were probably many more that didn't appear on that list for one reason or another, but it was a place to start. I printed it out and began to call each one. I reached a number of unhelpful people who hung up shortly after telling me that I must have the wrong person. A few times I got voice mail, and listened to the voices of the men who identified themselves as Daniel Singer. Most I could rule out because of certain accents or a gruffness that told me they were much too old to be my Dan. On the few that might be possibilities, I left a message with my name and office phone number. My brother would recognize the name, and I couldn't believe he would ignore me after all these years.

Once I had gone through the list, I felt no closer to finding him. I doubted somehow that he was one of the men I'd just called. I sat still at my desk, thinking over the possibilities. He had been in New Mexico the last time he wrote Della, and for some reason, I felt he might still be there, far away from the Midwest. I pulled up the Santa Fe phone book on the Internet again and began to go through the Singer listings once more, this time calling each one, no matter what the first name, to ask if they were related to Dan Singer. Many weren't home and the ones who were didn't know a Dan Singer with sandy-blond hair who'd be in his late thirties.

I had called more than half of the Singers in Santa Fe and was about to give up, but I made myself finish calling the rest of the list. *Follow every avenue, every lead. Look under every rock.* My father had told me this when I first started practicing, when every case seemed too difficult to handle. Keep fighting, he would tell me. You have to simply keep slugging.

So I did. There were two listings for S. Singer. I called the first one and reached an older woman who was anxious to be helpful and clearly lonely.

"I don't know any Daniels in my family," she said, her voice wavering, "but I knew a David. He was my brother-in-law."

"Okay, well, thanks for your time," I said, but the woman wouldn't let me go.

"I fancied David more than my Louis if the truth be told," she said. "Never told anyone that before."

I doubted that. I listened to another minute of the woman reminiscing before I excused myself.

A few more calls, I decided, looking at the silver clock on my bookshelf. It was five o'clock already. I needed to do a few more hours of work before I met Maddy for dinner. I dialed the number for the other S. Singer.

After four rings, a woman answered, out of breath.

"Hi," I said quickly, going into the same spiel I'd been giving everyone. "My name is Hailey, and I'm looking for someone named Dan Singer. Late thirties, sandy-blond hair, grew up in Michigan—"

The woman laughed, a harsh sound. "Did he meet you at a bar?" Her voice had a tired, resigned quality to it.

"Excuse me?"

"Is that where he met you? A bar or something?" the woman said.

"Oh, no." My thoughts bounced from confusion to elation that I might have found someone who knew Dan. "I didn't meet him. I mean, I have, but it was a long time ago. But—"

"Doesn't matter," the woman said, cutting me off. "It's not important. What is important is our daughter, who he was supposed to pick up on Saturday, over two weeks ago. Did you know he had a daughter named Annie?" The woman's voice bordered on angry.

"No. I didn't. I—" I stopped short. *Saturday, over two weeks ago.* The night Caroline disappeared.

"Well, he does," the woman continued, "and she's still waiting for the bastard to call. So if he didn't call his daughter, do you think he's going to call you?"

"Look, I'm an old friend from the Midwest," I said. I spoke fast, not wanting her to hang up. "I haven't seen Dan in a very long time. If you could just give me his phone number, I'll make sure to have him call Annie when I find him."

"He's hopeless. Don't waste your time, girl-friend."

"It's not like that." I could hear the pleading tone in my voice. I was desperate now for some real information. "If you could just let me know his address even."

"He's in Albuquerque now. And if you find him, you can tell him he's an asshole." And she hung up.

I replaced the phone on the receiver, my head buzzing. Dan hadn't shown up two Saturdays before, the same day Caroline disappeared. And I was an aunt. I had a niece in Santa Fe named Annie.

15

I pushed through the crowd at Veronica's, one of my favorite restaurants in the neighborhood, a dark, cozy place decorated with wood and warm colors of wine and mustard.

"A Stoli and tonic with lemon," I said to the bartender, throwing my jacket over a tall stool.

I was early, but I wanted to get a drink, to sit silently at the front bar for a moment. I knew when Maddy got here, there would be no quiet. These regrouping sessions, as Maddy and I called them, were the closest thing to therapy I had in my life. Maddy would spend hours with me deciding whether I should cut my hair one inch or two, whether I should shop for a condo or continue to rent, whether I was really depressed or just had PMS. I would do the same for her. She was the nearest thing to a sister I had found.

The minute I sat down, though, with my back to the door, I felt uneasy, as if I could be watched without knowing it. I tried to convince myself that the feeling I had lately of being observed was just paranoia from my overloaded mind. But I couldn't shake it, so I moved from my stool to another at the end of the bar where I could see Maddy when she came in. Or anyone else.

The bartender slid a thick, frosted highball glass in front of me. I took a long sip, letting the cool bitter of the vodka and the sweet tang of the citrus slide down my throat. After my drunken night in Woodland Dunes, I swore I would never drink another drop of alcohol again, but like other such promises, it had fallen away.

I stared down at the dark wood bar, thinking about the woman on the phone who'd clearly been my brother's wife or girlfriend. She'd said that Dan hadn't picked up his daughter last Saturday, the same day Caroline disappeared from Charleston. She hadn't heard from him since.

When I called Albuquerque Information, I had received a listing for Dan Singer in that city. I copied the number down, as well as the address, and I called the number at least ten times, but there was no answer. Not even a machine.

I was scared suddenly, more scared than I had ever been. It was as if I'd just realized that for my whole life I had stood on sand that was packed hard. Not a solid-rock foundation, but one that allowed me to walk and go about some semblance of a normal life. But after rummaging into the past, the sand had blown about and disappeared, until I felt there was precious little to stand on anymore. If I didn't have my father, my love for him, my belief in his goodness and judgment, most of that remaining foundation would be gone. It left only Maddy and whatever I had inside me.

I heard a call and saw that Maddy had entered the bar. I swiveled on the stool and fell into her hug. I held on longer than usual.

"You all right?" I heard Maddy ask, her words muffled by my shoulder.

"Yeah," I said, releasing her.

"You're sure?" Maddy's hazel eyes squinted as if trying to read my face. Her dark curly hair was pulled back, a few tendrils escaped at the sides of her face. She wore a lilac suit, cut snug to show off her curves.

"Let's get a table. I'll tell you the whole saga."

We ordered two entrées—the sea bass and the mushroom risotto. I launched into the story, telling Maddy briefly about the McKnight arbitration, then moving on quickly to the weekend in Woodland Dunes.

When I got to the part about getting drunk with Ty on Saturday night, Maddy held up her hand. "Okay, first things first. We're getting you off the vodka right now and switching to wine." Maddy flagged down the waiter, and ordered a bottle of Chardonnay.

"The next issue," Maddy said, leaning forward on the table with her elbows, "is this Ty person. Let's talk about him."

I groaned. Maddy was the dating queen of New York. She was forever giving me hell for not going out with enough men.

"There's nothing to talk about."

"You told me twice he was cute," Maddy said, pausing to okay the bottle of wine the waiter proffered. "And he sent a tray with wine and cheese to your room with a nice little note that I bet you read at least three times."

I burst out laughing. Maddy knew me implicitly, and that felt so damn good.

"I knew it. And then to top it off, you act like an intoxicated fool, and yet he doesn't leave you in the street like he should have."

I accepted a glass of wine from the waiter. "So?"

"So? He sounds like a gem. Why didn't you kiss him and see if the whole world disappeared?"

I shot her an exasperated look. Maddy knew about my flimsy test for true love. Sometimes, I wished I'd never told her about it. "I'd just met the guy!"

"When is the last time you had sex?"

"Oh, no. I'm not having this conversation."

"Okay, fine. You don't have to sleep with him anytime soon."

"Gee, thanks."

"But," Maddy continued, "you should at least think seriously about dating him. He sounds like a prince."

"Maddy, he's a hotel owner in Michigan, and I'm an attorney in Manhattan. Does that sound like it's going to work?"

"Never know until you try."

I shook my head and fell silent while Maddy sipped her wine. I would never win the argument.

"When are you going to see him again?" Maddy said.

"Never? I don't know."

"Look, I'm not trying to bug you."

I gave her another look.

"Okay, maybe I am." Maddy gave me a devilish grin. "But just promise me you won't dismiss this. Not yet. See what happens when you go back to Chicago."

"Fine," I said to get her off my back. The entrées arrived, and I cut the sea bass down the middle, putting half of it on Maddy's plate. I let myself think about Ty for a second. It wasn't that I didn't like him. If he lived in Manhattan, I'd probably be all over the guy. But the long distance seemed too great an obstacle, when I already had so many others.

"All right," Maddy said, a pleased little look on her face. "Glad we got that settled. Now keep going with your story."

I told her about the letters from Della and the dinner with the Mannings.

"Oh, God. That must have been horrible," she said when she heard about the abuse suspicions Chief Manning had considered.

I didn't let myself linger on the issue, because the truth was that the thought made me sick. "It wasn't true, though," I said. "That's what Ty's dad decided, he…" Something snagged in my mind.

Maddy looked up at me as my words trailed away. "What?" she said.

"I was thinking of my conversation with them." I went quiet, making myself review that night and the exact words Chief Manning had said.

Maddy waved a hand in front of my face.

"Now that I think about it," I said. "I don't remember him saying he decided the abuse allegations weren't true."

"What did he say exactly?"

"She fell down the stairs."

Maddy pursed her mouth in a suspicious smirk.

"I know, I know. It's the classic line to cover up abuse, and Manning said he suspected my dad. It's crazy, right?"

"Ridiculous! They obviously cleared him."

"That's the thing," I said, returning in my mind to the Mannings' snug kitchen and their painted wood table. "I asked Ty's dad if they'd ruled him out, and he said, 'I guess you could say that.'"

"What's that supposed to mean?"

"I'm not sure." I pushed my plate away, not hungry any longer. "At the time, I took it to mean that my dad was cleared of those suspicions. I mean, that's how the conversation seemed, but now that I'm remembering it, Chief Manning didn't really say that."

"Well, this isn't a deposition, Hailey. He wasn't precise with his words, but I'm sure he meant he ruled your dad out. Otherwise they'd have pressed charges."

"Right," I said, wanting to believe her. "Right." But something about Chief Manning's response irked me.

"So keep going with your story," Maddy said, pouring more wine.

I dragged my mind away from the Mannings' kitchen and told Maddy about Portland, meeting Matt, and finally my conversation with the woman in Santa Fe, as well as my phone calls to the Albuquerque home of someone named Dan Singer.

"Geez," she said. "You've been busy. So when are you going to Santa Fe?"

"What?"

"No one answers at Dan's house, right? So you don't even know if he's in Albuquerque anymore. And that woman who had a kid with him isn't going to talk to you on the phone. She's hostile, and she's had enough. If you happened to go to Santa Fe on business, though, if you just happened to call from your hotel and say you're stopping by, maybe she'd tell you what she knows."

I thought for a second. "I like it, but I'm too crazy with the McKnight case."

"You can work on planes. You can work in a hotel room. You'd probably get more done if you're by yourself without the phones ringing and everybody around your firm talking about the partnership election."

Maddy had a point. "Would you go with me?" I said, excited. "We could make it a girls' trip."

"Oh, sweetie. I would. You know I'd do anything for you, but I've been kind of busy myself." Maddy wore a coy expression.

"What is it? I'm sorry I've been dominating the conversation."

"Oh, shut up. My story's not half as interesting." But Maddy looked very interested. "I think I might be falling for someone."

"What?" The word came out louder than I expected, and I noticed a few other diners turning their heads toward me. "You mean just *one* guy?"

Maddy had a big smile on her face now. "Yep."

"Tell me!"

"Well, he's older."

"Of course." Maddy had a thing about older men, and as long as I had known her, she had mostly been interested in guys that were anywhere from five to twenty years her senior.

"A little older than usual, actually."

"He's not seventy or something, is he?

Maddy laughed. "No. His name is Grant, and he's in his fifties. Married once a long time ago, no kids."

"Any issues with the wife? Was the divorce recent?"

"Oh, no. They were married and split before they were even thirty. He found the love of his life after the divorce, but something happened with her. I think he's still trying to get over it in some way."

I held up my glass to her. "And you're the perfect girl to help him with that."

"Exactly!" she said, toasting with me.

We made our way through the bottle of wine, and Maddy gave me all the details about Grant, a business consultant from Boston who came to Manhattan often.

I let the warmth of the wine and the conversation fill me. I let Maddy's familiar smile shine a light into my heart. And as I threw my head back and laughed with Maddy, I realized this was the first time I'd felt safe since I'd gone back to Woodland Dunes.

The rest of the week flew by. Magoo Barragan and I worked long into each evening, preparing a budget and trial analysis for Sean McKnight, while Natalie Decker focused on research. I had returned to dealing exclusively with Beth Halverson at McKnight Corporation, making my life much more pleasant. By Thursday night, we'd finished the budget and analysis, and the three of us met to strategize.

"All right, what next?" I said to them.

Magoo had pushed the files off my couch and stretched himself across it, his tie loosened to the point that it hung in a circle around his neck. Natalie sat on one of the chairs facing my desk.

"You pick," Natalie said, running her hands through her black, razor-straight bob. "There are two million things to do." Her face was bland, though, as if two million tasks weren't necessarily insurmountable.

"I don't know how we'll be ready in three and a half weeks," Magoo said, throwing an arm over his face to block it from the light overhead.

Three and a half weeks. My stomach flipped. The thought of a big trial still sent a charge of panic through me as the days drew nearer. During my first few years of practice, the firm had always made an older partner try any case with me. After a number of them, they agreed I could handle the cases by myself, and for the last two years, each trial was my own, although sometimes one of the attorneys from the group second-chaired it with me. It wasn't as if I had been doing this for twenty years, though. I was even more nervous this time because I didn't have my normal focus. Instead, I had spent half my brainpower wondering about my mother, the whereabouts of my siblings and the conversation I needed to have with my father.

I had tried to talk to him a few times since Tuesday, yet he was always at a meeting or running out to a deposition. But I knew that tonight he was having dinner with a client at his club in the city. He would be nearly done now, and I planned to head there as soon as I wrapped up the meeting.

"Let's just break it down," I said to Magoo and Natalie. "We'll go over each task, we'll prioritize, and divide them up."

"Sure," Natalie said, as if discussing whether or not to have breakfast tomorrow morning.

"Sounds good," Magoo said.

We talked for another twenty minutes, listing the jobs that needed to be completed, debating which were more important than the others, until

I had a neat, orderly inventory that made it more manageable. Magoo and Natalie volunteered for various jobs, and I printed each of them a copy of the list so we could all keep track.

By the time we were done, it was nearly nine-thirty. I knew my father would probably leave the club in fifteen minutes in order to catch the ten o'clock train to Long Island.

"I've got to run," I said, grabbing a stack of file folders off the desk. "I'll finish up at home tonight."

"See ya," Magoo said with a wave. Natalie shrugged.

Soon, I was in a cab, headed toward midtown and the Van Newton Guild, a stuffy, antique-filled private club that admitted only men until about a decade ago, when a lawsuit forced them to accept women, as well. As far as I could tell, few women had taken advantage of the new membership policy. My father found the place as pretentious and old-fashioned as I did, but many of his longtime clients dined there, so he kept his membership current and made appearances when needed.

A liveried doorman dressed in a crimson jacket with gold epaulets opened the door. Inside, a long stretch of gray and white marble led to a desk where members and guests were required to check in. As I walked down the hall, I felt as I always did when I was here, as if I was sneaking into a museum after hours, and any minute someone would politely ask me to leave. I tried to step lightly, but my heels kept making succinct clicks on the marble.

"I'm here to see Will Sutter. I believe he's in the dining room," I said to the man behind the desk. He was a bespectacled guy about my age who was probably getting a doctorate in medieval poetry during the day. The Van Newton Guild always hired academics with no personal skills.

"Name?" he asked with no hint of a smile.

"Hailey Sutter."

The clerk barely gave me a nod before calling the dining room. He turned his back and spoke in low tones as if imparting a state secret to the maître d' upstairs. I glanced at my watch: 9:45 p.m. Hopefully, I hadn't missed him.

"Mr. Sutter will see you in the bar," the clerk said, turning to face me again. "I'll call someone to escort you."

"I know where it is," I said. I moved toward the elevator hidden in the side wall.

"Miss!" the clerk called out. "Club rules!"

I groaned and waited a full minute before another bespectacled academic took me into the elevator and upstairs to the bar, which was more like a library. Paneled with inlaid bookshelves that housed leather-covered tomes, the room was my favorite in the club since it actually seemed somewhat inviting rather than pompous. I saw my father immediately, sitting at a game table with another man at the far side of the room. When he spotted me, a wide smile formed on his face.

"I'll take it from here," I said to my escort. But he insisted on walking me over to my father and formally announcing me.

"Miss Hailey Sutter," the man said, before he gave a short bow and disappeared.

My dad laughed at my annoyance. "Hi, sweetie," he said. He stood to kiss me on the cheek.

He introduced me to Mack Randall, the head of a trading operation, which my father had represented for about fifteen years. Mack excused himself almost immediately, saying he had to get home to his wife.

"You came to have a chat with your old dad?" My father gestured toward the chair Mack had vacated.

I sank into it. "Yes, actually, I did. Are you trying to catch the ten o'clock?"

"I can get the next one."

"Great," I said. But didn't know where to start. Luckily, a waiter came over, and I ordered a coffee with skim milk.

I shifted in my chair, and as I did so, I noticed that a glass with ice and amber-colored liquid sat before my father. Whiskey, I realized.

This was truly odd, a sign of something off, because my dad never drank. He had grown up in Kansas on his parents' farm. It was an ideal childhood until one particularly bad flood killed the farm, and his parents started drinking. The alcohol wrecked them, he had told me. It had wrecked their family, and he wouldn't continue that legacy.

I looked at the glass again, then met his gaze and raised my eyebrows. *What's up with that?* Sometimes we didn't have to talk to communicate.

He shrugged, then again. *Nothing. Nothing important.*

I let it go. While I waited for my coffee, we made light conversation, my father telling me about a lawsuit Mack's company was involved in. My coffee seemed to arrive too fast, and my father stopped, waiting for me to begin.

"I have some questions," I said. I took a sip from the porcelain cup and tried not to make a face. The Van Newton Guild was not known for its culinary excellence.

"Okay. What's this about?"

I fell quiet. How to summarize this? Just start at the beginning. "It's about Mom."

My father didn't respond immediately. The word *Mom* hung in the air.

"All right." His voice sounded wary, or maybe I imagined it.

I took another sip of the coffee, but this time, I

barely noticed how horrid it was. Instead, I was simply happy to have something to do with my hands, anything that could pass a little time until I figured out how to broach this topic that had been hidden for so long.

"I guess the first thing I want to know is how she died." There. I'd said it. I stole a glance at my dad over the rim of my cup.

He blinked once, then twice, then again. He slid his hand across the game table and touched my upper arm. Something about his touch startled me. I put my cup down immediately, looking from his hand and back to his face.

"Honey," he said, his voice agonized, "you know this."

"What? No, I don't. We've never talked about it. You never wanted to."

He sat back, and the spot where he'd held my arm suddenly felt cool without his hand there. "Well, I don't know if that's true."

I felt a flash of anger. "Yes, it is true. You wouldn't ever talk to me about this, and so I stopped asking. I'm an adult now, though. I want to know."

He shook his head. "Of course. I mean…well, I know we didn't talk about this often. For so long, it was too painful for me, but I thought we'd had some conversations along the way." Absently, he picked up his glass and jostled the ice around.

Suddenly I began to doubt myself. Had we had these talks, and had I somehow pushed them out of my mind, the same way I had shoved away my memories of that night?

"Maybe we did, Dad. But I just can't remember, and I've been wondering. So please, tell me."

He made a sound, like a coarse breath escaping his lungs. "Your mother fell down the stairs. She hit her head and died of internal bleeding in the brain." He took a small sip of his drink.

There it was. The same story. The story that Chief Manning had settled on, the story that I, myself, had apparently told the police.

When I didn't say anything, my father put his glass down and looked at me directly, his eyes full of concern, grief, and, if I wasn't mistaken, that wariness again. "Are you remembering now?"

Remembering now? What did that mean? I could feel my father watching me, waiting for me to answer. "No. I don't recall anything about it."

It sounded so simple. My mother had fallen down the stairs. Tragic but simple, so why couldn't I remember it like that? Why couldn't I remember it at all?

My father sat back, his face clearing a little. Why did he look relieved?

"Were you there?" I asked. I knew from Della, and from Chief Manning's version of events, that my dad was out of the house, separated from my mom by then. But I had never heard my father say that. I wanted to see if he would be honest with me. I prayed he would.

He hung his head. "I wish I was. But no."

"Where were you?"

He sighed. "I don't know if you knew this, if you remember this, I mean, but your mom and I had taken a break."

I took a quick breath. I was asking and my father was telling. It was the truth, as far as I knew it, and the realization sent relief coursing through me. "I don't remember that."

"Well, we'd had some problems, and we decided it would be better if I moved out for a while."

"Where did you go?"

"The apartment in Chicago."

I nodded. I'd assumed as much. "And so how did you find out about Mom?"

"Find out what?"

"About her death. Her fall or whatever." What had he thought I meant?

"Your brother called me. It was about seven in the morning on a Saturday, and I was getting ready to go to the office for a while." He paused for a second, then said in a low voice, "What a terrible day that was." And I could tell he was reliving it. I could see from the way his eyes stared at the table without really focusing that he was back there again.

"What did he tell you?" I couldn't bring myself to use Dan's name, as if it might startle my father too much.

He was quiet for a moment, then looked at me. "He said your mother was dead. That he'd found her in bed. You and your sister were in the room with her."

Your sister…your brother. I wondered at my dad's use of these terms instead of calling them Dan and Caroline, but I couldn't place any significance there. It had been so long since we had talked like this at all, since we'd talked about the family that had once been.

A clap of laughter rang from the bar where a few guys in their forties had planted themselves, suit coats off, ties loosened. My father flinched at the noise, and I found myself thinking that he looked older now than I had ever seen him. His posture, normally ramrod perfect, sagged at the shoulders, his eyes slightly unfocused.

"And what did I say when you talked to me?" I asked. This was what I wanted so badly to know. What had *I* seen that night?

Again, he didn't answer the question right away. He sat up straighter. "You said she fell. She just slipped and fell down the stairs. After that, she wanted you to help her into bed. You did, and you fell asleep. She must have died sometime during the night."

I felt tears sting my eyes. I wanted so badly to remember this. It seemed a disservice to my mom not to do so, but none of it was familiar except the image of her standing at the front door with her hand to her head, the recollection of being in bed with her that next morning, Dan calling from outside the room.

"And what did Caroline tell you?"

"The same thing. Your mother fell." He sounded as if he'd said these words a hundred times. As if he'd been answering these questions over and over. His voice was even, practiced.

"What did the police say?"

My father flinched again, almost imperceptibly this time. "Why do you ask that?"

"They must have looked into it."

"They did."

"And what did they find?" I asked.

"Nothing. Your mother fell. There was nothing else to find."

We were both quiet for a second, my father seemingly lost in thoughts of the past, while I tried to screw up the nerve to ask where my brother and sister were now, and why I hadn't seen them. I decided to start with what happened after that day.

"So, afterward, Caroline went to boarding school, right?"

"That's correct. Brighton Academy. It was one of the best in the area."

I nodded. "And Dan?"

My father looked down at the table, then back at me. "College. At Michigan State. You remember that."

I nodded again. That I did remember. "Did Dan graduate?"

A small smile lit my father's mouth. "Yes," he said, his voice tinged with pride. "A degree in business."

"Why didn't we go to the graduation?"

The grin died away. "He didn't want us there."

"Us?" I said. "He didn't want *us* there?"

My father dipped his head, almost a nod, a gesture he often made in court when he was about to clarify a point. "I should rephrase. He didn't want *me* there."

"Why?"

"Oh, Hailey, do we have to get into this?" His eyes were strained, and I watched him as he picked up the whiskey and sipped it again.

"Dad, I'm sorry, but I have to get this out of my head. I have to know." I didn't say that it was dysfunctional never to have spoken about my mother's death, that I had received a strange letter that seemed to refer to my mother being murdered. I didn't say that I'd been in Caroline's house, that I was thinking of traveling to the Southwest to look for Dan. And it made me feel awful to hide something from my father while at the same time demanding painful answers from him. I had never deceived him before. But something new had snuck into my feelings about him—a suspicion brought on by the fact that he had kept me away from people who were important, information that was important.

Another dip of the head from my father. *Continue.*

"Why didn't we go to Dan's graduation?"

"Your brother was very angry about my separation from your mother. He thought I had abandoned her."

"Did you?" I said this in a quiet voice, afraid to stop the flow of words coming out of his mouth.

He shot me a look, annoyance, maybe hurt, but then it was gone. "Of course not. If you must know, your mother asked for time apart."

The group at the bar became boisterous again. My father sent them an irritated glance before he turned back to me. He seemed impatient now, rather than sad, like he wanted to take his medicine and leave.

"So you just let Dan go? You never kept in touch with him?"

"I tried, Hailey. I tried. But he moved away, first to Detroit and then out West, and he really wanted nothing to do with the Sutters anymore. I believe he even changed his name."

"To what?"

"Singer, if I'm not mistaken."

I felt a wash of relief. The truth. All I'd had to do was ask. "And what about Caroline? Did she go to college after boarding school?" I said, still testing him.

He took another sip of his whiskey. It was almost gone now, although he didn't show any signs that it was affecting him. "Yes, Caroline went from Brighton on to school out East."

I sank back in my chair. "She went to a university?"

My father nodded and signaled the waiter for a new whiskey. "More coffee?"

"No." I sat very frozen, praying that I was somehow mistaken, that my father wasn't lying to my face. "What school did she go to?"

"Yale."

I almost laughed. Yale? Caroline had gone from a boarding school to a psych ward to a community college in Portland. Nothing Ivy League about that. I felt a hard shield form over me. "And what did she do after that?"

"We lost touch. Like Dan, she wanted to create

her own world. She didn't want to be reminded of your mother. I think she moved to Paris. She's in the arts if I'm not mistaken."

"Really? Paris?" My voice got loud and my father looked at me quizzically. "Where did she live in Paris? On the Left Bank? Maybe by the apartment that we had there?"

"No." His voice was soft in comparison to mine. "She actually lived by the airport, I believe."

I felt like crying now. He was painting an entirely false picture of Caroline—an East Coast school, a move abroad to Paris to be an artist—giving the impression that he knew few details, since he didn't keep in touch with her.

"Well, I'd better go." I pushed back my chair just as the waiter arrived with my father's whiskey.

He looked startled. "So soon?"

"I have work to do." I crossed my arms over my chest, as if I could hold in the battle of emotions inside me.

His face carried a helpless expression I'd never seen before. "We could talk some more. About Caroline and Dan, if you want."

"All right. Why don't you tell me if Dan ever hit Mom? Tell me if *you* ever hurt her."

A second went by. Then another. And another. The only movement in the room seemed to be the blinking of my father's eyes.

"Why would you say that?" he said.

He hadn't denied it.

"Why would you say that?" he repeated.

My throat felt as if it was closing, and I had to stop the tears I felt coming. I wanted to say, *It doesn't matter because you wouldn't tell me the truth anyway. You'd lie to me, just like you have all my life.* Instead, I stood, and murmured an excuse about the McKnight case. I turned and walked away then, my heels sinking into the thick, plush carpeting, making me feel as though I might stumble. I gripped my briefcase more tightly. When I got to the doorway, I looked over my shoulder.

Will Sutter sat alone, oblivious to the cries and shouts of laughter from the men at the bar, staring at my chair, as if he hadn't yet registered that I was gone.

16

Friday dawned with growls of thunder rolling through the city and rain pelting my windows. Usually, I was up by six, often taking a run before I jumped in the shower and hurried to the subway, but that morning I couldn't make myself move from the bed. I rolled over and curled myself into a ball, pulling the comforter up to my ears. My limbs felt leaden, my mind dull, but when I let myself focus, one thought pierced through. *He lied to me.* All my life and last night to my face, my father lied to me. This realization made it seem as if my whole life was at an odd angle, one where I couldn't get my footing, where I couldn't trust anyone.

Except Maddy, I thought. I looked at the clock: 7:20 a.m. She would be up and getting ready for work. I dragged myself over to the side of the bed and lifted the cordless phone off the nightstand. But there was no answer and none on her cell phone, either. For a moment, I wondered if I should be alarmed. Then I remembered Maddy's new man. She'd probably spent the night at the corporate apartment he had in the city. The thought brought a faint smile to my face. Maddy deserved to find happiness with a guy. She and I couldn't be the terrible twosome forever. But that thought restored the frown. I turned over on my side again and let myself drift back to sleep.

When I woke again, it was after nine.

"Shit," I said, sitting up. By the time I showered, I wouldn't get to the office until at least ten, even if I took a cab. I hated the thought of strolling in at that hour. It looked terrible to anyone who might be paying attention in preparation for the partnership election. I reached for the phone and dialed Amy's direct number.

"Are you all right?" Amy said. "I was just starting to get worried." Since I was usually at the office by eight—Amy got there shortly after—I knew she had probably been watching the clock, checking the diaries over and over, wondering if I had forgotten to mention a court call.

"Sorry. I'm not feeling well." I didn't have any guilt saying this, since it was true. I didn't mention that it was my emotional health that was in jeopardy, not my physical well-being.

"I'm not surprised. You've been running yourself into the ground. Why don't you stay home?"

"I think I will work from here today."

Amy tutted. "I wasn't talking about *working* at home. I'm talking about ordering soup, watching soaps all day."

I managed a little laugh. "I've got files with me, and I've got to get some stuff done, but I'll try to log in at least two hours of television, okay?"

"Okay, but take it easy. And I'll keep everyone away. I promise you won't get even one phone call from the office."

"Perfect," I said, because I wouldn't be home anyway. I was going to Santa Fe.

I found a last-minute Internet flight, and I landed in Santa Fe at four o'clock. As I stepped outside the airport, I felt a rush of arid heat that told me I was in the desert.

"Oh, that's right off Canyon Road," said the woman at the car-rental desk when I gave her S. Singer's address. "That's where the majority of the galleries are." The woman circled the area on the map.

It took me only twenty minutes to reach the Canyon Road area. Along the way, I passed adobe houses that blended with the red-dirt ground and the mountains in the distance. Even the gas station and pharmacy I drove by were rounded adobe buildings. I turned up Canyon Road and saw that

the woman at the rental desk had been accurate.
The street was lined with art galleries, a café or two
sprinkled into the mix.

When I reached the street where S. Singer lived,
I turned again, and easily found the small house.
It was also adobe, the color of sand, with red-
painted trim along the top. A large cactus served
as the centerpiece for the otherwise plain front yard
where straggles of grass tried to grow in the dry cli-
mate. Although it was far from fancy, the house
looked neat and well cared for. I glimpsed a small
pink bicycle leaning against a sidewall. My niece's,
I thought. That bike belongs to my niece. *My niece,
my niece, my niece,* I repeated in my head.

I walked slowly across the quiet street, no passing cars to stop me from reaching the other side in
a second, and then there was nothing to stop me
from walking up the short path to the unadorned
wood door. A bronze knocker in the shape of bull's
horns hung high on the door. I raised my hand and
used it. Once, then again and again. My anticipation had been running high, but I felt it flatten. No
one was home. God, I hoped they hadn't left town
since I'd called and hung up this morning. I looked
up the street, then the other way, wondering if I
should ask a neighbor. No, I decided. I didn't want
to tip off the woman that I was looking for her.

It was still light out, so I decided to take a stroll.

Narrow concrete walks flanked either side of Canyon Road, and I made my way from one gallery to the next, studying the lifelike paintings of the Southwest landscape, picking up the Native American pottery and jewelry. Every so often, I pulled out my cell phone and dialed the number for S. Singer, which I now knew by heart. Still, the woman wasn't home.

A gallery owner recommended that I have dinner at Celebrations, a small restaurant across the street. I sat at an outside table next to others filled with couples or bunches of friends. I was overly aware of the fun going on around me. My eyes kept straying to the front sign and the name of the place—Celebrations. My mood was anything but celebratory. Every time I got excited that I might soon meet my niece, that I might gain some information that would bring me closer to my brother, I would recall my dad, sitting across from me last night at the Van Newton Guild, looking me in the eye, telling me lies about my sister, and God knew what else. I picked at the food. Finally, I threw some money on the table and left.

The sun was lower as I approached the Singer house again, and I saw lamplight in the windows. My pulse picked up. When I reached the front door, I raised my fist and gave a quick rap.

I heard the patter of feet inside, and then the door swung open. I let my gaze fall and met the light brown eyes of a girl with curly chestnut hair that hung to her chin. She must have been about six years old. I searched the girl's face—full pink lips, a small smear of something that looked like chocolate at the corner, high cheekbones and a small, button nose. She wore pink shorts and a white T-shirt. She didn't resemble Dan exactly, but I came back to the short swing of bangs on the girl's forehead and below that her eyes. Round eyes, the color of coffee after milk is poured in it. The exact color and shape of my mother's eyes. This was Dan's daughter. This was my niece.

"Hi," I said. "My name's Hailey. Is your mom home?"

The girl looked me up and down, and gave me a bashful grin, followed by a nod. "Mom!" she called, not turning her head away from me.

"What's your name?" *This is my niece. Family.*

"Annie." The girl said. She shrugged, as if she wasn't quite sure.

"Well, it's nice to meet you, Annie." I held out my hand.

Annie stared at it for a moment. She turned her gaze up to me, then back down again. At last, she reached out her arm and clasped my hand. Annie smiled shyly. I smiled back, liking the feel of the girl's small, warm hand next to my skin.

"Can I help you?" The woman's voice was sharp.

I dropped Annie's hand as if I had been caught touching the girl inappropriately. I looked up to see a woman, probably ten years older than me, who resembled Annie except that the woman's eyes were muddy brown and her wavy hair was cut close around her face. She wore khaki shorts and a black, sleeveless sweater designed to show off her tan, toned arms.

"Who are you?" the woman demanded.

"I'm Hailey. I spoke to you on the phone earlier this week."

The woman made a bitter sound. "Oh, for Christ's sake. Annie, go to your room."

Annie shot me another bashful grin before she took off in a run toward the back of the house.

"You called me about Dan, didn't you?" the woman said.

"Yes."

"You're the girl from the bar. I knew he was probably off the wagon."

"No. I tried to tell you that day. It's not like that."

Off the wagon? Did Dan have an alcohol problem?

I thought a moment. I hadn't exactly planned out everything I would say, and it didn't appear this woman would give me a chance if I didn't grab her attention soon.

"You know what," the woman said. "Just get out. I don't have the—"

"I'm his sister," I said.

The woman's mouth opened, like she was about to say something, but then it stayed open and silent as if she had forgotten what words to use.

"Caroline?" she said, her voice somewhat tentative now.

"No. I'm Hailey."

The woman narrowed her eyes. "Dan doesn't have a sister named Hailey."

I wanted to cry. He hadn't even mentioned me to her, the woman he had a child with.

"You look like him, though," the woman continued. "I didn't notice it at first."

I nodded, then held out my hand again. "I'm Hailey Sutter."

"Sutter. Right. Dan's old name." The wariness on her face seemed to soften. "I'm Sharon. Maybe you should come in."

The house was furnished simply but neatly with ruddy Aztec-print sofas and rustic wood tables. A few prints hung on the walls—charcoal drawings of mountain plains.

"Did you get those on Canyon Road?" I asked Sharon, gesturing toward the drawings.

She handed me a glass of water and laughed, almost under her breath. "No. They're mine."

"They're great." We both sat, me on the love seat, Sharon on the couch.

"It's just a hobby. Not much time to do it with my sales job."

Sharon's voice was level and conversational, and I wondered what had caused the sudden shift.

"So you're in sales?" I wanted to keep the discussion mundane for now, establish some kind of rapport.

"Pharmaceutical sales. It's how I met Dan."

"Oh." There was Dan's name, sitting between us now. "And you're obviously not together any longer?"

A rueful smirk took over Sharon's face. "Divorced about five years now."

"Did he always use the name Singer? I mean, as long as you'd known him?"

Sharon nodded, and I noticed how quiet the house was. Somewhere in the back, Annie was playing, but there were no sounds to confirm this, and although Santa Fe was a city, I couldn't hear any passing cars or blaring horns. No shouts or sirens.

"He changed his name from Sutter to Singer when he moved to Santa Fe. Something about wanting to cut ties with his family. It was symbolic for him. Not that I knew this back then. It only came out when we got divorced. I kept the Singer name for Annie's sake."

I tried to ignore the bitterness that had crept back into Sharon's voice. "And he never mentioned me?" I said.

"Dan didn't mention much. That was part of the problem. He always kept secrets from me, and it made me crazy. I only found out about Caroline because I found a receipt that showed he wired money to her. I went nuts. I thought he was cheating on me, but then he tells me that he has a sister named Caroline in Portland who needed cash."

"When was this?"

"God, it had to be the first year we were married." She put her water glass down on a rough-hewn side table and gave me an appraising look. "You're obviously younger than Dan."

"Ten years younger."

"And so, are there any other brothers and sisters I should know about?"

"Just Caroline and me."

Sharon gave me that appraising stare once more. "There's no estate battle or something like that, is there?"

"What do you mean?" A breeze blew through the open windows behind my head. My hair lifted and swirled into my face. I grabbed it with one hand and pulled it over my shoulder.

"I'm not Dan's biggest fan anymore, but as I said, he is Annie's father. I don't want to hurt him or anything. So if you're here to dig up dirt for some legal battle or something…"

"No, no. It's nothing like that. I've just never known Dan, or Caroline for that matter, so I want to get in touch."

"Well, I wish I could help you, but like I told you on the phone, we haven't heard from Dan in weeks."

"And is that typical?"

Sharon shrugged. "It's not totally out of character. He used to have a mean drinking problem, and sometimes he'd disappear for days, but since we split up, he's never missed a date with Annie. Every Wednesday and every other weekend and one holiday a year, he drives up from Albuquerque like clockwork. So I am getting a little worried now."

"I'm flying out of Albuquerque tomorrow, and I was thinking of stopping by his house."

"I can give you directions there, but you're probably wasting your time. If he was home, he'd pick up Annie. I know that much."

"Have you called his friends to see what they know?"

Sharon laughed. "You really don't know him, I guess. Dan doesn't have any close friends."

Just like Caroline, I thought. "Why?"

"Oh, he's got lots of acquaintances. He's got the typical sales personality." She made a wistful face, as if remembering something. "So he's got buddies in the business. I know some of the guys at his company, and I figured if he didn't show up tomorrow again, I'll give them a call on Monday."

"What's the name of the company he works for?"

"Rider Pharmaceuticals."

I nodded. I knew of it. It was a large, publicly traded corporation. I thought of Dan and how alone he must feel sometimes. No wife, a child he saw only on prescribed days, no real friends. I wondered if he still wrote the way he used to, filling those lined notebooks with his stories. I asked Sharon if he was still a writer.

"You know about the writing, huh?" Sharon said. She sipped her water again, her face suddenly sad. "I think I might be the only person he let read those stories."

"What were they like?"

"They were usually about men or boys who ran away from home and experienced freedom on the road. They used to piss me off."

"Do you have any of them?"

"No. He let me read them, but he always kept them close. Too close. I was always telling him to send them to literary magazines, but he never would. He did write a short essay for one of the papers in town."

"Do you still have that?"

"I think I might. Do you want to wait while I look for it?"

"Yes, thanks."

Sharon began walking out of the room. She stopped under the door frame and turned around. "Would you like to see some pictures?"

"Oh, that would be great." I could hear the excitement in my own voice.

"There's an album right there," she said, pointing to the lower shelf of the coffee table.

I leaned forward and found a small, maroon, leather-bound album. Photos of my family.

The room had grown dimmer as the darkness outside crept in. A light was on in the kitchen, and a lamp was lit across the room, but I still needed to switch on the barrel lamp on the end table.

In the first photo, Dan stood with his arms at his sides, smiling into the camera. It must have been moving day, because he was in the very room where I now sat, but none of Sharon's drawings hung on the wall and no drapes covered the windows. Dan's hair was much shorter than I remembered it, his blond bangs pushed up in front. I stared at his face, the white flash of his teeth and the dots of his eyes, but the photo had been taken at least ten feet away from him. So while I tried to read something there, all I saw was a man I once knew, who looked very pleased to have his own house in Santa Fe.

The next few pictures were of Sharon and Dan together. Some were clearly taken at a wedding or some other function because they were both dressed up, Dan in a suit. The others appeared to have been taken around Santa Fe—at sidewalk cafés or parties where there were crowds of people in the background. Those were closer shots, and I noticed that Dan was smiling in each, his arm usually tossed over Sharon's shoulders. The smile never really left his mouth, though. Instead, his lips seemed set, while the rest of his face was flat. Had he always made such a face in pictures?

I moved on through the album, the rest of it devoted to the decorating of their house and the birth of Annie. She had been an adorable baby, with fat, rosy cheeks and curly tufts of hair. Her light brown eyes, my mother's eyes, had been large at birth, making her look startled.

"That's me," I heard, and I nearly jumped. Annie had come into the room and was standing at the other side of the end table, peering at the album.

"You were a very pretty baby."

Annie just nodded as if this was obvious.

"Do you want to look at these pictures with me? You could tell me where some of them were taken."

Annie nodded again. She climbed onto the couch and settled in next to me so that our legs touched. I tried to act as if this happened all the time, as if I sat this close to a child to whom I was related. But in reality, I'd had little exposure to kids. I felt inadequate around them.

Annie clearly knew how to entertain herself, though, because she was soon pointing at pictures, naming people, telling me how old she was in various photos. As I listened to her, asking a few questions for clarification, I realized that my niece was a lot like myself, an only child who couldn't rely on others for amusement, who had to learn to play by herself or not play at all.

"That was my fourth birthday," Annie said. She gestured to a photo of herself in a pointed red birthday hat, Dan at her side, holding up a white frosted cake for the camera. "They were already divorced then, but Mom let him come to my party, even though it wasn't a Wednesday or Saturday."

"Oh." I wasn't sure how to respond to that. I had grown up without any siblings, just like Annie, but I never had to deal with warring parents. I wondered if having no mother at all was better somehow than having a father who disappointed you, who didn't show up, who made you worry.

I looked closer at the birthday shot. While Dan

was lifting the cake for the benefit of the picture, his eyes were on his child with a look of adoration. He certainly didn't appear to be a parent who would go on a drinking binge and not show up or call for weeks, but then what did I know? Maybe it was as simple as that. Yet in the corners of my mind, I knew it couldn't be that easy. Dan had seemingly disappeared on the same day as Caroline, a few days after I'd received the letter, one week before I went to Chicago and Woodland Dunes.

"Do you miss your dad?" I asked Annie, to fill the silence of the living room. I had never been comfortable with open spaces of quiet, certainly not with a young girl who seemed so foreign and yet familiar.

"Yeah," Annie said with a little tilt of her head. "But he's fine. He's coming back soon." She sounded very sure of her words, and I wondered if she was mimicking the lines her mother had fed her since Dan failed to show up.

"I'm sure he will."

"Do you know my dad?"

"Yes. He's my brother."

She looked at me for a moment. She seemed to have her mother's talent for appraising people.

"Well, he's probably coming home soon," Annie said, turning another page of the book. "He won't be gone very long. He misses me too much."

She kept turning the photos over, not bothering to stop any longer to explain them.

Something about the deliberation of the girl's movements, the precise way her little fingers with their delicate nails continued paging through the album, made me wonder. And after a second, I said, "How do you know?"

The small fingers kept moving, flipping pages, until Annie reached the end. Without a word, she started over at the beginning of the book again, with Dan surrounded by boxes, before she was even born.

I didn't push. I watched Annie turning and turning the pages until she put her hand over one picture, as if saving her place on the page. She looked at me. "Promise not to tell?" she said in a soft voice.

I leaned closer. "Promise," I said, matching her whisper.

The girl moved toward me, until her mouth nearly rested on my ear. I could feel her faint breath. "My dad's not drinking again. He's just on a vacation."

I tried to stay very still as if Annie were a deer that could be startled back into the forest. I strained to hear toward the back of the house, for any signs of Sharon advancing to the room and finding me, again, in close physical contact with her daughter.

When Annie didn't move, didn't say anything, I turned my own head a little, so that I could angle my words toward her. "How do you know?"

"He called me when Mom was still at work. He had to take some time off, but he'll be back. He can't not come back because he misses me. He'll only be gone a little while."

Annie sat back away and smiled as if it were all just that simple.

I wanted to ask her—*When did he call? Where is he staying? Did he give you a number?*—but I only said, "Does your mom know?"

Annie shook her head. "She doesn't like Dad much." Her face looked stricken. "You won't tell her, will you?"

"No," I said, the word coming fast. "Of course not."

"I finally found it," Sharon said, coming into the room. "And I wrote down the directions to Dan's house." Her face held a pleasant cast, but when she looked from me to her child and back again, her expression became more wary.

"Great, thanks." I stood from the couch, the album falling off my lap. "Sorry." I bent to pick it up, but Annie had already scooted to the floor and grabbed it. I stood again, and let my hands fall to my sides, flustered with Annie's confidences.

Sharon watched me another moment before she crossed the room, holding out a fluttering piece of newsprint.

I took it, glancing at the title and byline. A Midwesterner Searches For Uncommon Beauty, by Dan Singer. It was a short piece with no accompanying photos. "Should I go somewhere to copy this and bring it back?" I asked Sharon.

"That's not necessary. I had a couple of them tucked away."

"Well, thank you so much." I didn't want to leave Annie. I wanted to see the girl's room and her treasures, to talk to her more about her dad, not just about his call but what she knew of him in general, what she thought of Dan Sutter Singer, but Sharon stood still, waiting, it seemed, for me to go.

"Thanks for everything," I said.

"I'll tell him you're looking for him," Sharon said. "Whenever he turns up, that is."

Both Annie and Sharon walked me to the door, Annie hanging back a little.

"It was really nice to meet you both," I said as I opened the door. Just then the phone rang from inside.

"You, too," Sharon said, glancing over her shoulder toward the sound of the phone. "Drive safe."

Sharon turned and disappeared into the house. Based on her speed, I bet that it was a man calling, maybe someone she was dating.

"Bye," I said to Annie, daring to ruffle the girl's hair.

Annie smiled up at me, then crooked a finger,

gesturing for me to bend down. I did so, and Annie whispered in my ear, "He went to Orleans."

"What?" I said.

"He went to Orleans," she repeated in a louder whisper.

"New Orleans?"

She nodded.

17

I got lost trying to find my way out of Santa Fe, my head too full of information, senses, images, like Annie's light breath in my ear, Dan's adult face in the pages of the album, his call to Annie from New Orleans. I wished I could fly there right now. But where would I look? Who would I talk to? Plus, I'd packed only a small bag with a pair of jeans and a T-shirt, and more importantly, hadn't done any work on the McKnight case. The other problem was that my return flight wasn't until tomorrow afternoon, and I was scheduled to fly out of Albuquerque, since I had planned on going to Dan's house tomorrow. But maybe I could switch and get a flight home tonight or tomorrow morning.

I called the airline from my cell phone, while driving in circles around Santa Fe, continually winding up, again and again, on a street called Paseo.

"No available direct flights out of Santa Fe to New York until tomorrow night," said the agent.

"How about to New Orleans?" I said.

A pause, the sound of fingers on a keyboard. "Not unless you want to pay a thousand dollars. You're better off just driving to Albuquerque and getting the flight that you're booked on tomorrow."

The night sky was totally black now, and I strained to read the street signs. Finally, I pulled over at a convenience store and got directions to the hotel I had found on the Internet and reserved for that night. It was located roughly between Santa Fe and Albuquerque, about an hour away. I would still get to see Dan's house tomorrow, on Saturday, and get back to New York by tomorrow afternoon. Sunday, I would work, and Monday, I needed to meet with Beth Halverson at McKnight Corporation in Chicago. And maybe New Orleans from there?

As I drove away from the city, I was struck by a feeling of immense space. A few lights twinkled in the distance, occasionally illuminating the side of a mountain face, but otherwise it was sheer black. The desert stretched out all around me.

The Tamaya Hotel & Spa was a large property set in the middle of nowhere. I drove under a long portico and gave the rental car to the valet. At the front desk, a cheerful hotel employee had me checked into a club-level room in a matter of seconds. After the time spent with Annie, the thought of another impersonal hotel room left me feeling bereft. I asked the desk clerk to have my bag sent up to the room and got directions to the bar.

I ordered a Baileys and decaf and took my mug and purse to the limestone patio outside, where two adobe fireplaces stood on either end, deep chairs in front of them. One set of chairs was occupied by a couple who were kissing and laughing softly, a bucket of champagne in front of them. I felt a flash of envy. It had been so long since I'd been part of a couple like that. I still went on dates here and there. Maddy sometimes set me up with friends of the guys she was dating, but they were usually much older than I, and although Maddy enjoyed that age difference, I never really connected with any of them. Occasionally, I met men when I was out. Sometimes I dated attorneys I knew from my cases. But for the last few years, I had simply been more interested in my career than my love life. Now, though, with this search into my family, with the separation I felt from my father, I wished I had a boyfriend or some family member who knew all about me, who would understand what I was doing, who would help me if I wanted, who would only listen if I wanted that, too.

I swear, as I sat there, craving companionship, craving family, I could almost feel the warmth of Annie's hand in mine. *My niece, my niece,* I kept saying in my head. *Family.* And yet, when would I see her again? Would I *ever* see her again?

I sat in the low leather chair in front of the other fireplace and took a sip of my drink. Maddy, I thought. I didn't have a boyfriend, I didn't have much of a family, but I did have Maddy. I reached into my purse and pulled out my phone, hitting the speed dial. She wasn't there, and she didn't answer her cell, either. This was getting to be a habit, one that left me feeling lost out here in the desert by myself.

I took Dan's article out of my purse, and moved my chair under an outdoor light.

A Midwesterner Searches For
Uncommon Beauty
By Dan Singer

When a Midwestern boy from Michigan relocates to Santa Fe, his definition of beauty changes. Beauty, once an obvious companion, becomes a playful vamp, one he must find in uncommon places.

No longer does he find beauty in the Midwest's wrenching changes of season—the golden autumn crashing into three months of a white-covered world, which stumbles suddenly into a too-short spring and then a blazing hot summer. Instead, he looks for the subtlety of the Santa Fe weather. The flat stretches of dirt brown don't change, nor do the salmon-colored curves of the mountains or their dotting of green bush. Instead, he keeps a watchful eye on the first prickling of vibrant blooms in early April, waiting for the flowers to dress up the Plaza like a woman putting on her makeup, when she knows visitors are about to arrive. And he waits for the crowd of canvases and sculptures to appear on the street, letting him know that the gallery shows have started and summer has emerged. The August rains whisper in his ear, telling rumors of a coming fall, and when the wildflowers make their appearance, he knows the rains were telling the truth. Christmas, for him, isn't symbolized now by pine and holly but by the burning farolitos lining the rooftops.

The Midwestern boy can't find beauty in his family any longer, for they lead different lives thousands of miles away. Now he watches his new wife lifting a pan out of the oven or arranging yellow buds in a coffee can converted into a vase, and he thinks that this is more lovely than the family reunion he will never have. The Midwestern boy and his new wife have created their own family during this search of his, and the baby girl who has entered their lives shines with an internal beauty, one her father hopes never dims, never has reason to.

His old Michigan landscape, hilly and forest green, crisscrossed with highways and roads and covered with lakes that reflect the navy blue of the sky, is no longer there for him. Now he turns to the single lonely byway connecting Albuquerque to Santa Fe. He finds comfort in the stillness of the vast expanse, in the lighter blue sky that is bigger than he could have ever imagined, in the brown trickle of the Rio Grande.

He no longer looks for redbrick, black wrought-iron railings and patrician columns to tell him a house is beautiful. He turns, instead, to the rounded corners of squat blond adobe, to the flat roofs, and the blue window frames.

Santa Fe has changed the boy from Michigan. It's changed his thoughts and the places he seeks comfort. It has told him of an uncommon beauty lingering in its corners, and in doing so, it has found him a home.

I read the article twice more, struck by the spare loneliness, the use of the word *boy* to refer to himself, and the mention that Dan had been searching

for something. The article seemed intent on showing that he had found it, that he had located whatever he was looking for, but I didn't quite believe
it. I didn't know my brother any better than I knew
molecular science, but there was a lingering feeling there in the article, one of desperation, one
that I thought I could relate to. I'd been trying to
convince myself that I belonged in Manhattan
since I moved there at the start of law school, and
yet, I still felt like an outsider, one who wanted
badly to fit in. Maybe I did have something in
common with my brother after all.

I scheduled a massage for Saturday morning at
the hotel spa, and as the therapist rubbed the knots
and stiffness out of my body, I wondered why I
didn't do this more often. After the massage, I sat
in the outdoor hot tub, letting the bubbles swirl
around me, the sun strike my face. I ordered a
breakfast of fresh fruit and yogurt, which I ate on
the deck of the spa, swaddled in a thick terry-cloth
robe. By the time I checked out an hour later, I felt
better than I had in weeks.

I decided to drive by Dan's house, and then I
would head to the airport. Now that it was light out,
I could see, rather than simply sense, the desert
spreading around me. I passed sandy hills with
occasional outcroppings of flat-roofed houses

nearly camouflaged into the landscape. Sprout-
ings of barely green tufted sagebrush and washed-
out khaki-colored trees lay below the peaked
outlines of the craggy brown mountains in the distance. I began to understand Dan's article and his
concept of uncommon beauty.

A woman on an old, low-rider Harley drove next
to me for a while. She wore black-fringed chaps and
a helmet painted in a black-and-white cow pattern.
She looked to me like a woman who knew herself,
knew her place in the world, but then what did I
know? I was judging her by her appearance. Once, I
had heard two summer associates at the law firm talking about me in the bathroom. I had frozen inside the
stall when I heard my name, scared that it was Paige
or one of her crew ready to skewer me, to start some
nasty rumor, but it had been very different. The two
women, whose voices I soon recognized, were very
kind, complimenting my clothes, my work at the
firm, even commenting that I seemed to have so much
confidence. It was that last comment that depressed
me. Sure, I was glad that I presented that image, but
sometimes I felt so alone, not confident or proud, and
the saddest thing was no one seemed to recognize it.
Maybe Maddy, maybe my dad sometimes. But I
knew the bigger problem was me. I wasn't letting anyone in on those occasional not-so-proud moments.

As the woman in the chaps rumbled past on the

motorcycle, I noticed a green four-door about two car lengths behind me. It was in the same lane as the motorcycle, but as the motorcycle sped away, and the car had an opportunity to pass me, as well, yet it dropped into the lane behind me, keeping a reasonable distance. I sped up and began passing cars, but the green four-door stayed with me, always a short distance away, making it impossible to see the driver by looking in the rearview mirror.

Soon, I reached the Albuquerque exits. I turned off at the first one, even though it wasn't where I planned on leaving the highway. The green car did the same.

I drove to a gas station and quickly pulled up to a pump. The green car slowed as it approached the station, then sped up again. I got out and stood by my car, pretending I was studying the gas prices, but behind my sunglasses, I watched the car drive a short way down the road, pull into a parking lot, turn around and come back toward the station. The car's left blinker went on. It was about to turn into the station, but a number of passing cars in the other direction forced it to wait.

It was the opportunity I needed. Paranoia or no, I was going to lose this guy. I jumped back into my rental car and sped away from the tanks, back down the road, making my way toward the highway exit. Roaring up the ramp, I kept shifting my gaze to the rearview mirror. No sign of the green car, but I felt hot and flushed all over. I cranked up the air-conditioning, ignoring the decreasing speed limits into the city. I kept my foot on the gas until I was sure the car hadn't followed me.

Finally, I found the exit I had originally intended to use. By then I had cooled down and I felt foolish. I began paying attention to navigating my way to Dan's house.

If Santa Fe was a hamlet posing as a city, Albuquerque was a metropolis. There were Western designs on a few of the buildings and some American Indian decorations, but mostly it seemed like many other cities. Skyscrapers, winding byways, ghettos.

Dan's house was easy to find with the directions Sharon had given me. I'm not sure what I had expected, but it wasn't this. A large, aluminum-sided house painted gray-green that was identical to the other houses in the subdivision. They were all nice homes, but there was barely anything to distinguish one house from the other. A different car in the garage maybe or a baby stroller waiting outside another front door. And Dan's house was barren of even those effects. Maybe I had anticipated something with more character, because I always pictured Dan as a writer more than a salesman, or maybe I was remembering the proud look on his face in that picture when they had just moved into the Santa Fe home.

I parked in the driveway and walked to the front door. I looked around a few times when I reached it, but there was no sign of the green car, just a couple of kids riding their bikes. I wondered if Annie had friends in this neighborhood. Did she like visiting her dad?

My knock made a hollow echo inside the house. I wasn't surprised. The mail was stuffed in the box next to the front door, some of the envelopes and magazines spilling onto the concrete stoop where the postman had started stacking the rest of the mail.

I knocked again and again. Nothing. I walked around the house, but all the blinds were closed tight. No sign of life. It was time go.

When I reached my apartment, I collected my mail and flipped through it in the elevator. As soon as I came to the fourth envelope, a large, manila one, I stopped and smiled.

Ty Manning, the return address said.

I went into the apartment and let my bag fall onto the floor. I stuck my finger in the small opening at the end of the flap and pulled. Inside was a stack of paper.

The top sheet was plain but for a few handwritten lines.

Thought you might want to see this. It's a copy of the police file on your mom's investigation. Let me know if I can do anything else to help. Hope you'll come back to see us soon. Ty.

I set aside the top page and flipped through the others. Sure enough, they were police records. I was used to reading such records occasionally for certain cases, but now my mother's name was on the face sheet, accompanied by phrases like "cause of death" and "severe head injury." At the bottom there was a stamp that said, "Case Closed."

I riffled through the other pages, noticing typed witness interviews and handwritten notes, but I couldn't focus on the content.

I pulled out my Palm Pilot and looked up Ty's number. No answer at his house. I called the front desk at the inn. He answered, and we chatted for a few seconds, but I was too anxious for small talk.

"Ty, how did you get these records?" I asked. Whenever I wanted a police report for a lawsuit, getting it was usually a lengthy, detailed process that involved subpoenas and court appearances.

"I just asked the records clerk. Everyone knows me, so it wasn't very difficult."

"Does your dad know?"

Silence for a second. "I did ask him first, and

he said he'd dig them up, but I knew he'd never get to it."

"So you went around him."

"I guess." Ty sounded uncomfortable now.

"I don't want you to do anything that could affect your relationship with your dad." I was feeling bad about my own relationship with my father. I didn't need to hurt Ty's, too.

"Well, there isn't much to affect," Ty said in a wry voice.

"I thought you were close."

"My dad is close to my mom, and that's pretty much it. He was a good father in some ways. He brought home the money, went to a few football games, but he's not going to win any father of the year awards."

"Oh. I didn't realize." I thought of the feelings of affection I'd had when I was in the Mannings' kitchen for dinner, the desire to have a family like that.

"It's no big deal," Ty said. "He just got beaten down by the work over the years. He's seen too much, I guess. Too much ugliness. At least that's what my mom says. Because he wasn't always as hard. It's why my brother and sister live away from home, though. They can't deal with him on a regular basis."

"I'm sorry to hear that."

"Like I said, no big deal."

Ty and I talked for twenty more minutes. I filled him in on my trip to New Mexico. *I have a niece named Annie,* I said. I told him the things I'd learned about Dan, and he told me stories about a group of rowdy guests that had stayed at the inn that week. The conversation was natural, easy.

"Are you coming back to Woodland Dunes any time soon?" he asked.

"Oh, I don't know." I surprised myself with a coy tone to my voice. "I'm not sure if there's anything there for me."

"Well, there are about three kegs at the bar that you didn't drink last time."

"That's a low blow." We both laughed. "I am coming to Chicago this week. For a case."

"Call me when you get here, and if you can't come over to our side of the lake, I'll come to you."

"You'd do that?"

"Definitely."

Before I read the police records, I tried Maddy once again. The number of beeps on her answering machine told me that she hadn't checked her messages in a while. Must be staying at Grant's place. Or maybe they had gone out of town. I felt a little pang of envy. I'd gotten messages from Maddy, but they were quicker than usual. She was always running out the door to meet Grant. I hadn't even met him, and yet she always seemed to be with him these days. I tried her cell phone, but got no answer there, either.

I unpacked my small bag, which took only a few minutes, and made some pasta with sauce from a jar. Once I'd eaten and watched an hour of mindless TV, there was nothing keeping me from reading the police records. I was anxious to get to them, and yet fearful of what I might find.

I could hear an increase in the volume outside, car horns and stereos and voices, signaling that the city was priming up for another long Saturday night. But I had no plans. Maddy was nowhere to be found. I didn't want to call my father, despite the number of messages he had left on my machine, so I was holed up in my apartment with a stack of old records calling to me from my coffee table. Finally, I settled on the couch with a mug of cinnamon tea, a far cry from the martinis and scotches that were being drunk around the city.

I picked up the face sheet of the police records. Its lines and boxes contained typed factual information. "Assistant Chief Manning" was listed as the investigation officer. The cause of death was there—"severe brain stem injury/hemorrhage"— as well the date of death, "May 20, 1982." I felt that date like a thud to my chest. The anniversary of my mother's death was only a few days away.

I made myself continue through the rest of the information. The time of death was stated as "Approx. 1:20 a.m." How had they determined that, exactly?

I flipped through the stack until I found the coroner's report. Authored by Dr. Charles Winnaker, the autopsy was a clinical description of every organ of my mother's body, every limb and nail bed. There was a rush of sickness in my stomach, the pasta I'd eaten seeming to slosh and churn. I was vaguely familiar with autopsies from the one or two medical-malpractice cases I'd worked on as a summer associate. I knew that they involved a literal carving of the body, the skin split from pelvis to neck, the ribs cut with a saw, the heart and liver weighed and documented like a butcher slaughtering livestock. This was all necessary, I knew, for the physician to determine exactly what had happened to the body, what had caused the eventual shut down, but the thought of my mother's body undergoing that was grueling.

I put the records down for a moment. *Just read it all quickly,* I thought. *Skip the morbidly detailed inventory of body parts and get to the conclusion.*

I lifted the autopsy report again and scanned it, trying to pretend this was just another case I was working on at the firm, that this wasn't about someone I knew. Finally, I reached the end. There, Dr. Winnaker stated that a massive hemorrhage in the brain stem had caused the death of Leah Sutter, and, based on the decomposition of the body, he believed she had expired at approximately 1:20 a.m. He did not conclude what had caused the bleed but stated that it was consistent with either a blow to the back of the head or a fall.

A blow to the head, I thought. That could mean physical abuse, just as Chief Manning had originally suspected. A fall was the other possibility that the doctor had decided on, though. I knew I should be relieved that a cruel but simple fall down the stairs might very well have been the end of Leah Sutter. Nothing sinister about it. Certainly not murder. But why couldn't I get myself to remember it? Why didn't it sound right?

It was the letter, I decided. The damn letter suggesting murder. I went into my bedroom, dark but for the streetlights outside, and without turning on any lamps, I found it in my briefcase, bringing it back to the couch with me. *There is no statute of limitations on murder. Look closely.*

For the first time, I wondered if maybe I had misinterpreted the thing. It had been addressed to me, no doubt about it, but maybe it hadn't been referring to my mother after all. It had simply been an immediate, gut-level conclusion. But if not my mother, then who? I ran my mind over past clients, possible extended-family members. But I couldn't think of any clients who had passed away, and as for family members, I didn't know any. My father had taken care of that.

I took another sip of the cinnamon tea that had grown cool. *Enough musings,* I decided. *Quit putting it off.* I picked up the police records again.

The most interesting records were Chief Manning's handwritten notes and the dictated, typewritten summaries of his interviews with various witnesses. He'd been diligent in his note taking, making mention of the day and time whenever he jotted something. His first few notations were often similar, such as "high suspicion of domestic abuse." The next ones indicated he had interviewed William Sutter, the husband of the deceased, as well as Dan Sutter, son. According to the note he'd jotted afterward, *"The statements of Mr. William Sutter and Mr. Dan Sutter appear rehearsed and strikingly similar. Covering for each other?"* Then he wrote, *"Physical abuse—husband, son or boyfriend?"*

The sickness riding my insides deepened. Had my father or my brother struck my mother? Had they hidden it together? I'd never seen Dan again, after all. Perhaps he had been told to run, to stay away, the same thing he was doing now in New Orleans. Had they done it because they had discovered the relationship with her boyfriend? That man on the beach, the man at the front door on the night she died?

I flipped through pages looking for the dictated summary of the interrogation of my father. Upstairs, my neighbors kicked off a party. Blaring music and pounding footfalls came clearly through my ceiling. I found the interview and began to read. William Sutter and his wife had been separated three weeks, he had told Chief Manning, but they'd not yet filed for divorce. He was hoping for a reconciliation. The reasons for the separation, he said, were his need to live in Chicago during the week and his wife's affair. He had just found out about the infidelity. She admitted this to him and told him it had been going on for less than a year. She refused to tell him the name of the man she was involved with, and Mr. Sutter indicated he did not have any idea as to who that person might be. Mr. Sutter denied any suggestion that he had abused his wife. He was described by Chief Manning as distraught. The interview had to be stopped on more than one occasion because Mr. Sutter was crying.

I felt a wave of sympathy for my father. If he had told Chief Manning the truth, then in the span of a month, he'd found out his wife was having an affair, become separated and endured the trauma of her death. But Manning hadn't believed my father, because he made that notation after the interview wondering whether the abuse had been caused by William, Dan or the boyfriend. Was that why my father had been crying?

I turned next to the interview with Dan. My brother was portrayed as quiet and aloof, telling Chief Manning that he had been out drinking beer with his friends, since he believed both parents would be gone from the house that night. He did not know where his mother had been intending to go, but he thought she might have been planning an evening with her boyfriend. Dan claimed not to know the identity of his mother's male friend. He denied physical abuse in the family household. At the end of the report, Manning indicated his belief that Dan was withholding information and that his story appeared rehearsed. He also noted that Dan had been arrested one year prior on charges of battery with another student following an incident at a high-school bonfire.

I tucked my legs under me on the couch. So Dan had added to Manning's suspicion about domestic abuse. He'd been arrested for battery before.

I flipped back to Manning's notes and followed them down the pages, looking for the date of my own interview or that of my sister. I came first to Della's. Della had said she was aware, of course, that the Sutters were separated, but she knew nothing about an extramarital affair on the part of Leah Sutter. On the night in question, she had left after making dinner for Leah, Caroline and Hailey Sutter. Leah had seemed happy and excited. She told Della that she had plans for the night and that Caroline was going to stay home and babysit Hailey.

I continued to read Chief Manning's notes. He hadn't been able to interview Caroline or Hailey Sutter right away, he said, because Caroline was under the care of a doctor, who recommended that the interview be put off. In addition, my father had requested that I be spared unless it was absolutely necessary. A brief telephone interview was held with Caroline's physician, Dr. Randall Wainer, a family practitioner in Woodland Dunes. He confirmed that Caroline was suffering from post-traumatic stress syndrome and was being medicated.

What had Caroline seen? What had she done?

I had a mild memory of Dr. Wainer as a kind, older gentlemen who saw the Sutter family for colds and shots and ankle sprains. I wondered if he was still in Woodland Dunes, if maybe he could be convinced into telling me something about Caroline and what she had said during those few days after my mother's death. On a whim, I went to the computer and logged on to the Internet, then began searching for Dr. Randall Wainer on the Web site of the American Medical Association. I found one physician with that name, but he lived in Newark and had graduated from medical school just a few years ago. The Dr. Wainer I remembered would be at least eighty by now, probably older.

I ran an obituary search and found what I feared: Dr. Randall Wainer of Woodland Dunes, Michigan, had passed away in the early 1990s.

Another idea occurred to me. I wouldn't be able to speak to Dr. Wainer, but there were other doctors who had treated Caroline—those at the Crestwood Home in Connecticut. Maybe I shouldn't leave for Chicago so fast. I was only a short drive from Connecticut. I pulled up the Crestwood Home Web site and copied down the address and phone number. I would call them tomorrow on Sunday and leave a message.

It was almost midnight by the time I picked up the police records again, my eyes growing heavy. I decided to take them to my bedroom, and, after changing into a pair of old, worn pajamas, I plumped the pillows against my headboard and went back to reading.

Chief Manning had finally been able to interview Caroline a few days after my mother's death. He described the interview as very difficult, due to Caroline's insistence on one-word answers. Like Dan, Caroline was accompanied by a criminal lawyer from my father's law firm, and even her attorney had requested on a few occasions that she be more forthcoming, but Caroline remained withdrawn and quiet. Because of this, the interview took numerous hours and two sessions until Caroline became more cooperative. Eventually, she confirmed that her mother had been preparing to go out on the night in question, and Caroline had intended to babysit her younger sister, Hailey.

According to Chief Manning, he believed Caroline's version of the events up to this point, but when she was asked who my mother had been intending to see that night, her eyes turned downcast, and she withdrew again. She didn't know, she said, and she refused to change her answer. When asked about her mother's injury, she said Leah had been talking to her and Hailey at the top of the stairs when she had stumbled and fallen. When asked about her mother's body positioning and exactly how she had moved leading up to the fall, Caroline's answer changed subtly, causing Manning to doubt her description of the events. Caroline's lawyer finally protested, calling the interrogation "police harassment," and Caroline was allowed to leave.

I leaned my head back against the headboard, letting the papers fall to my lap. The top of the stairs. According to Caroline, we'd both been standing there with my mom when she fell. I could envision the stairs clearly since I'd just visited the old house. I tried to put myself back there in my mind's eye, before my mother staggered to the door holding her head, before that next morning. I forced my thoughts away from the sounds of the party above me and tried to dial my memory back. I had a spark of recollection of my mother in the powder-blue suit, dressed up for the night as I had rarely seen her. Her face was nervous and slightly flushed, her milky-brown eyes wide. She said something to Caroline and me, some explanation. Caroline gave a harsh laugh, like a dog's bark, a foreign, ugly sound coming from my sister's throat.

I was startled away from the memory by a sudden pounding, like someone falling, which came from directly above me. The neighbors' party. I squeezed my eyes shut, but I couldn't bring it back, and I felt taxed by the effort. I would read the rest of the records tomorrow.

I pulled a pillow over my head to block out the sounds of the city, but it didn't matter. All I could hear was Caroline's coarse, ugly laugh over and over.

18

I took a shorter run than usual on Sunday morning. The city was relatively quiet, since many people had already started their summer sojourns to the Hamptons, and the rest of the population was sleeping off their hangovers. But still, the ever-present smoky exhaust, along with the stale-beer smell from the alleys, made me claustrophobic today. Instead of taking my usual jogging path, replete with packs of cars and people, I ran down side streets to Washington Square Park and did small loops around it.

The run didn't calm me the way it normally did. I was overly aware of the couples who shared the Sunday *Times* on benches and the three girlfriends who walked with paper coffee cups, laughing about their evening escapades.

After a quick shower, I dressed in light khaki pants and a white T-shirt. Gathering the police records and my cell phone, I left the apartment. I simply couldn't spend another hour in there. I should enjoy the city, even if I did it by myself.

At my local coffee shop, I bought the *Times*, a large latte and a cranberry scone. I managed to score one of the outdoor metal tables and settled myself there, making sure to keep my back to the wall. That feeling of being watched had made me cautious.

I nibbled the scone and sipped the coffee. I tried to read the paper first, focusing on the business section and the book reviews, but my thoughts strayed to the police records. I was nervous to read the summary of my own interview with Chief Manning. I had a prickling of fear that I might not like what I found.

But it was no use being fearful of a piece of paper, so I put the *Times* aside and lifted the stack of records from my bag, locating Chief Manning's notes first. Once again, I followed them as he recorded every step he took on the case and the date he performed the action. Along the way, he continued to make indications that he strongly suspected abuse and that he was intent on finding Leah Sutter's boyfriend. However, despite pleas in the local news for this man to come forward, no one had admitted to dating Leah Sutter. According to Chief Manning, this made him even more suspicious about the involvement of the boyfriend. I couldn't blame him. Why wouldn't the person show himself and help the police? An affair was tricky information, something that could destroy whole families, but it wasn't akin to murder.

I kept reading Chief Manning's notes until I found one that stopped me—"Interview with Hailey Sutter, daughter, age 7, May 24." I took a sip of my coffee. I crumbled some of the scone between my fingers. Finally, I thumbed back through the rest of the documents until I found the typed report. Manning wrote:

Hailey Sutter is a seven year old Caucasian female. She appeared with her father and John Matchman, a criminal lawyer with Mr. Sutter's law firm in Chicago. She was cooperative and forthcoming with her answers and speaks in the manner of a child her age. However, she had little, if any, recollection of the night in question, except to say that her mother just slipped and fell down the stairs. She recalls events from earlier that day in detail, including attending riding lessons with a friend named Patsy. (Her father volunteered that this child is Patricia Nawden, also of Woodland Dunes). She also remembers that the Sutter housekeeper, Della Castaneda, retrieved her and Patsy from the stable and drove Patsy home, and then transported Hailey to the Sutter house. She could not identify the time (confirm this with Ms. Castaneda). Hailey could also recall Ms. Castaneda preparing a snack when they arrived home. She then states that she played in her room for the next few hours. The child insists that she recalls nothing after this point, except when asked what happened to her mother, she states simply, "Mama fell down the stairs," and "She just slipped," but could not elaborate any further. She does not yet seem to grasp that her mother is gone, but this is not uncommon in deaths of parents of young children.

And that was it. Nothing more. Nothing illuminating really. Just a little recollection about riding with Patsy and a statement that my mother had fallen.

I set the records on the table and took a bite of my scone, not really tasting it. I felt disappointed somehow. It was odd that I would have remembered so little, especially if I'd been with my mom when she died. Had I been a good liar, trained already by my father to tell falsities to cover for the family? The thought was repugnant, but there it was, and after the half truths I discovered lately on my father's behalf, it seemed horribly plausible.

The crowd going in and out of the coffee shop

had increased. There was too much traffic around my table now to be relaxing, but I was determined to get through the rest of the records. I pushed the scone away and began skimming the notes and other interviews, looking for anything of importance. It seemed that Manning had canvased the community, asking for any information on the identity of Mrs. Sutter's male friend. A few people claimed to have seen Leah on the beach with a dark haired man, but no one knew his name. One of the witnesses suggested that it "must have been a summer person."

I continued skimming Chief Manning's notes. Near the end, he wrote, *Mr. William Sutter called in for additional interrogation. May 31.*

I scrambled until I found the typed summary of the second interview with my father. It was brief.

William Sutter presents the same as the last time interviewed. That is to say he is an attractive, well-dressed gentleman who appears distraught by his estranged wife's death. Mr. Sutter reiterates that a fall was the cause of death and not any domestic abuse on the part of himself or his son. Mr. Sutter continues to disavow any knowledge of the identity of his wife's companion. The witness appears credible in his assertions. This interviewer is inclined to close this case in order to bring an end to the suffering Leah Sutter's death has caused this family and the community.

I read it over once more. Strange how short it was and how abruptly Manning had decided to believe my father. It also seemed peculiar that he would refer to suffering on the part of the Sutters or the community. Wasn't it the job of the police to find who had caused the pain, not just to sweep a case under the rug so it couldn't show its ugliness anymore? Maybe I was expecting too much. When I had read police reports in the past, they were usually authored by the Manhattan authorities who couldn't give a damn how much suffering their investigations caused. But Woodland Dunes was a small community after all. Maybe things played out differently in such places. Still, the thought that someone may have hurt my mother—whether my father, my brother or someone else—and gone unpunished, angered me. It must have angered whoever wrote that letter to me, too.

I read again the summary of my father's last interrogation, trying to discern any other information that could have led to Manning's change of mind. After all, why should he believe my father's version of Leah falling down the stairs when he supposedly wasn't there that night? I was about to put the summary back in the stack, when two small typed annotations at the bottom caught my eye: D: 6/3/82. T:6/3/82.

I knew from reviewing documents at work that this meant the interview was both dictated and typed on June 3, 1982, three days after it took place.

I reviewed the dates of the other interviews. Without fail, Manning had dictated every summary on the day the interview was conducted. On a few occasions, the summary was actually typed a day or two later, but Manning, himself, had performed his dictation with immediacy. So why had it taken him three days to dictate William Sutter's last interview?

It was possible that Manning had simply come to believe my father and had, therefore, lost interest in the case. He might have been put on some other project. Or maybe he'd made up his mind, closed the file, and then remembered to go back and document his thought process. But really, there wasn't much there in terms of his thoughts. Just a short summary of an interview and a conclusion that the case would be closed.

I moved back to his handwritten notes to see if there was anything else. After the note about my father's second interview on May 31, Manning hadn't made any notes at all for two days. This was also odd, since he'd made numerous comments every day since the death. There was only one left after my father's last interview. It said simply, *Death Accidental. Case closed.*

Had I been off base in looking for some other reason for my mother's death? After reading the records, I didn't think so. This quick labeling of the death as "accidental" seemed abrupt, dubious. And my brother and sister had seemingly disappeared soon after I'd received the anonymous letter. Matt had believed that Caroline's disappearance was somehow connected to a call from our father.

Which reminded me, I'd promised Matt I would contact him after I had spoken to my dad, and yet I'd been putting it off, not wanting to admit that I'd realized my father was lying. I gathered the police records and left the newspaper on the table for the next person. Heading back to my apartment, I realized that Matt's wasn't the only phone call I needed to make. I had the number for Crestwood Home, as well.

I called Crestwood Home, telling the receptionist I was looking for information about my sister, Caroline Sutter. But I didn't expect to learn anything that day. It was Sunday, after all. Yet within twenty minutes, I received a return phone call.

"Dr. Adler will see you today," the woman said,

"this afternoon in fact, if you can make the trip to Connecticut."

"Dr. Adler?" I asked.

"Yes, he'll speak with you about your sister. Can you get here today?"

"Today," I repeated, not sure whether to be thrilled or wary. Finally, I recovered. I got directions and grabbed my car keys.

It took me no time to drive to Holly Knolls, Connecticut. Following the directions I received, I turned off the highway and glanced at my odometer. Thirty miles since I had left Manhattan. It would have been sixty or so miles from Long Island, which meant that during part of her stay at Crestwood Home, Caroline had been only sixty miles from where my father and I had lived in Manhasset. I'd never had any concept of what had happened to Caroline after we'd left Woodland Dunes, but my father had known. That was clear now. He would have paid Caroline's bills, probably spoken to Caroline's doctor. Had he visited her, leaving me at home with one of the nannies? Why had he kept Caroline away?

I slowed the car and turned right by a small, tasteful sign that read Crestwood Home. I pulled into the parking lot and turned off the ignition.

Crestwood was a Victorian home made of large brown stones, with two turrets on either side like mountain peaks. On the vivid green front lawn, a few men played croquet, while a woman sat in a chair watching them, her hands flat on her knees. If I hadn't known better, I might have thought it was a private club.

I got out of the car and walked the pebbled path to the front doors. Inside, the place was like a hotel lobby, decorated with soothing Monetesque oil paintings and thick gray carpeting, which blocked out any sound. I gave the receptionist my name and took a seat in an upholstered, high-backed chair.

After a minute, the woman rose from her seat and called to me, "Dr. Adler will see you now. Third door on your right." She pointed down the center hallway that led away from the reception area.

My footsteps fell silent on the carpeting. I pricked up my ears, listening for any noises. I wasn't sure what I expected to hear. Screams or cries maybe? Laughter or discussion? According to their Web site, Crestwood Home usually housed a hundred residents. But only an unnatural quiet rang back. I stopped and knocked when I reached the third door, which was closed and unmarked.

"Come in," I heard.

Dr. Adler's large office was furnished with over-stuffed leather couches with worn, flannel blankets tossed over them. A wood desk with numerous nicks and scratches sat at the far end of the room.

Above it, prints with bleak landscapes hung on the wall. If the rest of the home seemed like an up-scale hotel or a club, Dr. Adler's office appeared more like a lodge in Colorado.

A man stood from behind the desk, buttoning his tan jacket. I had expected a bookish, older man in a white lab coat, but Dr. Adler was tall and lean, his high cheekbones and pointed chin giving his face an elfin appearance. His brown hair was beginning to gray at the temples, and I guessed that he was in his late forties.

"Miss Sutter." He moved around the desk and clasped my hand. "I'm Dr. Adler. It's a pleasure."

"You, too. I really appreciate your seeing me on such short notice."

"Of course. This is one of my working week-ends, so I was here when you called." He raised a hand and gestured toward the couch along the far wall. "Would you like to lie down?"

I looked at the couch and back to his face again. "I don't think that's…I'm not here for…"

He gave me another half smile. "Just a little psychiatric joke."

"Oh." I laughed a little then, startled by the attempt at humor.

"Please," he said, this time pointing to one of the leather chairs in front of his desk.

I sank into it, the soft chair engulfing me until

I felt ten inches lower than Dr. Adler, who was now back behind his desk. I shifted, trying to position myself higher, wondering if he had bought the chairs like that on purpose.

"Dr. Adler," I said, scooting forward. "I'm here to talk about my sister, Caroline Sutter."

He gave a slight bow of his head. "My assistant mentioned that, and that's why I agreed to see you today. The Portland police have contacted me, as well, so I know that Caroline is missing."

"Really?" I remembered what Matt had said about the police being relatively unhelpful.

"Yes. I'm very concerned about her, as I'm sure you are, but I wanted to explain to you in person that, without Caroline's express permission, I can't divulge anything about her or her care to you."

"And why is that?" Jesus. He had gotten me all the way out here, and he wasn't going to give me anything?

"Because of physician/patient privilege. Are you familiar with what that means?" His voice held a trace of condescension.

"Yes, I'm an attorney. I know what the physician/patient privilege is."

Dr. Adler spread his hands wide as if to show the futility of my being there.

"Well," I said, "I'm sure you know the cases which say that a physician who fears his patient might harm themselves or others can break the privilege for the safety of the patient and the other people."

Dr. Adler placed his elbows on his desk, forming a steeple with his fingers and leaning his chin on them. "Ms. Sutter, I cared about Caroline very much, and I was extremely proud of her progress. I still worry about her from time to time, but I keep in loose contact with her, and the letters I've received indicate nothing like what you're suggesting."

"When did you last hear from her?"

Dr. Adler pulled open a lower desk drawer that I couldn't see. He turned his body and flipped through files. He lifted a sheet, glanced at it, then returned it to the drawer. "Six months ago."

"Before she disappeared."

"That's correct."

"Was she ever suicidal?"

"I can't tell you that," he said.

I tried not to show my frustration. Why was I here if he wasn't prepared to tell me something? I decided to try again.

"Then just think the answer to yourself," I said. "Ask yourself, was Caroline suicidal? Does the fact that she disappeared in the middle of a wedding and left a note for her husband telling him that she needed time away indicate that she might have had some kind of relapse? Does the fact that she is still missing mean that she might have harmed herself or be thinking about doing so?"

My voice raised slightly, despite my best efforts to remain calm. I didn't want to anger Dr. Adler, but the more I talked, thinking about my sister out there somewhere, alone, when she had already spent so much of her life by herself, had given me real worry. This wasn't just about me anymore and satisfying my need to discover what had happened to my mother. This had to be about Caroline and Dan, too.

The office was silent for a long time. Dr. Adler's eyes narrowed as if he was going through a mental exercise. I tried to sit perfectly still, tried not to tap a foot or even blink my eyes.

Finally he said, "Yes. It's possible that Caroline may try to hurt herself."

"Then you can break the privilege. You can help me to help her."

Silence again. And he nodded.

Dr. Adler had me wait in his office while he left the room to gather Caroline's files, and then again he left me waiting while he sat at his desk and reviewed them. It seemed an interminably long time.

I crossed and recrossed my legs, struggling to stay upright in the cushy chair, holding in an impatient sigh. It occurred to me that if the Portland police had contacted Dr. Adler, then the police must have learned about the clinic from Matt, which meant that Caroline had told him about her stay here. The thought that they were so close, that Caroline had someone in her life she could talk openly with, comforted me.

At last, Dr. Adler took his chair again and looked at me. "First, I should start by telling you that I was a psychiatric resident when Caroline was first admitted here. She was technically under the care of Dr. Sammeth, who is no longer with us, but because of the nature of my residency, I was the physician who saw Caroline most often."

I nodded, eager to get straight to the point. "And why was she admitted to begin with?"

"Caroline was admitted to Crestwood following a suicide attempt."

"Oh," I said, the sound slipping out of my mouth before I realized it. I had taken a stab in the dark when I asked Dr. Adler if Caroline had been suicidal, thinking that it might get him to help me, but hearing that she had actually tried to take her own life sent a surge of sadness through my body. It threatened to exhaust me.

Dr. Adler continued in a flat voice. "She used a kitchen knife to slit her wrists on the day she was supposed to graduate from high school. A place called…" Dr. Adler flipped through some notes.

"Brighton Academy," I said, my voice flat.

He gave me a glance, then returned his eyes to the file. "That's right. When we did an initial intake exam we found that she had been engaged in self-mutilation for a period of approximately five years."

"Self-mutilation," I repeated, finding my throat suddenly dry. "Can you tell me what that means?"

Dr. Adler put the file folder down on his desk. "It's just what it sounds like, hurting one's self, usually by cutting or slicing the skin, sometimes burning, in order to relieve one's feelings. It's often associated with unexpressed and unresolved loss or anger."

"But if she'd been doing this—this mutilation—for five years, wouldn't someone have noticed?" *Please,* I thought, *tell me someone noticed.*

Dr. Adler shook his head no. "It's quite easy to hide, really. In Caroline's case, she used safety pins, sometimes broken glass, but she took extreme care to ensure that no one could see the wounds. She cut herself in places like her armpits, inner thighs, behind her knees, that kind of thing."

Dr. Adler paused, as if giving me space to ask a question, but I was momentarily overwhelmed. Finally, I found my voice. "Why? Why did she do that?"

"As I said, this type of behavior is often associated with anger and loss. In Caroline's case, it appeared to be related to a few things. One was the loss of your mother. Another was a deep anger toward your father. Instead of expressing these emotions outwardly, she would harm herself in order to achieve some kind of relief."

"And did she talk about why she was so angry with our father?"

"Of course," Dr. Adler said. "Caroline was here for a good number of years, you know. It was very hard for her to stop the mutilation, and so she was considered a threat to herself for a long time. She underwent intensive therapy of many forms—individual, group, art therapy, meds. During that time it came out that she felt abandoned by your father."

A little rush of relief. "And is that it? She simply felt abandoned?"

"I'm not sure what you're getting at."

"Well, our mother died very suddenly, at least as far as I know, and from what I can tell, there was an investigation into her death. My parents were separated at the time, and apparently my mother was involved with someone else. I guess I'm wondering if Caroline ever talked about that or about anything specific that our father had done?"

Dr. Adler seemed to think for a minute. "Caroline was very reluctant to talk about the circumstances surrounding your mother's death. After your mother died, she was sent off to boarding school, leaving her to fend for herself. She was only fourteen, if I recall correctly, and there were apparently very few visits by anyone in your family. She essentially felt discarded and neglected, and that was layered on top of what already was a somewhat depressive personality in her case."

It made sense, I thought. But was that all there was?

Dr. Adler continued, "Now, as for your father, I should mention that Caroline was often reticent in her revealing her feelings and her past. It's one of the reasons she was here so long. However, it was obvious to me that there was something she was holding back about your father, something that had angered her deeply."

"Did she ever tell you what it was?"

"I'm afraid not."

"Do you know, generally, what it concerned?"

"I believe it may have concerned your mother, but I can't say for certain."

We both sat in silence. My mind stewed with thoughts of Caroline, of what she may have seen my father do.

"You mentioned her feelings of loss about our mother," I said. "Can you explain a little more about that, about how she felt?"

His forehead creased, his thumb stroked the

side of his jaw absently. "Caroline was, of course, experiencing a great amount of grief about the loss of your mother." He looked up at me. "You were very young at the time, I take it?"

"I was seven."

He continued rubbing his jaw. "Caroline would tell us that your mother fell down a flight of stairs, but she refused to give details past that point, which made us wonder if she was telling the truth. We never did get an answer from her that the staff was satisfied with. All we could determine for sure was that she felt an utter destruction of her world, as well as some guilt."

"Guilt?" I pushed myself forward in the too-soft chair. "Why would she feel guilt?"

"It's not uncommon in adolescents to feel a certain sense of helplessness following the death of a parent, a certain sense that if only things were different they could have prevented the death."

"Is that how Caroline felt?"

Dr. Adler gave me another one of his calculating stares. "You must be a trial lawyer."

"Why do you say that?"

"You notice the use of generalities in semantics."

I didn't respond.

Dr. Adler made a barely audible sigh. "This topic—your mother's death, I mean—was somewhat of a bone of contention with the staff here at the time. Dr. Sammeth and the counselors felt Caroline was reacting typically to this event..." He trailed off.

"But you felt differently?"

He gave a slight nod. "To me, her feelings on this issue seemed to be closely tied to another strong emotion."

"What was that?"

Dr. Adler shifted in his seat, and for the first time, I sensed he was uncomfortable. "Caroline had a certain irrational hatred."

"Toward a certain person?"

"That's right."

"Was it my father?"

"No."

"Who then?" I was beginning to get exasperated.

"I'm afraid," he said, placing his hands on the desk, "that it was you."

19

My foot lifted off the brake and stepped on the gas. I signaled a left merge onto the highway. I saw the outlines of the city in the distance. But I was removed from all of it. In my mind someone was chanting over and over, *She hated you, she hated you, she hated you.*

Dr. Adler had explained it well enough, I suppose. Her emotions about me had to do with the fact that I was taken care of by my father, he said. I had been sheltered, while Caroline was sent off to a boarding school alone, unprepared. It was perfectly natural, he said. He was sure Caroline no longer felt like that.

"She was making me a quilt," I said stupidly. I was slumped at the back of that cushy chair by then, unable to keep my rod-straight posture, unable to care anymore that the height difference might give Dr. Adler some kind of intellectual advantage. What did it matter? My sister hated me.

"Excuse me?" Dr. Adler said.

"I spoke to her husband, and he said she was making me a quilt."

"Well, that's excellent. As I said, Caroline had stopped focusing on that irrational hatred of you by the time she left us. When I've corresponded with her over the last few years, she seemed very happy with her husband."

My eyes met Dr. Adler's over his desk, the unspoken thought between us—if Caroline was so happy, why had she gone missing?

Keeping one hand on the wheel now, I fumbled through my purse for my cell phone. I hit the speed dial for Maddy's number. Not home. Again. No answer on her cell phone, either. The shock was growing into something more panicky. My sister hated me! I had to tell someone.

Matt. I should call Matt. I owed him a phone call anyway. I called Information for his number and stopped to pay a toll while the call was connected.

He answered almost immediately with a gruff "Hello," like the first time I called.

"Matt, it's Hailey," I said. "How are you?"

"Same."

"No word?"

"Nothing." He said the word so quietly that it broke my heart. There was a pause, then he said, "Have you talked to your father?" He had so much contempt in his voice now that he made the words *your father* sound like "that serial killer."

"Yeah, I have," I said.

"What did he say about Caroline?"

"We talked about her going to boarding school and stuff like that, and—"

"Hailey, I'm sorry to be rude, but I don't care about that. I want to know what he said about Caroline's disappearance."

Oh, God. How to tell him that I'd never even gotten to that topic because I'd been too upset about the fact that he was lying to me, telling me pretty tales about Caroline at Yale and in Paris. "We didn't exactly get there," I said.

"What? You didn't even ask him? You promised me!"

"I know, but I—"

"What?"

"I didn't think he'd tell me the truth. But look," I said, rushing on to a different subject, "I just found out something else about Caroline. I went to Crestwood Home. You know about her stay there, right?"

"Yes. But how do *you* know?"

"I saw some letters from there that she wrote to a family friend. I went to Crestwood today and talked to one of her doctors."

"And they actually talked to you? I mean, they

told you about Caroline's treatment?" His accusatory tone was impossible to miss.

"Yeah, they did. And I would think you'd want to know about it. I think you'd want to know anything that can help us find her."

"Well, did you find anything other than she used to cut herself and she tried to kill herself? Jesus, how could you do that? How could they do that? That's an invasion of her privacy! I don't want to know anything unless she's called them in the last few weeks, which I assume she hasn't."

"No," I said simply. I got off the highway and started making my way over the bridge into the city. Matt's palpable anger was making me shaky, unsure, and I was glad to hit a patch of traffic so I could slow the car.

He was quiet for a second. "I'm sorry. I'm taking this out on you, when I shouldn't be. I guess I've been hoping that you'd find something out from your father."

"I'm not sure he knows anything about Caroline or Dan, and if he does, I'm not sure he'd tell me."

"Dan? What do you mean he doesn't know anything about Caroline *or* Dan?"

Traffic had started moving again. My car growled as it slowly inched over the steel grid lines of the bridge. The closer I got to the middle, the more anxious it made me, just as my search into my mother's death made me more uneasy all the time. I explained as quickly as I could what I'd learned about Dan's life, about how no one had heard from him since that Saturday, the same day Caroline disappeared. I didn't tell him what Annie said about New Orleans. I had promised her after all, and it was something I hadn't been able to follow up on yet.

"Christ," Matt said. "This is too fucking weird. I mean, excuse my language, but a brother and sister both walking off into the sunset on the same day? Your goddamn dad has to know something."

"You're right. Look, I'll go over to his house tonight, okay? I'll find something."

"Please," Matt said, his voice soft once more. "Do whatever you have to do. I miss my wife. I miss her so much."

My father's house was dark. It was a large, Georgian home with redbrick, white square columns holding up the portico over the front door, and black shutters framing the windows. The setting sun cast a sinister orange glow behind it. The front-hall lights were off, a sure sign he wasn't home. After thinking about it all afternoon, I had decided to drive out here and simply confront him, ask him what he knew about Caroline and Dan. I procrastinated at first by halfheartedly working on the

McKnight case. I took a walk around the neighborhood. Finally, I got up the courage to drive out to Manhasset. But where was he? Maybe out of town for a deposition? Or maybe just out to dinner? Despite the messages he'd left me, I hadn't spoken to him since that night at the Van Newton Guild.

I would just go inside and wait for him, I decided. But even as I thought it, I knew that I wouldn't simply wait. I wouldn't lie on the plump couches in the den and watch TV, the way I used to in high school, nor would I sit on the sunporch off the kitchen. Instead I would go into his study. The place my father kept all the documents and bits of information that made up his life. Maybe I'd find something there about my siblings.

I drove down the street and pulled my car into the lot of a small park, where I used to make out with high-school boyfriends. Tucking my keys into my pocket, I walked back down the darkening street to his house. Once there, I reached under the shutter to the right of the front door and felt around the windowsill for the spare key. My fingers brushed over the stone of the sill that felt sandy to the touch. Where was it? Maybe he didn't keep a spare key outside anymore. I pushed my arm back farther, my cardigan sweater catching on a shrub, and finally I felt the cold metal of the key.

I glanced around guiltily as I put the key in the

lock, but there was no one around. The houses were set far apart, not the kind of place where neighbors looked out for each other. The door swung open, and I breathed in the clean, woodsy scent the house always had. As I shoved the key back onto the sill, a tinny *beep, beep, beep* came from inside the house, making me flinch.

The alarm. Shit. I'd forgotten about it.

I stepped inside and quickly crossed the marble foyer to the alarm panel, praying that he hadn't changed the code. I pressed the numbers that corresponded to my birthday—1013—but the alarm kept up its insistent beeping. Probably only thirty more seconds until it went off. What could he have changed it to? I entered 0102 for my father's birthday. The alarm continued its warning beep. Was it getting louder? Think, think, think! Caroline's birthday? What was it? I put in 0418. At least that's the date I remembered, but the damn thing kept beeping. I knew I had precious few seconds left. What was Dan's birthday? It was in June, but I couldn't remember the date. What about Annie? Would he have used her birthday? Did he even know he was a grandfather?

Any second a piercing scream would bring cops running to the house. *Think.* He always used dates of some sort. At least he had in the past. And then I thought of a date that had been looming in my mind, one that was fast approaching. May 20, the day of my mother's death. I punched in 0520, and the alarm went silent.

The house was eerily quiet, except for the thump of blood pumping through my body. A deep blue-black had settled over the rooms now that the sun was gone from the windows. A few breaths restored my heartbeat. I cut through the formal living room that we never used, down the long marble hallway to the right, and into my father's study.

The far wall, made all of glass, overlooked the English garden in the backyard. The two side walls held floor-to-ceiling bookshelves, lined with an array of books—legal and commercial fiction, leather-bound first editions and paperbacks. My father's decorator had suggested that he keep his paperbacks and the more "user-friendly" books somewhere else in the house, but he wouldn't hear of it. He loved all of them, he said. All the different volumes mixed and mingled. His books were the one part of his life that my father didn't keep meticulously organized.

I went to his desk, the place I used to sit when he traveled for work and some babysitter spent the night with me. I would climb up in that red leather chair, careful not to send it flying on the wheels, and I would touch the things he always used—the leather cup with the embossed logo of the University of Chicago Law School, the iron hammerhead from his father that he used as a paperweight, the heavy silver letter opener. These things were all still there. I picked up the hammerhead that was sitting atop a stack of faxes, turning it over in my hand, seeing the words painted on the bottom in red—*For Billy.* As always, I marveled that my father had ever been called Billy.

I flipped through the faxes and business letters. I vaguely read the trial notes on his desk, the half-written client letters printed out with his pencil-marked corrections. It struck me how few personal documents my father had here. I opened the large file drawer and found his household bills, scrupulously reviewed and filed alphabetically and by date, but there was little else. No postcards from friends, of which he had few, no magazine clippings or journals.

I went through his Rolodex and his address book, but there were no numbers for Dan or Caroline that I could see. Nothing that mentioned Portland or Albuquerque or New Orleans. I pawed through the rest of his drawers distractedly, wondering if he was about to come home any minute, dreading the talk I planned on having with him. One of the bottom drawers was difficult to view, since I'd turned on only the small desk lamp. I moved the lamp over to see in the drawer more clearly. Nothing exciting, just stacks of legal pads and some other office supplies.

I sat up, glanced around the desk once more, feeling achy and tired from too much driving, too much thinking, and the adrenaline rush of the alarm scare. I was about to move the lamp back, when I noticed a scrap of paper about one inch long and three inches wide. It must have been under the lamp. I lifted the scrap and read the number printed there in black ink. It was a phone number, one which began "504." New Orleans. I'd had a trial expert there last year, and I'd dialed his number often enough to remember the area code. There was no name on the paper, but I knew my dad had written it. I recognized the way he put the little slash through the seven, the flat top he gave his threes.

I started to feel hot, my scalp itchy. A scribbled number on a scrap of paper might have been an everyday occurrence for many people, but it was completely unlike my father. He always carried around a small notebook in his jacket pocket, and every desk he owned had its own address book. And he wasn't the type to meet women at bars, especially ones who lived in New Orleans. Or was he? What did I *really* know about him anymore?

I lifted the phone and dialed the number. It took an eternity before it began ringing. Agitated, I stood from the desk and paced with the cordless phone. The ringing continued, unanswered. I jiggled my leg. I blew my bangs away from my forehead. Finally, I sighed and sat back in my father's chair. After nine or ten rings, I hung up and tried again, just in case I'd dialed incorrectly. Same thing. A distant, ringing phone with no answer, no machine.

I felt deflated, tiredness overtaking me. I copied the number on a Post-it and carefully tucked the scrap of paper back under the lamp. I stood from the chair, surveying the room in case I'd missed something. Then I heard the rumble of the garage door. My father was home.

My first reaction was to hide. I switched the lamp off and ducked under the desk, tucking myself into a ball and pulling the chair in to conceal myself.

I held my breath, safe for the moment. But then a rush of panic swooped in. He would notice that the alarm had been turned off! I almost crawled out, but then it dawned on me that he might simply wonder whether he'd forgotten to arm it. I heard him entering through the kitchen and walking the rooms. I heard him flipping light switches.

Just get up, I told myself. *Talk to him, like you promised Matt you would.* But I reminded myself that what I'd actually promised Matt was that I would find something, and now I had. This odd scrap of paper with a New Orleans phone number. The words of my niece whispered themselves in my ear—*He went to Orleans.*

I didn't know if this phone number had any connection to Dan, but I did know that my father had already lied to me. I couldn't believe anything he said anymore. So what would be the point now of asking him? He would lie again, and then if the person who was at that New Orleans number had anything to do with my mother—or my brother or sister—he would tell them to run. I might never find out if it was Dan at that number. I would never find out if the piece of paper meant anything at all.

My father's footsteps approached the study. I prayed it was too late for him to work. But then the overhead lights blazed on. I imagined the meticulous way he stood there, letting his eyes roam over the room for anything amiss. I tried to envision the hammerhead. Had I put it back squarely in the center of those faxes? And the University of Chicago cup—had I moved it back to the right place?

The front of the desk, where I was crouched, faced the far wall, so he couldn't see me. If he decided to make a call, though, or take some notes, it would be over. The blood began to pound in my ears as I waited, listening to him. This was so bizarre, but I didn't trust him anymore.

Suddenly, he shut off the lights and moved down the hallway. A moment later, I heard his light footsteps on the stairs up to his bedroom.

If I ran out now, the alarm would go off again the minute I opened the door. And if I disarmed it, he would hear those tones, too. Either way, he would know someone had been in the house. Despite everything, I hated to think of his jolt of fear when he heard the alarm, but I wasn't prepared to face him, not now when I had a small piece of information that might get me somewhere. I waited until he was surely in his bedroom, then I slowly pushed out the chair. In the dark, I tiptoed out of the study, past the living room and into the marble foyer again. The tapping of my shoes sounded inordinately loud. I waited for a moment, straining my ears toward the upstairs, and I heard the sound of running water.

I put my hand on the front door, saying a silent *I'm sorry.* I opened the door then and ran down the street, the persistent warning bleat of the alarm following me.

20

"I'm here to see Madeline Kennedy," I said to the doorman.

"Name, please."

"Hailey Sutter." I smoothed my hair, trying to look composed, trying not to sound out of breath, but I couldn't shake the feeling that I was being chased.

I had called Maddy from the car, and once again, she didn't answer her cell or her home phone. I was desperate to talk to someone. I actually called Ty at Long Beach Inn, but got only a night receptionist, and finally I'd come to Maddy's apartment on Eighty-sixth and Lexington, hoping that she would come home sometime tonight.

The doorman dialed the house phone. He listened for a few moments. "Ms. Kennedy," he said. "There's a visitor here for you. Ms. Sutter." A pause. "I'll send her right up."

Maddy opened the door in her pajamas. Her

dark curly hair was wet, her cheeks flushed, and she had an unmistakable glow. "Hey!" she said.

I stepped into her apartment. "Did you just have sex?"

She winked. "He just left."

"Well," I said. "At least one of us is having fun these days."

"Oh, yes, I'm having fun." She gave me a hug. "But I'm sorry I haven't been around much."

"New relationship. I understand."

"I'm glad you came over, because I have those sandals I bought you at Saks. But what are you doing here on a Sunday night?"

The main area of Maddy's apartment was shaped like a long, rectangular box. The kitchen, which was at the far end, was inexplicably bigger than the minuscule living room, and yet the kitchen was cold and impersonal with its black-and-white tiles and white paint layered a thousand times over. Maddy's bedroom, on the other hand, was the coziest room in the place, the one where we always hung out. She led me in there now, and I curled up on the overstuffed chair she had in the corner. She stood at the mirror over her bureau, combing gel into her long curls. In the center of the room, her ivory sheets were twisted and shoved aside.

"I think I'm going crazy over this stuff with my

mom," I told her. "I don't know if I'm paranoid or smart or just a complete freak."

"I vote for freak," she said, smiling in the mirror.

"Thanks. Do you have any wine?"

"Sorry. Grant and I finished the last bottle." She grinned again, and I was happy to see her so content. "Now, tell me what happened," she said.

"Oh, God, Maddy, I don't know what I'm doing anymore. This whole thing is making me insane. I'm not even sure that there's anything to find out, but I'm running around like a nutcase. I even broke into my dad's place today."

"What?" She spun around from the mirror. "What happened?"

I told her about New Mexico and about Annie. I told her how my niece seemed to be clinging to my mind. And I told her about the police records, my visit to Crestwood Home, and finally my covert trip to my dad's house and the New Orleans phone number I found there.

"Wow, hon," Maddy said. "You've got to take a step back. I mean, I was all for New Mexico and everything, but sneaking into your dad's, and running out without talking to him? What are you thinking?"

"I'm thinking that he knows something!" My voice got loud. "He definitely knows *something* and not only won't he tell me, he'll hide it." I dropped my forehead onto my hands. "God, I've got a headache."

"I'll get you some aspirin." Maddy went around the corner into her bathroom. "Have you called that New Orleans number again?" she called out.

"Not yet." I rubbed my head some more, and then reached out and began playing absently with the stuff on Maddy's nightstand—her big silver watch, her tiny diamond earrings—things obviously taken off before she and the new boyfriend had twisted up the sheets.

"Well, keep calling the number and all," she said, "but you've got to concentrate on work, too. You've got partnership elections coming up."

"I know." I picked up one of Maddy's rings, spinning it around my index finger, thinking about my niece, about how she said her dad was in Orleans.

As Maddy came back into the room with my aspirin and a glass of water, I went to put the ring back on the nightstand, but for the first time, I really looked at it. It wasn't one of Maddy's after all. It was a man's ring. I raised it closer, and I felt that pounding of blood in my ears again.

The ring was gold and oval, with the shape of a black diamond on its face.

"Hailey," I heard Maddy say, but I couldn't look at her. I kept staring at the ring, and I saw it in my memory, resting on my mother's blue shoulder, while she stood at the door. The hand gripped her shoulder tighter, the man who wore it murmured something to her. My mother swayed, pitched sideways. The man caught her, the back of his dark hair bending over her.

"What's up?" Maddy said.

"Where did you get this?"

"It's Grant's."

"What? Are you sure?" I turned it around and around in my hand.

"Of course. He took a shower before he left, and he forgot it. Why? What's wrong?"

"Maddy, this is the ring," I said, ignoring the water and aspirin she was still holding.

"What ring?"

"That ring I saw on my mom's shoulder. Remember, I told you?" I was talking fast. "That night before she died, she had on the blue suit. She was talking to a man at the door, and he had a ring on just like this."

Maddy sighed and put the glass down on her nightstand. "Girl, you are getting way too into this."

"No, I'm serious. It was exactly like this."

"Well, so what?" She took the ring out of my hand. "This ring could be any man's. It's not that complicated."

"But that's exactly like the ring I saw. This could be the same one."

She sighed again. "Seriously, you've got to take a step back. I mean, c'mon, you're getting paranoid."

"Maybe." I had only been a kid, after all and I'd been yards away from my mom. I took the ring from Maddy's hand and held it close to my face. The gold back, the black diamond design—it was exactly how I remembered. In the center, there were four little etches, facing out, details I couldn't have seen that night because of the distance.

"I think this could be it," I said again. "Where did Grant get it?"

"Honey, please. You've got to take some time off."

"I can't."

"You have to." She reached over and squeezed my hand. "Hailey…"

I groaned. "I guess I am going crazy."

"Just a little." She took the ring and sat on her bed. "Listen, I think I know what this is about. I haven't been around as much since I've been dating Grant, and I'm sorry."

"No, it's not that. I want you to be happy, I want you to spend time with Grant. I'd like to *meet* him for once."

Maddy laughed. "That's fair. Look, I'll find out when he'll be back in town. The three of us will go out, we'll give him his ring, and you can see for yourself. You can get to know him. How does that sound?"

She flipped her wet hair over her shoulder, her face full of hope. She was probably right about me being paranoid. And I owed her—she'd always been there for me.

I nodded, and tried not to look at the ring as Maddy set it back on her nightstand.

On Monday morning, Lev Werner, the head of the partnership-election committee, stuck his shiny bald head in my office just as I was about to dial that New Orleans phone number again. I'd tried it at least five times that morning. Still no answer. I had even called one of my investigators and told him to find out who's number it was, the address it was associated with, anything.

"Hailey," Lev said, "got a second?" There was no mistaking his businesslike tone, making it clear that even if I didn't have a second, I had better make one.

"Of course." I put the phone back in the cradle and scooted around my desk, clearing the files from one of my visitor's chairs. "Have a seat."

He closed the door as he stepped into the office. Not a good sign.

"How are you?" Lev said, but it seemed a formality of a question.

"Fine, fine." I took in Lev's gray suit, half a size too small as usual. He was one of the few men

I knew who often talked about his weight, someone who made no bones about the fact that he struggled with it. That trait made him seem very human to me, unlike so many of the other older partners.

Lev shifted in the chair, as if it was a little tight, just like his suit. "Hailey, you know we have partnership elections coming up very fast here."

"Of course." I sat up straighter. "And you know how badly I want to be partner here." I sounded false, like a beauty pageant contestant talking about world peace.

"Yes, well." He coughed. "We still haven't received your essay."

I managed not to groan. I'd started the damn thing on the plane to Portland and never finished it. I was unable to bring myself to write the part about my father, about how I wanted to follow in his footsteps.

"I've started it, Lev, but this McKnight case is keeping me so busy."

He nodded, appeared unconvinced. "It was due over a week ago. Everyone else has turned them in."

"If you could just give me a few more days."

"I don't know. The election committee put off our first meeting until we could get your essay, but word got out. Some of the other attorneys who are up for partner are complaining about special treatment."

I didn't even have to ask who these other attorneys were. I was sure that Paige Amboy had learned I was the holdout and was leading the pack on this one.

"I'd like to work on it today," I said, "but I'm leaving for Chicago."

"Depositions?"

"I have a conference at McKnight headquarters first thing tomorrow morning. Then I'm meeting a potential witness." Amy had tracked down Eden Fieldings, one of the members of the Fieldings family, whose company had been taken over by McKnight so many years ago. Eden had told Amy that her father, the founder of the company, was too incapacitated in his advanced age to speak to attorneys, but she agreed to be interviewed herself. I needed to get the whole story on the Fieldings takeover before the trial. What I didn't say to Lev was, *I might go to Woodland Dunes; I might find out what happened to my mom; I might see a man named Ty.*

"You're not going to the cocktail party?" Lev said.

The firm had a monthly cocktail party in the reception area. It was that night, and I'd forgotten all about it. "I won't be able to make it," I said.

Lev shifted in the chair again, and tugged at his tie. "Hailey, I think you need to put in an appearance tonight. You need to convince everyone in this firm that you're serious about being partner."

"Isn't it enough that I make more money for this firm than any other associate?"

Lev raised both hands in the air, a futile gesture. Both of us knew that revenue alone wasn't enough. An associate had to kiss ass and grovel and attend all the necessary functions, which I had avoided lately, especially since I received that letter.

"I think you need to postpone your trip and make sure you come to the party," Lev said. His tone was grave, and I heard the message under his words—*You'd better do something or I won't be able to help you. You won't make partner, at least not this year.*

And yet for the first time in my life, I cared about something more than work. It had never happened to me before—boys, vacations, clothes, hobbies (what *were* hobbies, exactly?)—nothing had ever been as important as work. But now my career was taking an inadvertent back seat to my mother, my siblings, that damn letter.

"I'm sorry, Lev," I said. "But I can't be there tonight. I'll get the essay to you as soon as I can. Thanks for coming by." And then I stood from the chair, signaling the end of our conversation.

21

I was in Chicago by eight-thirty that night. I checked into the Ambassador East Hotel on State Street and wondered how to fill the next few hours. I'd already prepared for my meeting and witness interview tomorrow, and without the rest of my McKnight files, there wasn't much more to do right then. The only people I knew who might have a late dinner were the attorneys from the Chicago office. They were friendly people, a bunch of characters, but I couldn't bear the thought of talking about the upcoming partner elections. Instead, I ordered a salad and a glass of sauvignon blanc from room service.

As I waited for my food, I couldn't help thinking about Woodland Dunes, right across the lake, just sixty or so miles away. I got out my Palm Pilot and looked up Ty's number at Long Beach Inn.

"Oh, sorry, he's not here." It was Molly, Ty's friend, and she sounded decidedly unsorry that Ty wasn't around to talk to me.

"Do you know what time he'll be back?"

"Who knows? He's visiting his mom, and those two talk for hours."

"Okay, I'll call him tomorrow," I said. Molly hadn't even asked if she could take a message, and I doubted that Ty would get it if I left one.

"Great, thanks," she said, and she hung up.

I flipped through the channels. I tried to watch Court TV, but they were covering some depressing child-abuse trial. I gave a sitcom fifteen minutes, but found myself more irritated than amused. And I couldn't shake the feeling that I wanted to talk to Ty. I had his parents' number, but I didn't know if I should bother him there. Finally, I decided it was no big deal. At least I could tell him to call me later.

The phone rang at the Mannings' house. I felt consumed by an adolescent nervousness, like when I'd called a boy for the first time in high school.

But when I heard a deep, grumbled "Hello?" I got even more anxious.

"Chief Manning," I said. "It's Hailey Sutter."

A long pause. "Are you looking for Ty?" So much for chitchat.

"Yes, the person at the inn said he was here."

"You just missed him."

"Oh, well, I'll try him later."

Chief Manning grunted in what I assumed was assent.

"Say hello to your wife," I said, not wanting to let him off the phone. Why not ask him some more questions about his investigation? He was one of the few people who knew anything.

"Will do," he said. "Goodbye then."

"Wait!" I called out. "Can I ask you a quick question?"

Another pause. "All right."

"I was wondering if you'd ever found anything about the man who my mom was seeing before she died." I knew from his records that no one had been able to identify him, but maybe Chief Manning had learned something after the investigation was closed.

"You know about that?" he said.

"Yes." I didn't add that I knew most of it from his own records, the ones his son had copied for me.

"We could never identify him."

"Do you know how long they were together, or even if they were still together when she died?"

"Well, if I remember right, she told your father she'd been seeing him for a year, maybe less." His voice died off quickly as if there was more but he was reluctant to speak.

"Did you talk to other people, like her friends? You must have interviewed someone who saw them together."

A pause. "There was a neighbor that night who thought she saw someone pull into your driveway. She thought maybe a man was driving, but she couldn't say any more than that. I really don't know anything else."

A car in the driveway. A man at the wheel. I wanted to ask him why that wasn't in his records, but of course I couldn't. And something was tugging at my brain. A car in the driveway. A sound outside the house. The honking of a car horn. I remembered that. The car horn. I could hear it now. I could see my younger self standing near my mom.

It was evening, and I had walked out of my room to get a snack. I saw mom on the landing, standing still, as if she couldn't decide where to move. She turned and knelt in front of me.

"Hailey," she said, placing her hands on my shoulders. They felt as if they were pinning me to the ground. "I need to talk to you, and I need you to listen. I need you to act like a big girl."

I nodded, staring into her light brown eyes.

She looked down for a second, and I did, too. The shoes she wore were the color of sky in the summer, a powder blue to match her suit. I had rarely seen her in such clothes, even more rarely in high heels. I was used to her in jeans and T-shirts and brown leather shoes. I thought she looked better in the jeans.

As she stared at the floor, one of her ankles wobbled in the high shoes. The movement seemed to wake her from her thoughts.

She looked at me again and took a deep breath. "I'm going away tonight."

"Why?" I said.

"It's just for tonight. I'll be back in the morning." But she looked down the hallway, no longer at my eyes, and that look made me think she didn't mean what she had said.

"But Daddy isn't home."

She returned her eyes to me, and I think she knew what I meant. It wasn't just that he was away at the moment. He'd been away for longer than usual now. He hadn't come home the last few weekends. And now she was going to leave, too.

"Caroline is here. She'll watch after you." She gave me a warm smile, and for a second I thought maybe everything would be okay, but then came the sound.

My mother jerked her head a little so that her ear was toward the stairs, toward the door. It came again, and I recognized it as a horn from a car, but not Dad's car. He used to honk every time he pulled into the driveway on a Friday night. He hadn't done that in a long time, but I could remember the sound. Three short bleeps. These honks, though, were two long tones. Deeper sounds.

When my mother turned to me again, her face had changed. Her eyes were wide, her cheeks pink, as if she'd been running in the cold. "I have to go now, but I'll be back tomorrow, okay?"

"Sorry I can't help you more," Chief Manning said.

"No. Uh…no problem. That's…that's fine." I knew I was mumbling.

I kept hearing the two long tones of that car horn.

The machine picked up in Maddy's apartment. "Maddy," I said, in case she was screening. "It's me."

After talking to Chief Manning, I had nibbled at my room-service salad and taken a few half-hearted sips of wine. I called the New Orleans number again, but it only rang incessantly. I talked to my investigator, who told me the number was registered to a management company that rented less than stellar houses around New Orleans. The tenants rarely stayed more than a month, and so the company didn't do background checks or even keep good records about who was staying in the apartments, as long as the tenants paid weekly cash. The investigator had found the address, though, a place on a rough little stretch of Magazine Street. He'd asked if I wanted him to fly there and run some surveillance. It would be very expensive, I knew, and there was no case on which to write it off. I told him I would think about it.

Now, my mind was like a locomotive, running over new ground with a driving, fierce intensity. That night. Those car horns. It must have been my mom's boyfriend. She was going out with him that night. She was planning on staying with him. And my seven-year-old self hadn't believed that she would come back. I could see my mother crouching before me. I could see her holding her head and moving to the door. I could see her in bed the next morning, her hair like a curtain over her face. But what had happened in between those spaces? Had my father come home? Was Dan there? Was he in that house in New Orleans now? And that man with the ring, who was he?

Which brought me back to Maddy.

"Hailey?" she said, picking up in the middle of my message. She sounded distinctly sleepy. Or maybe in the throes of some sexual romp.

"Hi, hon. Sorry to wake you."

"No problem," she said. "What's up?"

"Is Grant with you?"

"No, he's traveling this week. I'm not even sure where. I didn't talk to him today."

"What's his last name again?" I asked.

"Mercer."

"M-E-R-C-E-R?"

"Yeah, why?"

"No reason. So, did you ask him about the ring?"

Maddy made a soft groan. "What would I ask him exactly?"

"Where he got it. How long he's had it. If he knows who designed it and where it came from. If he ever lived in Woodland Dunes." I said the last sentence lower, knowing it would probably piss Maddy off.

"Hailey, for Christ's sake! Grant has nothing to do with your mother. He's lived in Boston his whole life."

"Right. Right. How old is he again?"

"Midfifties, I guess. Can we move on?"

"One more question. Where did you tell me he worked?"

"I didn't tell you, but now that you're asking, he works for Renley & Associates, the business consulting firm. He's been there for over twenty years, okay?"

"All right. Sorry."

I got Maddy onto another topic, but as we talked, I reached over and grabbed a small pad of paper from the nightstand.

Grant Mercer, I wrote. Renley & Associates. Boston.

The next morning on my way to the McKnight headquarters, I called the Boston office of Renley & Associates, and asked for Human Resources. Posing as a mortgage officer who needed to confirm employment, I gave the woman Grant's name.

"I'm sorry," she said. "We have no employee by the name of Grant Mercer."

"Can you check to see if he was employed there in the past? Maybe I'm reading his application wrong."

She hummed while she worked. I could hear her fingers ticking against the keys of her computer. "Sorry," she said. "Grant Mercer has never worked for Renley & Associates."

22

As soon as I hung up I called Maddy. She would be annoyed at my meddling, and I couldn't say what it meant that Grant didn't work for Renley, but I had to tell her.

It was an hour ahead on the East Coast, already after eight o'clock there, so I tried her office. She was at a deposition, her secretary said, she'd be gone the rest of the day. I tried her cell phone, but I could tell it wasn't switched on from the way it went right to voice mail. I left her a message telling her to call me as soon as she could.

Feeling jittery and anxious, I reached the Mc-Knight office and was shown into a different conference room than last time, a smaller one. Beth Halverson and I were having a simple catch-up meeting about the status of our case and what needed to be done before trial. There were a million things, it seemed, and I felt exhaustion blanket my anxiety.

Beth came into the room, looking more rested

than me in a spring peach suit. "Hailey, how are you? Can I get you some coffee or something?"

"Coffee would be fantastic."

I got up and paced the room while Beth and I talked, waiting for the coffee to be delivered. I had the feeling that if I allowed myself to slow down, I might shut off completely. The image of that ring on Maddy's nightstand kept flickering in my mind, along with the fact that Grant Mercer had never worked for Renley & Associates.

Finally, the refreshments were delivered. As Beth cleared a place for the tray, I glanced at the photos hanging on the back wall of the conference room—a series of black-and-white landscapes. A windswept beach was pictured in one, a lake surrounded by tall dunes in the next. It was Lake Michigan, I could tell, probably taken on the other side of the lake, somewhere away from Chicago. I studied them a little closer, moving to look at the next picture in the series, which showed a square, white, monolithic house with a wall of glass.

"Hailey," Beth said from behind me. "Coffee's ready."

"Right. Thanks." But I remained motionless. I knew that house. "Who took these pictures?"

"Sean McKnight had them commissioned years ago, I think. Some kind of ego stroke."

"Ego stroke?" I kept staring at the photo of the house, mentally filling in the picture with a figure standing at the corner of the deck. A baseball hat, an orange windbreaker, binoculars held up to the person's face. And the binoculars pointed toward the lake, toward the beach, right at me.

"That's Sean's summerhouse," Beth said. I heard the tinkling of a spoon against a china cup.

"And this house is where?" I said. I knew the answer, yet I needed to hear it.

"Woodland Dunes."

I swung around to face her, my hands clasped behind my back to stop them from trembling. "Why did you hire me, Beth?"

She looked up at me over her coffee cup, surprised. "Because you were supposed to be the best in terms of cyber law."

"Well, how did you find me? Was it the American Bar Association article?"

"No, your firm sent that to us after we called about you. It was Sean who recommended you. Actually, he was pretty emphatic that he wanted you."

I took a deep breath to ease the tightness growing in my chest. "And how did Sean know about me?" I said.

"I don't know," she said, tapping a finger on her chin. "I really don't know."

* * *

I sat in the back of a cab going north on Lake Shore Drive, heading for my meeting with Eden Fieldings at the Fieldings family house in Evanston. Through the smeared, grimy window, I stared at the lake, a frothy light blue today, the wind whipping it into meringuelike peaks. But in my head, I was on the other side of the lake, seeing that white, monolithic house, that person in the orange jacket watching me through binoculars. That was the first day I had felt as if someone was following me, studying me. Had it been Sean McKnight? Had it been him the whole time?

I had gone to his office when I finished my meeting with Beth, but he wasn't in, his secretary said, wouldn't be in until this afternoon. And that was fine, I decided, because it couldn't have been him. I'd had that feeling of being watched in Portland, after all, and with that car in New Mexico. I couldn't imagine that Sean McKnight, the CEO of a large company, would have time to tail me, or have reason to hire someone to do so. Why would he?

Why? It brought me back to that other question—why had Sean wanted to hire me? Did he know my family from when we lived in Woodland Dunes? The thought came to me that he had been the man my mom was dating, but I couldn't believe that. He was sharp and mean, rude and unfeeling. My mother would never go for someone like that. Yet what did I know? I barely knew her.

The cab swung to the left onto Sheridan Road, and eventually turned into a short brick driveway, approaching a white wedding cake of a house. It had huge, twisted white columns and balconies from every room on the second floor. A fountain in front sent arcs of sparkling water into the air.

I asked the cabbie to wait, hoping that my meeting would take no longer than half an hour, and I headed for the front door. It was opened by a maid, who said very little as she showed me into a parlor off the front foyer. She disappeared for a minute and returned with a tray of tea and cookies, which she set on a low table. The room was pleasant, with a yellow porcelain-tiled fireplace at one end and pastel-colored Orientals on the floor. Works of the Impressionists, some of which looked suspiciously like originals, lined the walls.

A woman, who appeared in her late forties, strode into the parlor. She had short brown hair, and she wore a brown pantsuit, looking at odds with the light colors filling the rest of the room.

"Hailey Sutter, I presume," she said, stretching out her hand.

I rose and shook it, trying not to flinch at the

force of her grip. "You must be Eden Fieldings. Thank you for meeting with me."

She sighed and said nothing. The deeply etched lines around her eyes and mouth made her seem permanently tired, eternally unhappy.

We both took our seats. Eden gestured wordlessly toward the tea tray, as if to say, "Help yourself."

"Thank you," I said. "I'll get right to the point. I'm representing McKnight Corporation."

"Yes, so I heard," she said in a dry tone.

I cleared my throat, then busied myself with taking a legal pad out of my briefcase. "I'm here because I'd like to find out anything I can about the takeover of your company by McKnight Corporation."

She swallowed; she looked down, as if she was trying to hold something back. "What do you want to know?"

"First off, I'd like to know if you've been contacted by Evan Lamey, or someone from his office. He's the plaintiff's attorney on this case, and he—"

"I know who he is," Eden said, inflectionless.

"I take it to mean that he's tried to reach your family."

"Yes, but we've refused to see him."

"I see." But I didn't. "If I may ask, then why are you meeting with me?"

Eden began tapping the toe of her pointy suede pump. I had the feeling that she didn't even know she was doing it. "My father insisted."

"Your father? Walter Fieldings? My secretary said that you'd given her the impression he was rather aged and incapacitated."

Eden glanced over her shoulder toward the open doorway of the parlor. For a moment, she looked like a guilty schoolgirl. "My dad has had a number of medical problems over the years. I run the business now." She laughed, a sudden, caustic laugh. "Not really a business, actually, but I manage our holdings."

"Well, I'm sure that's very time-consuming." It came out condescendingly, which I hadn't intended, but Eden caught it.

She straightened up and gave me a hard look. "You've got five minutes. What do you want to know?"

Now what I really wanted to know was why Walter Fieldings had asked his daughter to meet me. But it was more important to learn the facts of the previous takeover, in case Lamey was able to get them from some other means. Despite everything else, I had a trial coming up.

"What I'm primarily interested in," I said, "are the events that led to your family selling your business to McKnight. As I'm sure you know, there have been vague allegations that there was some impropriety that caused your family to sell."

"Yes, *vague* allegations," she said. Was she mimicking me?

"Can you tell me how the decision was made?"

"I was only in my twenties then. I wasn't an integral part of the decision-making process, but it was a family matter, so we all discussed it. And McKnight twisted our arm, so to speak, until it broke."

"Can you be more specific?"

Eden made that caustic laugh again but stayed silent.

I decided to back up for a second, and ask the question I couldn't shake. "Can you tell me why your father wanted you to meet with me?"

She blinked a few times. She looked less angry, less sure of herself. Leaning over, she poured tea into a delicate white cup. "He's gotten sentimental these last few years. It was something to do with your name."

"My name?"

"Yes. Your last name."

Just then an elderly man in a golf shirt and khaki pants came into the room. He used a walking stick made of old, gnarled wood. "May I interrupt?" he said.

"Oh, Dad," Eden said. "You're supposed to be sitting down."

He ignored her. He walked into the room slowly, making good use of the walking stick, each step a labor of movement. And yet the whole time, his gray eyes never left mine.

"You are Hailey Sutter?" he said.

"Yes." I stood to meet him and offered my hand.

It took a long time for him to reach me, and I began to feel awkward, standing with my arm out. Finally, he took my hand in his. It was large, probably once a strong hand, and yet now it felt papery and soft. "I'm Walter Fieldings," he said. He had a head full of thick gray hair that contrasted with his heavily wrinkled face and the frail stoop of his shoulders.

"Dad, here," Eden said, pushing her chair toward him. Once he sat, she took a seat on the couch. "Ms. Sutter and I were just talking about McKnight Corporation, but I know this is a tough subject for you. Why don't you let me finish this, then we'll have lunch?"

"I was just trying to find out exactly what happened when McKnight took over your company," I said, sitting again. "From what I understand, there was some early disagreement, but you decided to sell, is that right?"

Mr. Fieldings smiled. "In its most rudimentary form, that is what happened."

"Can you tell me the not-so-rudimentary version?"

"Dad," Eden said. Just that one word. A word of caution.

Mr. Fieldings glanced in the direction of his daughter, but seemed not to see her. "How do you spell your last name?" he asked me.

"Sutter. S-U-T-T-E-R."

"And your family? Where are they from?"

The question threw me. I paused for a moment. "We're from... Well, we're from all over. My father and I have lived in New York for many years now."

"I see," Mr. Fielding said. "And your father's name?"

That tightness in my chest that I felt this morning came back. "William Sutter," I said, my voice coming out low.

"And he goes by Will, does he?"

"Do you know my father?"

"Yes," Mr. Fielding said. "I knew him once. I'm surprised you didn't ask him about the McKnight takeover."

"Excuse me?"

"Your father was our attorney."

I'd heard wrong. I was sure I'd heard him wrong.

"Dad," Eden said again in that warning tone.

"Your father," Mr. Fieldings said, leaning forward in his chair, his right hand still gripped tight to that stick. "Your father is the reason I lost my company."

No more than ten seconds of silence could have passed, but to me it was an eternity. *Crazy old man.* That was my first thought. He had to be mistaken. But then the doubt and the anger rushed in, adding to the already long list of emotions about my father. Something else he'd kept from me, apparently, probably hoping desperately that I wouldn't dig too far into the McKnight case.

My throat felt parched, my mouth too dry to talk. I moved forward in my chair to pour a cup of tea, spilling my legal pad from my lap in the process. "Sorry," I said. "Excuse me."

By the time I picked up the pad and retrieved my pen from under my chair, Mr. Fieldings had poured me a cup of tea, which he offered to me on a saucer. I mumbled a word of thanks as I took it and sipped. It was a smoky black tea. Exotic and foreign-tasting.

"I wasn't aware my father represented you," I said. "Are you sure it was him? The name isn't that uncommon."

"He's with Gardner, State & Lord?"

"Yes."

"Then it's the same Will Sutter. Of course, this was a long time ago, twenty-some years ago now."

I took another sip of tea, the cup clattering as I set it back on the saucer. *Calm down.* So what if my father had represented Fieldings? So what if he hadn't told me? I didn't know all of his past cases.

What would be the point? I glanced at Eden on the couch, who was watching her own father with a strange look, a mix of fear and anticipation.

"Mr. Fieldings," I said, my voice stronger now. "I take it from your comment that you weren't happy with my father's representation."

"Not happy?" he said. "Maybe you didn't hear me correctly. Your father is the reason I lost my company. He gave confidential information to that bastard McKnight. And your client then blackmailed me with it."

"Dad!" Eden said. She got up from the couch. "I think that's enough."

"Sit down, Eden!" He said this as if he was scolding a dog. "I've kept quiet long enough. I want to get this out before I die. And you don't know what I'm talking about anyway."

Eden was silent. She slumped back on the couch.

"I am quite sure that my father would never give away privileged information," I said. "You must be mistaken."

"How old are you?" Mr. Fieldings said.

"Almost thirty." My birthday was five months away. I sounded like a toddler who says they're "three and a half."

"Will Sutter represented me twenty-two years ago. I highly doubt that you know anything about it. Shall I tell you what happened? I find it ironic that you're representing McKnight now, although maybe I shouldn't be surprised. For all I know, your father was in his employ the whole time. Either way, you should know what I have to tell you."

It was hard to concentrate on what he was saying. Twenty-two years ago, I kept thinking. The year my mother died. "I don't think my father has even met Sean McKnight," I managed to say, but it came out weak, unsure.

Mr. Fieldings chuckled. "I can assure you, my dear. They knew each other well enough."

He started to talk then. He leaned forward on his walking stick to make a point, never even glancing at his daughter, who seemed as shocked as I did by his tale. It occurred to me that she might be hearing this story, most of it anyway, for the first time.

According to Walter Fieldings, my father had been hired to represent them against a takeover bid from McKnight Corporation. Mr. Fieldings had started his company, he said, and the family had decided long ago that it would never become publicly held, it would never be owned by anyone but the Fieldings family. At first they were pleased with my father's work. Will had defended them well. Mr. Fieldings got the impression that my father had a personal vendetta against Sean McKnight, but that was fine with him.

But then one day, Sean McKnight called Walter Fieldings. At first, Mr. Fieldings wouldn't talk. He told McKnight to contact his attorney and was about to hang up, when McKnight said a few words that changed everything. "Your son, Laddy," McKnight had said. "I know about his extracurricular activities."

Eden sat forward on the couch at that point. "Dad, I think that's enough."

Her father snorted, waved her away with a quick gesture of his walking stick. "I'm not talking about the drugs, Eden. We could have gotten over that."

"Ms. Sutter," he said, turning his gaze back to me. "What I'm about to tell you is private family business. I have no reason to trust that you'll keep this confidential, since your father couldn't, but I'm old now, my company is gone, and frankly it doesn't matter anymore who knows. So I'll tell you."

I made a barely perceptible dip of my head, unable to tell him to stop, unable to encourage him to continue.

"My son, Henry, who I called Laddy in private, was a sweet boy." He rubbed the top of his walking stick, his knuckles turning pink from the tight grip. "He was a little too sweet, unfortunately. Took everything personally, if you understand me. He was very sensitive. His mother and I managed to get him into a university out East. We were hoping that college and some time away from home would toughen him up. He was supposed to help me run the company one day. But he didn't handle college well, either. Got mixed up with the wrong folk, started taking drugs. Cocaine, they tell me, which I consider a fool's drug. But then it turned out that my son was a fool."

Mr. Fieldings took a breath. He rubbed his hand over the top of his walking stick some more. "Goodness," he said, "this is tough, even after all these years."

I didn't say anything. I couldn't. I was still waiting for my father to come back into the story. When I glanced at Eden, she was looking down, twisting a napkin in her lap.

"We got a phone call one night from the police station near the university. They'd arrested Henry. He was involved in some…" Mr. Fieldings rubbed his lips together, seemingly searching his mouth for the right words. "I don't know what you'd call it. A ring, I suppose. A prostitution ring for men who like other men."

Eden made a tiny gasp. Her father looked at her implacably. "Not now, Eden."

"Will Sutter," he said to me, "was the first person I called. He was doing well for me, so I thought, and I asked his advice. And he handled the Henry situation for me. He had the charges dropped, the records sealed. We got Henry into a drug center. We still had hopes for him. We thought he could clean himself up and get his act together. And life returned to normal for a while, until McKnight called me that day. He knew about Henry."

"Mr. Fieldings," I said, relieved to find my voice and a point that I could argue. "That doesn't mean my father told him the information. Mr. McKnight could have easily learned about your son's arrest from an investigator."

"I'm not a fool, my dear," he said. "Obviously, I thought of that. But you see, it was that first phone call from McKnight that made me realize he had learned this from your father. He called my son Laddy. That was my nickname for him, no one else's, and I didn't use the name in public. But I'd told your father that when I called him upset that night. Your father knew."

"I'm sorry, but I still don't think that's enough. I'm sure you're mistaken."

"I confronted your father. He admitted to me what he'd done."

"What?" I said. My voice was too loud, echoing through the parlor.

Mr. Fieldings's wrinkled face seemed to tighten around the jaw with the memory. "He would never tell me why, but he admitted it."

"Then why didn't you call the Attorney Disciplinary Committee if you were so sure? Why not turn him in?"

"My dear, don't you see? If I turned in your father, then I would have to come clean about my son. And if I did that, my family would have been ruined. I still had hopes that Henry would take over the reins from me. McKnight promised that he would keep me on after the sale. He led me to believe that he'd always have a Fieldings on the board, that kind of thing. I wanted to believe him. I wanted my son to have the chance to follow my legacy. So you see, I couldn't tell anyone. I did what I had to do. I sold the company."

"And your son?" I asked.

Mr. Fieldings was quiet for a few long seconds. "Laddy died seven years ago of an overdose. That's why it doesn't matter anymore. I've lost my son, I've lost my company. My wife is gone. I have nothing left, you see?"

On the couch, Eden cried softly. *And what about your daughter?* I wanted to ask. But all I could do was thank Mr. Fieldings for his time and for sharing his story. When I left the house, the sky was dove-gray and thick with rain. I walked to the cab, ignoring the drops that splashed my face, and I told the cabdriver to take me to McKnight headquarters.

23

As the cab sped south down Lake Shore, heading back to the Loop, I dug frantically through my briefcase for my cell phone. I dialed my father's office. I missed a number and got a message for someone named Glenn. "Shit!" I said, squeezing the phone tighter, dialing the numbers again with more caution.

The phone rang and rang, and finally my dad's voice mail picked up. I hit zero and waited for Barbara, my father's longtime secretary, to answer. But I got her voice mail, as well.

"Shit!" I yelled again. The cabbie eyed me in the mirror.

My frustration made me weepy, a few tears clouding my eyes. I hit zero again, and rolled the window down, letting the damp breeze blow on my face, wiping my eyes with the back of my hand.

I finally reached the Gardner State receptionist and asked her to page my father. After what seemed like ten full minutes, he came on the line. "Hailey, sweetie," he said, "where are you?"

"Did you give Sean McKnight information to blackmail the Fieldings family?"

Silence.

"Dad?"

"I'm here."

"Answer the question." My voice came out hard and even, as if I was talking to a witness at a deposition.

"It was a long time ago."

"So what?" I yelled.

More silence. I had never raised my voice around my father.

Finally, he said, "You know as well as I do that it shouldn't be admissible in court."

"Are you admitting it then? You used confidential information and gave it to the opposing side?"

"Leave it alone, Hailey."

"Leave it alone? What are you talking about?"

The rain was coming harder in the taxi window now, but I didn't move to close it.

"Miss?" the cabbie said, "are you all right?"

"All of it," my dad said. "Just leave it alone. Please." Was he crying or was it the sound of my own tears?

"Please," he said. "Please. Please." And he hung up.

"Oh, my God," I whispered. I rolled up the window. I wiped my eyes. I lifted the phone and tried my dad's number again, then went through the same five-minute process of getting a message, waiting for the receptionist and having him paged. As each second ticked by, I felt as if I wanted to jump out of the cab, I wanted to scream. Instead, I tapped my fingers on the armrest. Tap, tap, tap, tap. But he didn't come to the phone this time.

Finally, I reached Barbara. "You just missed him," she said.

"Where did he go?"

"Out of town for a meeting. Didn't he tell you?"

"No," I said abruptly. My mind was so cluttered that I couldn't even dredge up any pleasantries. "When is he getting back?"

"I'm not sure."

"You're not sure? What do you mean?" Like my secretary, Barbara was exceedingly efficient and fiercely loyal to my father. Not knowing his precise schedule was unheard of.

"He's not sure how long the meeting will take," Barbara said. "Maybe a few days."

"A few days? Where is he?"

"I can't say."

"Barbara, it's me, for Christ's sake. I need to talk to him."

"I'm sorry, Hailey, but he was explicit. No one is to be given information about where he is. And to be honest, *I* don't even know all the details."

"Seriously, I need to talk to him immediately. This is important!"

"I'm sorry. I can't."

Time for a lie, I thought. Why not? There were so many out there already. "Barb, I need to talk to my father. I've just been to the doctor, and I've learned some bad news. Really bad. I can't go into it specifically, but this is grave."

"Didn't you just talk to him?"

"Yes, but I got cut off before I could tell him."

"Oh. Well, I'm sorry. Are you going to be all right?"

"I don't think so."

"Jesus," Barbara said under her breath. "If he wants to fire me, you'll have to find me a job."

I wished I could laugh, but the impulse only had the opposite effect—I wanted to cry again. I said nothing, made not a sound.

At last, Barbara said, "You know your dad doesn't have a cell phone. Makes me crazy. And I don't have hotel information, but I can tell you that he's going to New Orleans. And I've got a phone number. You ready?"

"Yes," I said.

As she recited the number, I knew I didn't have to write it down. I already had that number memorized.

"He's not in," McKnight's secretary said. She smiled at me sweetly. "Can I have him call you when he returns?"

I looked behind her to the light maple door of his office. It was closed, a crack of light at the bottom. When I had been there this morning, the door had been open, the office dark.

"No, no message," I said.

She smiled again and returned her attention to the computer. But instead of leaving, I charged around her, moving fast for his door before she could stop me. I pushed the door open, and sure enough, there was McKnight, ensconced behind a contemporary glass desk, looking up blandly from a stack of papers. Strangely, there was little else on his desktop except for that stack. A neat freak, I thought, apropos of nothing except my growing hatred of the man. Behind him, a huge window showed a skyscraper to the left and the lake behind that, gray now and turbulent with rain.

"I'm so sorry, Mr. McKnight!" the secretary said, bursting into the room. "I told her you weren't available. I said that—"

"That's quite all right, Mary," McKnight said, his eyes never leaving mine.

"Well, I'll call security." The secretary sounded nervous. "I'll have them waiting outside."

"That won't be necessary," McKnight said. "Ms. Sutter has been punishing herself enough, I believe."

"What's that supposed to mean?" I said loudly. Out of the corner of my eye, I saw the secretary tiptoe quickly to the door and close it behind her.

"Will you have a seat?" McKnight gestured to a white couch to the right of his desk.

"Why didn't you tell me you knew my father?" I crossed my arms and remained standing.

"You never asked."

"Did he give you information to blackmail the Fieldings family?"

McKnight drew his head back, a barely perceptible movement. He looked surprised. "Now that you mention it, yes."

"Why didn't you tell me that before? Why did you have me working for you if you were going to keep that information from me? Is this some kind of game to you?" I had a million other questions, a thousand other accusations, but I couldn't get them to form a logical queue in my mind.

"On the contrary."

"Tell me what is going on here!"

McKnight opened his hands wide, as if to show he was hiding nothing.

"Why did you hire me?" I lowered my voice.

"You're supposed to be the best, right? All those articles about the cyber-law wunderkind." He sat back in his chair and folded his hands on his lap. "And I suppose I wanted to meet you. I wanted to see how you'd turned out."

The personal tone of his voice chilled me. "You have a house in Woodland Dunes," I said.

He nodded.

"And you knew my parents when we lived there."

"Bravo, Hailey Belle," he said.

I coughed involuntarily. Hailey Belle was what my mom used to call me, a shortening of my full name, Hailey Isabelle. "You were involved with my mother," I said. A trembling in my stomach, spreading throughout the rest of my body. I crossed my arms tighter, fearing I might start shaking all over.

"Yes, I was," McKnight said.

"Oh, God." I remembered Walter Fieldings's comment about my father's personal vendetta against McKnight. "That's why my dad hated you."

"Does he hate me? Too bad."

"Of course he does! Doesn't everyone? Do you know anyone who cares for you, who even likes you?" I was yelling again.

"Your mother did."

The logical side of my brain clicked into gear. *My mother in her blue suit, saying, "Caroline is here. She'll watch after you." The sound of two long car horns.* "You were there that night. You came to pick her up on the night she died."

"Good work, Hailey Belle."

"Don't call me that!" I unfurled my arms and strained toward him.

He laughed. He actually laughed at me, and my anger zinged into something sharper. I saw more flashes from that night. *My mother clutching her head, answering the door. The hand on her shoulder. That ring with the black diamond inset. The man catching her as her knees buckled, his dark-haired head leaning over her.*

And then something else shifted into focus. Maddy. That same ring on her nightstand. "Have you been dating my friend, Maddy?" I said incredulously.

"Yes, she's quite lovely."

"My God! Don't tell me that's a coincidence."

"I wouldn't think of it, although I would call it a convenience."

"Are you sick?" I yelled. "Are you fucking sick?"

"Some might say. But no, I'm quite well."

"Did you use my mother, too? Did you seduce

her so you could blackmail my father and then blackmail the Fieldings?"

He looked surprised again, his eyebrows arched. "My. You *are* smart, aren't you? I haven't been giving you enough credit." He swung around in his chair and gazed out the window. Rain was pelting it now, fog starting to obscure the view of the lake. "It may have started out that way. I saw your mother walking the beach night after night. She was a very attractive woman." He glanced at me as if waiting for a reaction.

"And?" I said sarcastically, angrily.

"And your father was rarely around. I knew your father represented Fieldings, and so yes, I thought if his wife had an affair, he might want to keep it quiet. But you should understand one thing." He turned back and leaned forward on his desk. "I grew to love your mother very, very much. Her death destroyed me."

I scoffed.

He looked at me with eyes that could cut. "I loved your mother." He enunciated each word. "And the night she died I told her, very briefly, what I'd done. I told her that I'd set out to use her as a pawn, but I'd fallen in love with her."

"And Maddy? Why? Why did you do it?" I thought of Maddy's excited face, her happy eyes when she talked about "Grant." "Were you trying to keep tabs on me?"

"It was a nice way to find out firsthand what you were thinking about, Hailey. What you were doing. Besides, you've got to admit that your friend, Maddy, is quite the attractive girl."

"You disgust me."

He paused. "I'm sorry to hear that."

"You left the ring at Maddy's place on purpose, didn't you?"

"Why not? I didn't wear it anymore. I haven't worn it since your mother died. And you were taking so very long to figure things out."

"You were having me followed!" And then another piece shifted into place. "You sent me that letter."

"I thought it was time," McKnight said. "You're a big girl now."

My breath was coursing in and out, too fast, too shallow. I felt light-headed and then red with anger. "You sick asshole. Did you kill her? You just said you were there that night, and I wouldn't put it past you to brag about it. Did you hurt her?"

"You don't know yet? Maybe you aren't that savvy."

"Tell me."

"This is yours to figure out, Hailey Belle."

"If you call me that one more time, I'll—"

"You'll what?" he said incredulously.

"I'll call the police."

He laughed again. "And tell them what?"

He was right. It was an empty threat. I could say that I wanted the investigation of my mother's death opened again, that I suspected McKnight had had something to do with it, but what if he didn't? What if the real person at fault was my dad or Caroline or Dan?

I clenched and unclenched my hands. I felt like screaming so loud they would hear it across the lake in Woodland Dunes. Instead, I grabbed my briefcase from the floor, threw open his office door and ran for the elevator.

24

On the way to the airport, I called the airlines and booked a flight to New Orleans. My hands had a light tremor to them, as if an earthquake was rumbling a hundred miles away. I wanted to call Maddy, but she would still be in that deposition, and I didn't know how to break the news to her just yet. I could barely get it to sound real in my own head.

I called Ty. He answered right away at Long Beach Inn, and in that second after he said hello I could see him clearly. The coppery hair hanging over his forehead, his strong shoulders beneath an olive T-shirt, the hint of a smile.

"Did you get my messages?" he said.

The urgency of his voice scared away his image in my mind. "No, I'm in Chicago."

"Chicago? When did you get in? I would have come to see you."

"I would have liked that." I stared out the window at the bungalows lining the highway. Somewhere, inside one of those homes, someone was having an average day, a boring day. "I got in last night. For some business. But I've got to talk to you." I pulled my eyes away from the houses and stared at the back of the driver's bald head. "I've got to talk to someone."

"Yeah, sure," Ty said. "I need to talk to you, too. That's why I've been calling you all day. Something's happened over here."

"What do you mean?"

"My father resigned yesterday."

"Oh." I wasn't sure what else to say. I thought his news would be somehow worse. "Was it unexpected?"

"Well, yeah. My father could never quit that job. He loved it. That's why I bought the inn from them. But look, that's not the point. I don't know how to tell you this."

I closed my eyes. It was going to be worse. "What?"

"He started drinking last night. He used to have a problem, but he'd quit years ago. Anyway, Mom called me because he was getting out of hand and scaring her. When I got to the house, he was totally loaded. It was pretty out of control. My mom had left the house, and I tried to get him to eat something, but he was talking crap. At least I thought."

"What was he saying?"

"I didn't really pay attention at first. He was saying something about how he deserved it, but I had no idea what he meant. Finally, I realized he was talking about when he got promoted to chief of police. I kept saying, 'Yeah, Dad, of course you deserved it,' but he wouldn't listen to me. And then this was where it got weird. He grabbed my hand and said, 'Tell Sutter that I could have done it on my own.'"

"Sutter?" The cab was weaving in and out of traffic, the motion making me nauseous.

"Your dad," Ty said. "He kept repeating himself, but finally he told me that your dad had gotten him the promotion to chief of police."

"What do you mean?"

"You know your dad was corporate counsel for the town of Woodland Dunes? Well, apparently, he got my dad his promotion by having his predecessor fired."

"That's crap," I said, but my voice was weak, unconvincing.

"Maybe. But that's not the worst part. I don't know how to say this."

I rubbed a hand over my face. "Just say it." I hated the flat tone of my voice.

Ty sighed. "He might have been talking shit. He was stinking drunk."

"What did he say?"

"He said he knew the true story of what happened to your mom. He said your dad got him the promotion to keep him quiet, and he wanted the job bad enough to go along with it."

The cab had pulled into the airport now, and the driver stopped at the curb, waiting for me to get out.

"And?" I said, my voice anything but flat now. "Oh, my God, Ty, what? What happened?"

"I'm sorry, but he shut up then. I couldn't get him to tell me anything else. He just kept saying that he could have gotten the job on his own, he should have done it by himself."

The cabdriver had gotten out of the car and opened my door now. "Ma'am," he said.

"Ty, thank you for calling me, for telling me this, but I have to go."

"What are you doing? I could drive over there."

"I wish so badly that I could see you right now, but I'm at the airport. I'm going to New Orleans."

"New Orleans? Why? For business?"

"For my family," I said. "For my mom."

I had half an hour to wait until my flight boarded, so I sat on a padded bench, my cell phone at my ear. Ignoring the crowds and the announcements about gate changes, I called that New Orleans number—the one I'd found in my father's house, the same one he had given his secretary before he left town. Once again, it rang and rang. Yet what was I expecting? I had the address that the investigator gave me, and I would go there as soon as I landed.

I called Amy next and told her I would be out of the office for at least another day. I didn't know what I would find in New Orleans, but even if I could get a flight back to Manhattan that night, I couldn't imagine going to work in the morning. The thought of ever working on the McKnight case again was repugnant. I kept seeing Sean McKnight's face. I kept hearing his words—*This is yours to figure out, Hailey Belle.*

"Oh, no," Amy said. "You've got to be back tomorrow."

"I can't."

"You have to. The partnership committee wants to interview you."

"What? When did this happen?" But really, what did it matter?

"They started today. Everyone else was here, so they said they would take yours tomorrow. I already told them you'd be back."

"Tell them I can't." Two women walked by me, pulling black bags on wheels. They were both laughing. I felt a stab of envy for them, for an uncomplicated and benign moment.

"Hailey, I really think you need to get here tomorrow." Amy had a knowing tone to her voice, which meant she had heard something through the secretary gossip pool.

"Why?" I said, although again I found it hard to muster up any alarm or even interest.

"Werner's secretary said you're on shaky ground, and if you don't get in here and dazzle them, you're definitely not going to make it this year."

Dazzle them. It sounded as if they were expecting showy parlor tricks. "I guess this isn't the year for me to be partner," I said.

I shut off my cell phone.

Another cab ride, this one from the New Orleans airport to the address on Magazine Street. I felt exhaustion sweep over me with a few light brushstrokes, something I could put away for a while, but something that would claim me eventually. My cell phone remained turned off inside my bag. I was sure that if I switched it on, I would find a message from Amy and at least a few from attorneys at the firm. But there was no one I wanted to talk to right now. Except my father.

Twenty-five minutes later, the driver turned onto Magazine Street, an eclectic mix of run-down homes, upscale restaurants and kitschy antique stores. I noticed a cab in front of us, one that had been there for most of our trip. A tingling sensa-

tion went through my body. The back of the passenger's head in the cab. Why hadn't I looked
closer before? The thin gray hair, the ramrod posture, the perfect navy suit collar. The passenger
turned his head to watch something on the street,
and I knew for sure. There was no mistaking the
profile of my father's high, proud forehead, his
strong chin.

"Can you slow down?" I said to the cabdriver.

"We're just about there."

"Then stop, please."

And as I said this, I saw my father's cab halt in
front of a tiny white house with a flat roof and a
minuscule front porch. There were a few emaci-
ated bushes out front, and the house paint was
peeling, revealing that it had once been gray.

My cab pulled to the curb about forty feet behind my father's. "Here?" the driver said. At least
I think that's what he said. I could barely tell because of the blood hammering in my ears and my
head, giving everything a fuzzy, reddish fun-
house slant.

I watched my father get out of the cab in his
navy suit, with only his brown leather briefcase in
his hand. He looked calm, maybe even a little tired,
as if he was stepping out of a taxi in front of the
court building in Manhattan. Should I get out now
and call to him? Or should I follow him? No choice

was right. They were both odd, false; I could almost convince myself this wasn't happening.

I paid my cabdriver, and he got out to take my luggage from the trunk. I stayed in the car, watching my father trot up the front steps of the little house. He knocked, but apparently it was unlocked because he turned the knob and disappeared inside.

I thanked the driver, marveling at the businesslike tone of my voice, which I heard through the still-thumping blood in my ears. I tried to mimic my father's purposeful walk as I started down the sidewalk toward the house, but I felt clumsy, off balance. I stowed my overnight bag in the scraggly front bushes. I had a flash of a thought that this neighborhood might not be safe and my bag might get stolen, but it hardly seemed important.

I put my foot on the first of the steps. The house had shutters that were closed tight over the front windows. No sounds from inside. The silence made sense, though. My father and I had been silent for so long.

No choice but to climb the stairs, to put my feet one after another, to place my hand on the cool black iron of the doorknob and to turn it.

The door opened into a small front living room, empty but for a nubby green couch and an old TV. There seemed to be no hallways. From the living room I could see into the next room, a bedroom, obviously, from the double bed, neatly made with plain white sheets. There was another room beyond that and then another. A murmur of voices came from one of those rooms. The blood in my head pounded louder. Could my father hear it? Could he hear my footsteps on the softly creaking floorboards? Apparently not, because the voices kept talking, speaking words I couldn't make out but growing louder.

I passed through the living room; I walked through the bedroom. I noticed a woman's blouse folded at the foot of the bed, along with a quilt. A red-and-white quilt, half-made apparently, for there seemed to be squares missing. My pulse grew stronger; I could feel it in my fingertips, my stomach, my neck. *She was making you a quilt.*

The next room was another bedroom, this one with two twin beds. The voices became stronger. I could see the edge of a table in the following room, the kitchen. I could see a man's arm on the brown wood.

"It's over!" said an unfamiliar male voice. His tone was insistent, angry, but controlled. "We've got families, too. This has gone too far. Way too far! It has to end."

"You're right," my father said. It was his courtroom voice, measured, deliberate. "This is the last time. I've told you that before. But if we hadn't done this now, then all these years, they would be worth nothing."

"They *weren't* worth anything." This time a woman's soft voice. "Maybe it made sense at the beginning, but somewhere it got out of control. And it wasn't worth it."

"It was," my father said.

I stepped into the kitchen. Two people sat at the table. My father stood near it, his briefcase at his feet. His mouth opened in a small O. He looked as if he might break into song.

"Hailey," he said, his voice a rough croak.

The two people at the table were silent. A man and a woman. Caroline looked older than the wedding picture I'd seen. "Hailey," she said, as if mimicking my father. And then she began to weep quietly.

My brother, Dan, wore a yellow golf shirt and jeans. His sandy-brown hair was a little silver near the temples. He'll look like Dad, I thought.

We all sat there, like actors on a stage, waiting for our directions, for someone to call out our lines. But there was only a resounding silence that seemed louder than any scream.

Finally, I found words in my mouth. "Someone better tell me." It might not have made sense to someone else, but it was all I could say, and no one looked confused.

My father's shoulders sagged, as if he had just heard a guilty verdict from a jury. Caroline wiped her eyes but kept crying.

"You're all grown up," Dan said. A little smile moved his mouth.

"Someone better tell me," I said again.

My father looked aged and sick all of a sudden, like an old man talking to ghosts that no one else sees. "Hailey, I can explain—"

"Dad," Dan said, cutting him off. How strange that word sounded, coming from his lips. "It's too late. This has got to stop." He looked at me again, but this time it wasn't a look of pride for a little sister, but an expression full of regret. "Take a seat," he said, and he pulled out a chair for me.

"Do you remember the night Mom died?" Dan said, "when Caroline was supposed to babysit you?" He seemed to be the spokesperson of the group. My father just stared dumbly, as if he was only half there, in his body only, but not his mind. At the sound of her name, Caroline looked up.

I told them what I remembered—Mom in the sky-blue suit, telling me she was leaving for the night; two long car horns from outside; Mom answering the door, holding her head; the next morning in her bed.

My body grew cold with fear. I ignored my father, still standing. I kept staring at Dan and Caroline. They were adults. They were here in front of me. They were my family.

"But you don't remember what happened other than that?" Dan said.

"Daniel," my father said, a sharp word that he seemed to have dredged out of his chest.

But Dan just gave him a cautionary look and shook his head, the way you might warn a two-year-old not to throw his food. Dan was in charge.

But then Caroline spoke again. "I should tell her. I was the one who was there." She wiped her eyes again and looked at me. "You're so pretty, Hailey."

I wanted to cry but I only blinked a few times. "I... Thank you."

"Mom was going out with her boyfriend," she said. "I don't know if you understood that at the time, but I did, and I was angry about it."

She kept talking. And as she did, my picture of that night trickled in along with her words, an unearthing of long-buried, intentionally forgotten memories.

"Caroline is here," my mother said. "She'll watch after you." She gave me a warm smile, and for a second, I thought maybe everything would be okay, but then came the sound.

My mother jerked her head a little so that her ear

was toward the stairs, toward the door. It came again, and I recognized the sound as a car horn, but not from Dad's car. These honks were two long tones.

When my mother turned to me again, her face had changed. Her eyes were wide, her cheeks pink as if she'd been running in the cold. "I have to go now, but I'll be back tomorrow, okay?"

"No." I started to cry. I hated it. I knew I wasn't being a big girl, like she'd asked, but I also knew that she wouldn't be back tomorrow. She was leaving for good. Everyone was leaving.

"Stop that, Hailey Belle." Her voice was irritated now, and I tried to control my tears.

The horn sounded again, the same long tones.

Caroline came out of her room then. I didn't see her, but I heard the door close, and I heard her light tread. Caroline made very little noise and said even less, but I'd grown used to the sounds of her—the catch of the door when she opened it, the creak of the porch swing, the soft scrape of the brush through her hair.

My mother gave Caroline a strange look I had never seen before. It was the same expression Caroline wore the time she accidentally dropped Mom's favorite vase.

I glanced at Caroline, and it was as if they had changed roles somehow, because Caroline leaned against the wall and crossed her arms over her chest, staring at us, the way Mom stared when one of us had done something wrong. I moved my eyes back and forth between the two of them, but they seemed not to notice me. They seemed to be watching each other, waiting for one to drop her eyes.

It was my mother who did so. She squeezed me around the middle, then stood up. "I'm going now, Hailey."

"No!" I said, the tears falling down my cheeks again. "Don't go. Please don't go."

She started to back away. "I have to." She glanced at Caroline, who hadn't moved, then at me. "You'll understand one day. You both will."

I heard Caroline give a harsh laugh, like a dog's bark, a foreign, ugly sound coming from my sister's throat.

I saw my mother narrow her eyes at my sister, then the menace in her eyes fell away, leaving only hurt.

"Goodbye, girls." She bowed her head, and in that instant, I rushed to her.

I meant to hug her, to try to hold her there with us, but I was moving too fast. When my hands reached out to her, I pushed her instead. She wobbled on the high heels. I looked up and saw her eyes slide from sadness to panic. Her neck strained, her arms flailed. I grabbed the edge of her sky-blue jacket, and heard Caroline gasp, and in that instant, she disappeared, no longer in front of me. I didn't hear the sounds of her tumble down the stairs. For a second, I heard nothing. I just watched helplessly as she slid and bounced down the grand staircase, a vivid blur of blue. And then my ears worked again, and I heard the crack of her head on the marble floor.

She lay there, her body curved, her head slightly cocked to one side.

Caroline and I rushed down the stairs. Her eyes were closed, and she wasn't moving.

"Oh, no! Mom!" Caroline shook her, then raised her hands away from her body, as if maybe she shouldn't do that. "Mom, can you hear us?"

The grandfather clock in the drawing room began seven long chimes that seemed to echo through the house.

Caroline poked her in the shoulder with a finger. "Mom. Please wake up. Please be okay."

I stood up and moved a foot away, scared to touch her, scared of hurting her again.

Caroline looked over her shoulder at me, her eyes large and alarmed.

We heard her moaning, and Caroline hunched over her again. "Mom, Mom. Can you hear me?"

My mother's eyes fluttered open, an expression of bewilderment. Slowly, slowly, she pushed herself up on her hands, and glanced down as if sur-

prised to find herself in the fancy clothes. Then she looked at me.

"I'm sorry," I said. My voice was so small I didn't know if anyone could hear me.

"I'm fine," she said, but she held a hand to the back of her head and winced.

"Are you sure?" Caroline said.

She nodded.

The bell rang then. Whoever had been honking must have come to the door.

My mother looked at her watch. It seemed to take her a long time to read it. "You girls go upstairs."

"I'll get the door," Caroline said, moving toward it.

"No." She held both hands to her head now, flinching as she touched her scalp. She was quiet, her breath coming through her open mouth in short bursts. "I'm not going anywhere tonight. Now go upstairs and wait for me." Her voice seemed to catch on her last few words.

Caroline hesitated, but my mother gestured with a sluggish throw of her arm. "It's all right," she said again. "Go on."

Caroline took me by the hand and led me back up the stairs. We both stopped at the landing and looked down. My mother struggled to stand. She sank once back onto the marble, but the next time she was able to right herself. She walked slowly, oddly, holding the back of her head with her right hand until she was standing in the doorway, opening it, blocking it, it seemed. Her hand was at her head still, and she was talking softly to someone. The other voice was lower, much lower than my mom's.

"Let's go in your room," Caroline whispered in my ear.

I shook my head no, and so we stood there on the landing, peering around the post, Caroline's hand on my shoulder. And just then, I saw a hand appear on my mother's shoulder, as well. Large and tanned. Not my father's hand, but definitely that of a man.

Their voices rose for a second, and I heard my mother say, "Not now." I heard the rumble of a man's voice, but couldn't make out his words. "No!" my mother suddenly cried out, her voice perfectly clear. "Why? Why?" and then "No! That's not true!"

Something glittered then, reflecting off the porch light. I narrowed my eyes and saw that it was a ring on the man's hand. A gold ring with an oval face, something black set into the gold in the shape of a diamond. I stared at that ring, at the hand on my mother's shoulder, but then my mother swayed and nearly fell. The man caught her, and I saw the back of his dark hair bending over her. She righted herself. The man kept talking, whispering, my mother shaking her head no, her shoulders shuddering. Finally, she closed the door.

She leaned with her back to the door, her head bent. I heard her whimpering.

She raised her tear-streaked face and saw us on the stairs. "Hailey, come help me to bed."

I ran down the stairs as fast as I could and let my mother lean on me. Slowly, we moved across the foyer and began climbing. Caroline watched us from the landing, quiet as usual, but when I looked up, I saw something like fear in her eyes.

"I'll call a doctor, the hospital," Caroline said.

My mother leaned on me more. "I'm fine." Her words trembled.

"I think I should call Dr. Wainer," Caroline said.

My mother pressed harder on my shoulder. "I said, no, Caroline. I just need to rest."

Caroline opened her mouth, then closed it again. We'd reached the top of the stairs by this time, and she moved to allow my mother to lean on her, as well. We walked down the hallway like that, Mom between us, until we reached her bed. She slumped onto it, and seemed to fall asleep immediately, but then raised herself up for a moment.

"You girls," she said. "There's no need to tell anyone about tonight."

Neither Caroline nor I said anything.

"I want you next to me," my mom said. "Please come sleep next to me."

I looked at Caroline, who was staring at my

*mother. Caroline's forehead was knotted, her eyes
still scared. When she climbed onto the bed, I did,
too. We lay on either side of my mother, and I held
her hand, until I fell asleep.*

Epilogue

For my flight out of La Guardia, I upgraded myself to first class. I thought it was fitting. I put the seat belt into the metal opening and pushed it until it made a sharp click.

A flight attendant strode down the aisle. "Can I get you something before we take off?" she said.

I shook my head no. I turned to look out the window. Maintenance crews moved around the plane next to us, quickly unloading suitcases and duffels onto a trolley before they hurried away.

If only it was so easy to rid yourself of your own personal baggage.

I killed my mother. Not intentionally, of course, but there it was, an undeniable and hideous fact.

It was apparent in the first week after her death that I was quickly forgetting what had happened, my seven-year-old psyche doing what it could to protect me. My father decided it would be best if I continued to forget, if there was nothing and no one to remind me. So off Caroline went to boarding school and Dan to college. And they stayed away. Not intentionally at first. It wasn't part of an elaborate scheme. But when my father saw that I had truly blocked it all, that I was growing up like a young girl should—free from blame, free to be happy—he pushed them away, little by little. Caroline and Dan died in a sense. Certainly their family died a slow death over the years, as it became clear things would never change. But they went along with it so that I could live without guilt. So that I could live.

My father blackmailed Ty's dad with the chief of police position, and the case was quickly closed. And he let Sean McKnight blackmail him for information on the Fieldings Company because McKnight had been there that night, and my mother had told him exactly what had happened, how I'd inadvertently pushed her down the stairs. In fact, that evening was supposed to be McKnight and my mother's first time together in public, the first time they would spend the whole night together. McKnight apparently did love my mother very much, and he couldn't live with himself if he didn't tell Leah that, before he loved her, he'd been trying to use her. So he told her that night at the door. Later, he regretted it. He always wondered if she would have gotten medical attention if he hadn't devastated her with his news. But he blamed me more than he blamed himself.

My father and I moved around the country, around the world. Caroline and Dan crafted their own lives as best they could. But then I was hired by McKnight, who thought it was time for me to know, to remember, to understand what I'd set in motion. As far as McKnight could tell, his life, as well as the lives of all the Sutters, crumbled on that night my mother died. All those lives dashed, except for mine.

His letter had the intended effect—I started looking for answers. My father panicked, but he blindly hoped for the best, just as he had my whole life. Yet he knew this time was different, that I was more driven to discover the truth, and he had to protect me. He figured I would try to find Dan and Caroline eventually, and so if they weren't around for a while, if no one knew where they were, maybe I'd get tired and give up. He asked Caroline and Dan to step away from those lives they'd created, because if they didn't try to keep me from the truth now, then what had been the point of it all? But when I showed up in New Orleans that day, they knew their plan wouldn't work any longer.

* * *

The plane barreled down the runway. When the wheels finally lifted off the tarmac, I squeezed my eyes closed. I was heading for a new beginning. In fact, so many new chapters started after that day in New Orleans.

Perhaps calling them "new chapters" is too grand, because for many of us nothing changed outwardly. Dan, for example, went home to Albuquerque and found a new sales job. He made amends in the form of stepped-up child-support payments to Sharon, and once some extra cash was coming in, he was allowed to resume his weekends and his Wednesday nights with Annie. Most of the people who vaguely know him, his neighbors, for example, might have noticed that he was gone for a few weeks, but to them very little about Dan's life would look different. Yet, isn't that how it is? We rarely know what other people go through in their lives.

I'll soon get to find out firsthand what Annie is like. Dan is bringing her to visit my new home next week. My heart threatens to leap out of my body every time I think of it. Annie. Dan. Family. With me.

Caroline returned to her beloved Matt and their cozy house on Northeast Jarrett Street in Portland. They had to work through the secrets she'd kept from him and the agony she'd put him through. But again, their lives, to the unknowing observer, belie little change. In fact, Caroline has blossomed with the unearthing of the secrets. She's pregnant. If it's a girl, they'll name her Leah.

Ty's father decided to leave the police force. He still believes he deserved the chief position, but he can't stand how he got it. He's decided to work with his son at Long Beach Inn.

My father has faired the worst from all of this. It was as if the secrets were the steam that kept him going, and without it, he's wilted. He has gone into semiretirement, but he doesn't seem to know what to do with his free time. Luckily, he's met someone. A woman from his golf club. Will Sutter is dating for the first time in decades, and that puts a smile on his face every so often. For a while, he came to see my therapist with me, and we tried to work through what he did after my mom died, why he did it. The course he charted was flawed, but it was born of love. It's tough to fault someone who loves you so much.

I never did represent McKnight Corporation in the trial against Kingston Marketing. Magoo and Natalie tried the case, and to my internal chagrin, they won. There are rumors on Wall Street, though, that McKnight's board has grown tired of his high salary, his elitist ways and the company's lack of growth. If the rumors are right, there may soon be a McKnight Corporation without Sean McKnight at the helm.

As for Maddy, she was devastated about "Grant." Sean McKnight had beaten me to the punch, and by the time I returned to New York, she knew all about his deception. Maddy said she cried and screamed as he told her the story; she threw her college tennis trophy at him. She still regrets that she missed his head by a half an inch. But like the true friend that she is, her concern was for me. How was I doing? she wanted to know as soon as I got back. Did I want to talk about it?

I did want to talk, in fact, because I've learned something through this whole ordeal. I've learned that although I can control my professional life with a tight fist, something I'm very good at (probably too good at), I can't hold so tight to my heart. I've tried, God knows I've tried. I have rarely gotten deeply involved with men, and I pushed away the confrontations with my father that should have happened long ago. But none of that worked, did it? And so I talked to Maddy, and I talked to Maureen, my new therapist, and most of all I talked to Ty.

I won't say that I'm fine. I won't even say that I don't hate myself, violently, sometimes. All I can say is that I let the swings and sways of my emotions have at it. I've become moody instead of calm, unpredictable instead of centered. But strangely, these swings and sways have brought something into my life I've never had before—momentary episodes of euphoria. Often they occur at times I wouldn't expect, like when I get a whiff of fresh coffee as I push open the café door or I catch the sight of the morning sun making a series of yellow rows across my hardwood floor. These details appeal to me now, they make me want to sing in between the times I want to cry.

I suppose to my co-workers I don't seem so different than I did before. They know I'm moving to work at the Chicago office, and they assume that's because I failed to make partner in New York. They think I'm running away, but really I'm just running right into it.

The plane lands at O'Hare. It seems days go by before we reach the gate. It takes forever to get my small suitcase from the overhead bin and hurry down the concourse. The rest of my stuff, all my baggage, is coming later.

At last, I get to the arrivals sidewalk, hoping my hair looks all right despite the blustery Chicago wind. And then I see that monstrous green car of his driving down the ramp. He pulls to the curb next to me. I smile big. I feel kidlike and giddy. He gets out of the car and walks around to me. He wears faded jeans and a blue button-down shirt, which make his eyes more deeply indigo and the freckles on his face more prominent. Without a word, he lifts the bag from my grasp and sets it on the sidewalk. He takes my face in his warm hands. He kisses me then, and everything else in the world disappears.

If you enjoyed what you just read,
then we've got an offer you can't resist!

Take 2 bestselling novels FREE!
Plus get a FREE surprise gift!